The Last First Sunday

C.J. Lawrence

The Last First Sunday.

This book is a work of fiction. All of the characters, names, incidents, organizations and dialogue in this novel are either the product of the author's imagination or are used fictitiously. Any actual individuals depicted in the TLFS, are people that the author admires and/or are people that have had a positive influence on the author.
Inclusion in this book is the author's way of acknowledging these individuals.

FIRST EDITION
second printing

ISBN-13: 978-1468188462

PRINTED IN THE UNITED STATES OF AMERICA

In loving memory of my parents,
Elizabeth and Browne (B.E.)

You will always remain in my heart and thoughts.

ACKNOWLEDGMENTS

Thanks to Denise R., Dereck B. and Jeannette T, the three people that encouraged me to continue to write when I only had ten pages and no plans to write more, let alone a novel!
And thank you to my very good friend Valda H. whose experience, guidance and critique made me more determined to follow my heart. You helped make this happen!
Thanks to my sister Bari for your encouragement, help and invaluable input.
And to my sister Shelley for allowing me to read excerpts over the phone, again and again and for always wanting to hear more.
Thanks to Alesia, Chuck and Teresa for your wonderful enthusiasm and thirst for more.

Thanks to Linda Cashdan for an editing job well done. Your perspective and suggestions were insightful and on point.
Thanks Larry M. for putting up with me and using your amazing talent to give me the cover that I envisioned.
And thank you Barbara H. and Angele J. for taking the time to proof read.
And last but not least, thanks to Henry L. for being supportive and always ready to help and to the following who have inspired me and contributed in ways that only they can, Charles B., Kevin B., William D., Michael D., Noel J., Stan M. and Coco.

"We have everything we need,
to have whatever our heart desires."

A.B. Murray

"Go confidently in the direction of
your dreams.
Live the life you have imagined."

Thoreau

Prologue...

Would I join a book club? Hmmm, I doubt it, but if I did, it would probably be just for the experience. Would I *start* a book club? No. Nada. If I'm not planning to join one then I'm *definitely* not going to start one!

It began innocently, as a *one-time-only* discussion that somehow snow-balled and then eventually led to a second and now a third meeting. And believe me, this was *not* my intention.

The book that prompted my little monthly meetings was different — different because this was the only book that intrigued me so much that for the first time I actually wanted to sit down and discuss it.

This intrigue-turned-journey started on game night. Eight of us were playing Spades at a friend's house when I noticed a book next to the card table. I picked it up and after flipping through a few pages, it spoke to me. Not *literally,* but what I did read motivated me to go out and buy it the very next day. My friends, Will and Devin, had already read and enjoyed the book. So, after I read it, I suggested that the three of us get together to discuss it.

Basically, I just wanted to see if their interpretation was the same as or different from mine. And if it was different, I was curious to know in what way.

Before I knew it, the group for our initial discussion grew from the three of us to ten. Most of the others we knew, one or two we met while reading the book and one I met by just carrying the book! At the second discussion our group dwindled down to five and today our third one-time-only discussion-turned meeting, is now back to our original three. It was during our second discussion that we started doing the exercises in the companion workbook. Our meeting had just started when my friend Robyn called with a *tempting* invitation.

"C'mon Cyd it's gonna be fun! It's KYSS FM's annual singles brunch and from what I hear, there are going to be some fine ass men there. And, I'm not just talkin' fine, gu-url I'm talkin' Shemar, Taye and Mel Jackson FINE!! I even heard that some of the Knicks players are coming. And you *know* that's how I like them, tall with deep pockets!"

Just my friggin' luck!!! "Rob, I can't go. Will and Devin are here."...*And we've already started so it's too late to reschedule.*

"Oh gurl puh-leeze, not that *we-meet-once-a-month* book crap again," Robyn says mockingly into her phone's speaker.

"Rob, don't even go there. You know if I could I would. And by the way Ms. Thing, since when did reading to explore unknown areas of you become *crap*?" I press and then continue without giving her a chance to respond. "Areas that can connect you to a power that will help you with whatever your heart desires!" I can hear Robyn's breath through the phone preparing for her usual smart ass retort. "Please before you start, all I'm saying is don't knock it 'til you at least try it. Look at me; even though I love books, girl, you know I'm not a *let's-all-sit-down-and-discuss-this-book* kind of girl. So, all I'm saying is just take a walk outside of that little box of yours and be open to something new." I'm on a roll and can't stop my momentum, "and you can start by joining us next month. Girl, I really think, no, I *know* you'll be just as intrigued as I am!" I tell her as I switch the phone to my other ear.

"Are you done, O.J.?" she slipped in putting an abrupt halt to my momentum.

"O.J.? What the hell does O.J. Simpson have to do with anything?"

"Not O.J. O.J. gurl, Oprah Jr.! So now tell me "O" wise one, is this exploring crap gonna *assist* my ass in my *heart's desire* to get a man with some damn money?"

"I think you're missing the point, not that that can't happen, but Robyn, what's happening here is much bigger than finding a 6'3" walking ATM machine. We're exploring a remarkable revelation where the possibilities are not only endless, girl, they're mind-bog …" I stop mid-sentence because knowing Robyn this will more than likely turn into a lo-oong, drawn out conversation or in Rob's case, a long ass debate — a debate that, quite frankly, I'm not up to dealing with right now. Besides, I have company and can no longer ignore Will's loud, Neanderthal-like sighs signaling his obvious irritation with every word, breath and syllable that exits my mouth or *yap session,* as he's been known to call it.

"Sorry, Rob, I gotta go! But good luck at the brunch and think about next month."

"Sure, O.J., I'll think about it all right. I'll call you later."

Shaking my head, I smile while pressing the **END** button on my phone's handset. *Hmmm, a couple of the Knicks? Oh well, there's always next year.* "Sorry about that, guys. Now, where were we?"

Will repositions himself to get comfy on my couch, while Devin clears his throat before continuing from where he left off.

"I think that we can learn from the characters in the book as we examine the process used during their exploration. Then we can draw and hopefully apply the parallel to our own lives. So, let's begin by sharing what we feel is missing from our lives as we know it. Then for homework, we can apply the lessons from the book and draft steps for a resolution. So, if it's okay with the two of you, I'll go first."

"Knock yourself out, my brother!" Will says amusingly.

"Well, all in all, I have to say that I have pretty much everything I need, although I do believe that my life could be richer and somewhat fuller if I were to meet and marry a woman who's also on her spiritual path. This way we can not only learn from one another but ultimately grow together as well. Okay, Will why don't you go next?"

"Okay, but first I have a question for you, my brother. *Any* woman on her spiritual path or a *fine* woman on her spiritual path?" Will teases.

Devin laughs. "Well, *fine* would be nice and probably even preferred, but not at all necessary. Looks aren't everything. But enough about me, let's get back to you. What's the void in your life?"

"Truthfully, as I see my life, it's pretty complete with the sole exception of my mind, body and spirit not being in total alignment and that's something I'm working on daily. And to date, I would say that I'm about 78% there. What about you Cyd?"

"Really Will? 78%? Are you sure about that? See, I would have had you pegged at… hmmm… 79%?" I tell him poking fun at his precision.

"Nope, it's definitely 78%!" he says with confidence.

I shake my head. "You're too much! Okay, let's see, for me there are actually a couple of things that I need in my life; the first being resolution for whatever it is that's behind this nagging, ongoing emptiness that I've felt for what seems like an eternity. And the funny thing is that at one point I thought I knew what it was but now, I'm not so sure…"

"Well, what did you think it was?" Devin asks.

"I'm sure both of you will swear that I'm a hopeless romantic, but I thought that my heart was craving that true *I knew-it-from-the-moment-I-saw-you* kind of love."

Devin and Will smile in silent unison, intentionally not making eye contact with one another. Because, knowing them, if they even glanced at the other, one of them would probably end up saying something stupid or even worse, laugh. Whatever! I can't help it if I'm a romantic at heart. I really just want to smack those silly smirks off their faces! Instead, I just ignore them and continue.

"And the other thing is something that I really, really want and it's the only accessory I will ever need, this baa-ad *Gucci* shoulder bag with the trademark brass horse bit, antique brass studs and hardware with a great kick-ass strap that has—"

Suddenly a loud, thunderous roar interrupts me! How rude! Before I can even finish describing the bag of my dreams, Will and Devin burst out into a ridiculous, earsplitting laughter. Willie was laughing so hard that the boy was actually doubled over with a couple of tears slowly rolling down from those small, squinty eyes of his! It was one of those tear-rollin' cries that can't be controlled no matter how hard you try. Well, that's what his little butt was doing while rocking his flat behind back and forth.

"WHAT IS SO FRIGGIN' FUNNY?" I yell which really only seemed to intensify, if that was even possible, their already high level of amusement. After several minutes of their little laugh-fest, both Will and Devin finally calm down. We gradually get back on track and continue this common chapter of our journeys. Humph, and they have no idea of how close they were to having their brown asses kicked out! And even though I hate to admit it, I'm *still* in the dark as to what was so friggin' tear-rollin' funny.

One

Eight years later…

It's been a rough week at work and there was *no one* and I mean *no one* on this planet who was looking more forward to today, Friday, than yours truly. Whoever the hell coined the phrase TGIF had to have been a bona fide, hardworking, *I-need-a-damn-break* New Yorker!

I just hung up from talking with my girlfriend Shaye and there has been a change of plans: Mister J is out and Miss Lula Mae is in. *Lula Mae's* is the new hot spot in Manhattan that, according to Shaye, has a fly, sunken lounge and the best jerk wings and mac and cheese on this side of the hemisphere. Just Tuesday I overheard a sister on the subway talking about Lula somethin' and the way she and her friend were raving about it made me want to put my book down, butt in and ask at *least* two of the four W's. If their conversation had not been so good I probably would have. Actually, the book and my *page turning* served as a good prop, as I continued to listen while pretending to read James Patterson's most recent Alex Cross saga. I do love Alex Cross though; that is one strong and together brother! Although, I am still amazed by how a 60 somethin' White man can write about the life of a 30 somethin' Black man and be *so* on point…right down to Mary J., Spades and fried chicken. And trust me, JP's not stereotyping; he's just keeping it real.

I love walking up and down Seventh Avenue in New York's garment district. The energy is like none other as buyers, designers and salesmen rush to their next appointments, weaving in and out and in-between a million rolling garment racks. I've definitely covered some ground in the last ten years walking to and from appointments throughout the fashion district. But this time as I walk up Fashion Avenue I can't help but think of the many memories, which instantaneously flood through me like a mini tsunami… memories that take me from my very first internship with IZOD to my job now, as senior designer for the DK*Urban* division of Donna Karan.

Coming from the Midwest to the fashion capital of the world with wide eyed dreams and train track braces was, without a doubt, intimidating but from age ten I knew that I wanted to be a fashion designer and thankfully I've been fortunate enough to realize that dream. I absolutely love designing and find it extremely gratifying to have my idea or mental image transformed into a three dimensional structure. That *thought-to-form* process is not only magical but in an even deeper sense, I find it spiritual as well.

The tall, 12-foot door which has **LULA MAE'S** stenciled on it, is made of heavy, thick glass and to most is quite impressive although some might find it a little over-the-top. Shaye told me that they re-cut the door and frame taller so that the pro basketball players, past and present, don't have to duck when they come in. Hell, now the door is so tall that Dennis Rodman can walk through the entrance with a pair of 5" Louboutin's and *still* have plenty of head clearance! As I look in through the glass facade, I immediately start surveying the area, from left to right, square foot by square foot. With the skill and precision of a roving, robotic eye I zero in on a small intimate group of hard working men and women along the twenty foot marble bar. As I walk through the second set of doors and check them out one by one, I see a familiar face. Once I'm in, barely, the petite Jada-like hostess smiles and greets me.

"Welcome to *Lula Mae's*. Will you be dining with us this evening?" she asks.

I smile at little Jada. "No, actually I'm meeting someone in the lounge."

"Great. Enjoy your evening," little Jada tells me as she places the hand-held menu back on the podium.

"Thank you. I'm sure I will," I assure her as I wiggle out of my jacket and walk toward the familiar face.

I met James several years ago at that year's hot spot. As we make eye contact, I'm immediately distracted by a wild, waving motion from my right. I turn toward the "arm show" and see Shaye in the sunken lounge sitting next to a guy I don't recognize but who could easily pass for Boris *fine ass* Kodjoe. I do a double take just to make sure it isn't Boris (don't worry, Nicole, it isn't). Shaye and I smile at one another. Shaye's smile reads "*Check out my new man!*" The look on my face coupled with the smile I return clearly asks "*Gi-rrl, where did you find him*?" They look pretty cozy and I don't really want to interrupt, not yet anyway, so I continue to walk toward James.

"Hey lady, long time no see. You lookin' good Cydney, lookin' good!" James grins as he places his drink on the bar.

"Hi James, how are you, sweetie?" I ask while walking right into James' long open, waiting arms as he plants a firm, semi-wet kiss on my cheek. James is an okay-looking brother — tall, Wesley dark-brown, with an average build and one of the most beautiful smiles I've ever seen, although to me, his greatest asset is his brilliant sense of humor. James has the type of comedic style that has gotten him over, time and time again in the same way it has those big, triple D cup women who always have men fawning over them and their *I-paid-for-them-so-they're-mine* boobs. Although, James was *born* with his gift, he, like the *my-cup-runneth-over* ladies, uses it very much to his advantage. And while on the subject of gifts, I should also mention that James thinks that he is God's gift to women, *all* women. As we release one another from our embrace, I can feel James' hand brush slowly down the back of my sweater and over my bra's hooks. For a second I think the bra might unhook and free the twins. Now, I could be a tad sensitive because lately it seems as if *any* touch from the opposite sex is sexually stimulating and magnified to the umpteenth degree.

James smiles as he slowly feels the bottom front of my sweater. "I like that sweater; it's nice and soft… light-weight cashmere?"

"Ah, yep 100%," I fib, half impressed and half flustered…Uh oh, the magnification process is starting so I manage to muster up a smile while stepping back and making a full *Modeling 101* turn to escape his *this-ain't-all-I-wanna-touch* clutch. "Thanks James."

"Okay, *America's Next Top Model*, what are you drinking?" James laughs while applauding.

"I feel like a mojito but first I would like a *cold* glass of water."

James guzzles what's left of his drink then signals for the bartender while I re-adjust my cashmere/silk blend sweater.

"What can I get you?" the bartender asks James.

"The lady would like a glass of ice water shortly followed by a mojito and I'll have another one of these," James tells him, then turns to me. "You hungry?"

"No, I'm good, thanks."

"You sure? I'm gonna order the jerk wings."

"No thanks, I had a big lunch, but I did hear that the wings and the mac and cheese are pretty good."

The bartender returns with my water and James' rum & coke. James picks up the bar menu, licks his more than ample lips then looks at me while pointing to the jerk wings and macaroni. The bartender nods as he takes the menu and walks away.

James is an executive for a large television station and always has great stories about a lot of celebrities. He's like a walking 6'1" *People Magazine*. I will never forget a story he told a group of us about one of the Wayans' in a platinum blonde wig, striped mini skirt and strappy Manolo's strutting down Fifth Avenue. That day he had everyone at the bar doubled over in laughter. If you ask me, James truly missed his calling.

"So how's work, James? Are you still with the network?"

"Good, good, yeah still there. I just met with a new comedian this past Wednesday. He is one funny ass brother. He's cool too, short as hell, but cool. We're trying to put together a sitcom deal but the guy wants us to bring his entire family up from Ohio. Brothers, sisters, cousins, dogs, cat every damn body."

"Sounds like he's new to the business. I'm sure you'll school him."

"Yeah, school, dress, feed….Oh and speaking of feed, Cydney you will not believe what that brother did when I took him to the 21 Club."

James continues with his story as the bartender brings my mojito and places it next to my water. James is funny and it sure is nice talking to him after an incredibly long and crazy week. I sip my mojito and it's perfect, not too sweet, and not too sour. I look up and glance toward the entrance and notice another familiar face walking toward the bar. We immediately make eye contact while James, oblivious to my distraction, continues with his story. For a few seconds our eyes lock then I quickly turn my attention back to James while "my distraction" orders a drink. I laugh with James only because he is laughing, I have absolutely no idea what we're laughing at but whatever it is, I'm sure it must be funny. All I hear is "Wah, wah, w a h, WAH" as I reach for my drink hoping that once I take a sip that it will slow down my racing heart. I want to take another look to make sure it really is *"him"* but I'm afraid it might not be. It's been over a year since I last saw *"him"* and am a bit anxious to look, but if I don't, I may never know. I take another sip and casually turn to look and *"he"* is staring at me as he walks away from the bar. "*He*" nods to say hello and I smile back shyly while still pretending to listen to whatshisname. It's not that I don't *want* to listen; I can't because my head is too busy filling itself with questions. *Why did he leave? What was he saying on my answering machine? Why didn't he call back? Did he…?* The questions and my curiosity are taking over and I want some answers. I look over toward the lounge and *"he"* is standing in front of Shaye and "Boris" looking at me while sipping his drink. I laugh one last time as I turn my attention back to James just in time to hear the end of his story.

"Wah, w a h, wah WAH…and he acted out the entire scene playing all three parts! Cydney, *everyone* stood up and gave that brother a standing ovation, at the *21 Club*!!!"

"James, c'mon, please tell me that you're lying! Unfrigginbelievable!!!!" I half laugh as I finish the last of my drink. "And if you ask me, Mr. *King-of-storytelling, you* should be the talent pursued, not the other way around!! Anyway, thanks for the drink and the great story! Now, I need to go to ladies room. Will you excuse me?"

James smiles, proud of himself for yet another well told story.

"Sure, I actually need to go myself. Should I order another round?" he asks while getting up.

"No thank you. I'm good," I lie as I grab my jacket and start walking toward the ladies room just as "*he*" walks in front of me. I look at "*him*" and smile.

"Hello Cydney."

"Hi…Omar? Are you live or is this Blu-Ray?"

"Touché," he laughed. "Yeah, it has been awhile, so how have you been?"

"I'm good. Wow, I didn't think that I would ever see you again."

"Yeah, sorry about that, I had some stuff going on and needed a change of scenery. I called you and left a message telling you that I was leaving, but your machine cut me off."

"Yes, I got the first half of your message, but never heard the part about you moving. Black actually told me later that you were in Georgia. Are you still there?"

"No, I moved back several months ago, I'm up in Westchester now… Hey, I'm sorry you looked like you were uh…headed to the ladies room and I stopped you. I just wanted to make sure I spoke to you before you slipped by. Why don't you go ahead and if it's okay, I'll wait for you in the lounge."

"Okay, I won't be long."

My head is reeling! I can't believe that that is really "*him*" and that "*he*" is here. Wow. I met Omar several years ago at *B. Smith's* restaurant. Three of us were at the bar and he walked over to say hello to my friend, Black, who was conversing with my girlfriend Robyn and me. It was kismet. I knew it was because right before Omar walked over, I was telling them about the strange feeling I've had that something was missing from my life and that it's been driving me crazy not knowing for sure what the hell it was. Then of course, Robyn being Robyn jumped in and said, *"Gurl, I can tell you what's missing from your life: a damn man! That's what's missing and that's exactly what your ass needs!"* And then almost as on cue, Omar walked in! I knew the moment I saw him that there was something there. *Something special.* Then Black introduced us and it was a wrap. I had noticed him as soon as he walked in the door. I think everyone did. Omar is hot! He's about 6'4", with a deep golden brown complexion, succulent lips and a set of hazel brown eyes that see straight through to your soul. So, I didn't waste any time nudging Robyn especially when those big ole eyes of hers lit up after seeing his rock hard, chiseled body! Once I saw her reaction and before she could say anything, I immediately whispered, "Down, tiger, this one's mine!" Then once I called first dibs and got it, the four of us had a nice conversation along with a few good laughs. Then thirty minutes or so later, "*poof*" Omar was gone.

I saw Omar, or *Brown Eyes* as Robyn dubbed him, out at various hot spots over the next three or four months or so during which time we talked briefly and somewhat flirted with one another before he finally asked me to call him. On that particular night, he didn't leave my side. Omar stuck to me like Hillary did to Bill. I didn't mind because he's one of few men who has this way of making you feel special and like you're the only woman in the room, which to most women, including me, is extremely appealing. Several hours later when I left the restaurant, Omar ran after me in the rain to return my cell phone which I absent-mindedly left on the bar. While handing me my phone, Omar also gave me his phone number and asked me to call him. I smiled and told him that I would, and then jumped in the car then Robyn and I drove off. I called him several days later and we met for Brunch and had a pretty good time. Good enough for me to know that I wanted to see him again. Within a week after we had brunch, he called and asked me to dinner. He came over on a Friday night and didn't leave til Sunday! To this day Robyn can't believe that *nothing* happened! But trust me, nothing did. I refuse to be another notch on a man's belt, so before I agreed to let him stay over, I broke it down for him and told him that I don't kiss before two months and/or the sixth date and I most *definitely* don't sleep with anyone prior to that. He just smiled and said that he wouldn't expect anything less from me. Sooo, we ended up talking all night, through the night then watched the sun rise. It couldn't have been more romantic. That morning, shortly after the sunrise, he kissed me on my forehead and thanked me for one of the best nights he ever had.

After that weekend, I saw him every week for the next five weeks. It was during the 6th week of us seeing one another that Omar left the message on my answering machine (yes, I *still* have one) and was cut off mid-sentence. And all I was able to get was his name. I must have rewound that machine at least four or five times trying to squeeze another word out of the message but I got nothing. Not even a syllable.

Several weeks later I ran into Black and he told me that Omar had moved to Georgia. Needless to say, I was speechless. Black offered zilch. No explanation, no phone number, absolutely, positively *nothing*. The only thing he was giving up was that Omar relocated to Georgia. And now, tonight, "*poof*" he's back!

…I won't tell a soul, no one has to know, if you want to be totally discreet…." Luther croons through the speakers in the bathroom as I wash my hands, finger comb my hair and check my make-up. After re-applying my *Mac* lipstick I pop an *Altoid* then head back to the lounge.

I stop briefly to say hello to Shaye who's getting up to dance with her new boo. She and I hug as she introduces me to *Boris.* Aka Jackson. They dance to Luther as I walk over to Omar, who has been watching me the entire time. Omar puts his drink down and meets me on the undersized dance floor, takes my hand and slowly leads me to the center of the floor. "*…let me hold you tight if only for one night. Let me keep you near to ease away your fear. It would be so nice, if only for one night….*" Several more songs play as we catch up on what's been happening with one another for the last year and a half. I glance toward the bar and see James glaring at me. Omar pulls me closer as I turn my attention back to him.

"I'm glad I came in here," he whispers.

"I'm glad you did too, I still can't believe you're back," I told him returning his whisper.

"Maybe this will help," he says softly as he slowly moves his face closer to mine and kisses me. After several sensual pecks, Omar's tongue slips through my slightly parted lips and slowly begins to explore my moist mouth. I feel like someone has *completely* taken control of my being. My knees are literally weak and I feel like a 5'7" pile of euphoric mush while Omar's tongue takes command and masterfully continues to explore my mouth. I have no clue where I am or who, if anyone, is around me. All I know is that this is the best I've felt in a long time. I initiate my own exploration as my tongue sensually co-explores with Omar's. His mouth is warm and his tongue is eager although not overly. The pair are perfect together and are as much in sync as two Olympic synchronized swimmers. There is nothing awkward about this first kiss; it's as if we have been "swimming" together all our adult lives.

"After tonight I will be the only one you think of. After tonight you will never be the same," Will Downing sings through the large speaker next to us while the explorers wind down their expedition as we s-l-o-w-l-y pull away from one another still tenderly kissing and tasting one another's lips as we gaze into each other's soul. Beneath Omar's gaze is a layer of surprise and one of partial amazement at how incredibly perfect our kiss was. All I can do is smile. He takes my hand and leads me back to our seats. We sit and before I can say anything, he kisses me again and again.

Two

I roll over to see what time it is. *Damn, it's six friggin' thirty.* I swear, it doesn't matter if it's Saturday or Sunday, I still wake up at the same daggone time I do every day of the five day work week. Just *once* I wish I could sleep late on the weekend but no matter how many times I wish or how hard I try, my internal clock just won't allow it.

Then once *again* while trying to steal a few more minutes of sleep, I notice that my phone is flashing. See, this is exactly why I turn the volume off in the bedroom—for people like this who call at all hours of the morning!

"Hello," I say, trying not to sound too annoyed.

"Good morning beautiful!"

"Oh, hi Omar, I didn't expect to hear from you today," I tell him as I struggle to sit up, eyes still closed.

"I know, I know, last night I told you that I was spending the weekend with my brother and I am but when I got home last night I checked his arrival time and realized that I don't have to pick him up from the airport 'til noon. And, I thought if you didn't have plans that we could meet for breakfast at *Tom's*. So, are you free?"

"Hmmm, let's see…uh yeah, I think I can squeeze you in for breakfast," I say sarcastically.

"Okay, great," he says while laughing. "Is eight good?"

"It's perfect, I'll see you soon."

◊ ◊ ◊ ◊ ◊

Tom's is one of the oldest and most popular diners in Brooklyn and hell, probably in all of New York. And believe me, the décor reflects it. Any tacky trend or memorabilia from the 50's is well represented within these four walls. I remember the first time my sister and parents came here; I still laugh at mama saying, "*If it was made in the 50's and you haven't seen it, and for whatever reason you want to, then come to Tom's because there's no doubt it's here!*" But in all seriousness, I have to say as tacky as the décor is, with the twenty dozen plastic flowers and even more knick-knacks on all of its walls, the food more than makes up for it which is why hands down, this is my favorite diner.

I walk in and am immediately greeted by Gus (Tom's son who took the restaurant over when Tom died).

"Good morning Cydney. Do you want your usual table?"

"Hello Gus. No thanks, I'm actually meeting someone and I think I see him in one of the back booths."

"Okay, I'll give you a few minutes then I'll send a waiter over."

"Thanks Gus. How are the boys?"

"Driving me crazy!"

"Now if they didn't, then they wouldn't be boys."

"I guess you're right about that," he laughs.

Omar is reading the newspaper as I approach the booth. He smiles and gets up to greet me. We hug then Omar pecks me sensually on the lips.

"Hi baby, you look nice."

"Good morning. And thank you, so do you. I'm sorry, am I late?"

"No, I was early, it's only five after eight but it doesn't matter because late or not, you're worth it."

"Awww, aren't you sweet..."

"It's not even about being sweet, I'm just being honest. But I *will* tell you what was sweet and that was running into you last night at *Lula Mae's*. In fact, the only way I could be sure that I wasn't dreaming was by asking you to have breakfast with me this morning."

"Would you like for me to pinch you so you can *really* be sure?" I ask while smiling.

Laughing he asks, "Will it hurt?"

Just enough for you to know that you weren't dreaming."

"Thanks, but I think I'm good. Seriously though, I'm just thankful that we have a second chance at this, at us," he tells me while sliding his hand over mine. "And I'm not sure where your head is, but I know that I'd like for us to pick up where we left off. *If* that's all right with you?"

"Maybe, but before I give you an answer, I have a question for you…"

The apron-clad waiter comes over with his order pad.

"Welcome to *Tom's*, what can I get for you folks?"

"Yes, I would like a small stack of banana walnut pancakes and a side order of turkey sausage."

"And I would like the western omelet with a side order of pancakes, regular sized."

"Okay, coffee, tea?"

"Yes, I'd like Earl Grey tea with lemon."

"Black coffee for me," Omar tells the waiter.

The waiter scribbles, and then goes over to the hot drink station.

"Okay, so what's up? What's your question?" he asks while gently squeezing my hand.

"I'm curious, why didn't you call me when you first got back in town?"

"Well, I wanted to, but I didn't know what to say. I wasn't sure if you wanted to hear from me given my sudden departure. But I'll tell you this, when I saw you last night….it was like…like a sign; well anyway, that's how I took it…"

"Kinda like kismet?"

"Yeah, exactly!"

The waiter comes and places our hot coffee and tea on the worn linoleum topped table.

Omar smiles as he slowly raises his cup of coffee in the exact same way one would raise a champagne flute before making a toast.

I mimic his lead and raise my cup of tea and hold it next to his. Omar moves his cup closer so they clink.

"To picking up from where we left off," he toasts.

Smiling, I add, "And to new beginnings."

Three

And then yesterday we went to *Tom's* for breakfast…"

"Whoa hold up gurl, not so fast, we need to roll it on back to Friday! Now, did I hear you say that you were *making out* in the middle of crowded ass *Lula Mae's*?" Robyn asks as she begins her usual interrogation.

"THEY WERE KISSES," I tell her. "You make it sound so friggin' crude and it wasn't! It was actually very nice."

"Oh, I'm sorry. Okay, so what happened after the spit swap meet, did anyone yell GETTA DAMN ROOM?"

"Look, Robyn you know better than anybody that I have *ne-ver* done anything like that ever, not even when I was in my 20's! Hey, what can I tell you? We just kinda got caught up in the moment."

"No shit? Okay, so what happened after the swap meet?"

"We talked for another 30 minutes and then he invited me back to his place," I continue while extending my legs to admire the natural colored French pedicure that I just gave myself.

"Typical man-move. What does he think – that he can disappear for over a damn year, not call you, not even once, then waltz his golden brown ass merrily back into your life like nothing happened?"

"Didn't matter, I wasn't going. I pretty much told him what you just said but *nicely*. Then I told him that it was getting late and that I had to go. So he left with me," I recount while putting a coat of quick dry on my toes.

"That's it?" Robyn asks, hungry for more.

"Pretty much, we walked and talked for several blocks. He hailed a taxi for me. We kissed good-bye. He paid the taxi driver and then I went home. The End."

"Aw, how sweet. Can somebody please tell me why all this romantic movie *shit* always happens to you? What about me? Damn, did I just say that out loud? Sorry, I just had a *poor-little-me* moment. Okay, but seriously, I will give the brotha props for paying for the taxi. That was definitely point-worthy," Robyn acknowledges.

"Yeah, that was very nice. Okay, girl, I gotta go. I have clothes in the dryer not to mention color boards to go over for my big presentation on Wednesday," I tell her while carefully removing the zebra patterned toe-spacers from in between my perfectly pedicured toes.

"Okay, talk to ya later. Keep me posted. Call me!" Robyn says, sounding like a crack addict begging for another hit.

"Good-bye, Robyn!" I reply somewhat curtly, pressing the **END** button on the handset. "Somebody needs to get a life," I mumble while walking on the back of my heels to the dryer by the way of the kitchen.

While munching on one of my freshly baked cookies I head into my guest room/office to go over the preview part of my presentation. The preview segment is almost as important as the actual line because it's the perfect opportunity to excite the buyers with a sneak peek of what you're working on for the next season.

As soon as I start grouping the fabric swatches for my presentation board, the phone rings. I quickly chew the remainder of the macadamia nut cookie that I had just shoved into my mouth.

"Hello," I answer while trying to chew quietly.

"Hey Cyd, it's James, did I catch you at a bad time?"

"Hi James, no, just working. Why, what's going on?"

"I have a couple of invites to that listening party tonight. If you're free, I can put your name down plus one."

"Uh sure, I was just doing some work but that sounds great. Consider me there," I tell him as I push away from the desk while looking at all the work I had planned to do. *Work that will now have to wait*, I tell myself as I leave everything exactly where it is and rush to my closet to figure out what the hell I'm going to wear.

"Okay, cool, it starts in an hour so I'll text you the address and make sure your name is on the list."

"Thanks James, you're the best!"

BEEP.

"Sounds like you have a call coming in. Okay Cyd, get your call and I'll catch you later."

"Okay, thanks James, I'll see you soon."

I press **TALK** then switch over to my other call.

"Hello," I answer into the phone's speaker while hooking the phone onto the top of my leggings as I look through my closet.

"Hello baby."

"Hi babe. This is unexpected. I thought you would be out entertaining your little brother."

"Well, actually that's why I'm calling. He got in yesterday and we did a few things and now we're about to go bowling and I, uh we're calling to see if you wanted to join us?"

"I wish I could but I just made plans to go to a listening party," I tell him while pulling my sheer *Theory* shirt and backless *Donna Karan* vest out of the closet.

"Isn't that when a recording artist sings a couple of tracks from his or her new CD?"

"Yeah, usually for a small group of people mostly in the industry."

"That sounds cool…a lot more exciting than bowling."

"Well, if you want I can try to get another invite so that you and your brother can come with me. I just need to make a quick call then after that, we can head into Manhattan."

"Cool, we'll pick you up in, say, thirty minutes, is that good?"

"Yep, that's fine. See you in a little bit."

◊ ◊ ◊ ◊ ◊

Brendon looks tough and nothing at all like Omar. And from what I can tell that tough exterior is just that, an *exterior.* Initially he didn't say much, but after about fifteen minutes or so, neither Omar nor I could get a word in. I couldn't even *buy* a vowel!

I purposely didn't tell Brendon or Omar who the listening party was for. I knew Brendon would be excited once we got here especially since he told me in the car that rap music and skateboarding are his two favorite things in life.

"Omar, Cydney look there's Rev Run from Run DMC, one of the first rap groups," Brendon whispered, somewhat loudly.

Omar grins as we both smile at Rev and his wife Justine. They return the smile then continue their conversation.

There has to be at least seventy people here and it didn't take long before Brendon spotted every famous face in the place. With each celeb, his eyes widened almost as wide as his mouth did when we first walked in. First, he saw Russell and Sean (P. Diddy) huddled over in a corner. Then *Omar* pointed out L.A. Reid laughing with

Justin Bieber and his mentor, Usher. I have to confess, I was actually a little star struck too but I think I did a pretty good job of hiding it.

"Thanks Cydney, this is mad cool! And so are you."

"Thank you Brendon! I'm glad you're having a good time. And by the way, I think you're kinda cool too!" I tell him as I feel a tap on my shoulder. I turn to see who it is.

"Oh, hi James."

"Glad you were able to make it."

"Uh, 'scuse me Cydney, Diddy's by himself now, do you think it'll be alright for me to go over and ask him if I can send him a demo of my music?" Brendon eagerly interrupts.

"I'm sorry, James this is Omar, and his brother Brendon. And this is James, my friend who got us on the guest list."

"Wassup guys? Look, Diddy's my boy and I can introduce Brendon to him if you want," James offers.

"Thanks man, that's nice of you, I'm sure my brother would like that," he tells James before turning to Brendon. "Look Bren, just meet Diddy and don't even think about asking him if you can send your demo to him. This party is not about you," Omar lectures.

"Okay, okay, Brendon reluctantly agrees."

While James and Brendon are making their way over to Diddy, the lights are dimmed and the mistress of ceremonies asks for everyone's attention.

"Good evening everyone, my name is LaLa and it is my pleasure to introduce to you a very talented young man who comes from a family of music royalty. Ladies and gentlemen, please put your hands together for DIGGY SIMMONS!!!!!"

Four

I can't stand Mondays! Because whether they are or not, they seem like the longest friggin' day of the week. As soon as I got home from work I changed into my work-out pants and my favorite Michael Jackson t-shirt then did some work on my upcoming presentation. Now, that that's done I'm about to dig into these leftover pork chops and head into the bedroom to watch a little television before calling it a night. Just as I bite into a nice crispy chop, the phone rings. I quickly wipe my hands on the side of my pant leg then answer the phone.

"Hello."

"Hi baby, how you doing?"

"Hey handsome, I'm good, a little tired, but good. Did Brendon make it home ok?"

"Yes, he called about an hour or so ago. He said to tell you goodbye and thanks again for the listening party. He still can't believe that he met Diddy *and* Diggy! And you're going to *love* this; he also told me that I better not screw up because as *he* put it, you're what he calls *platinum,* or how we say, *a keeper!"*

"Well, I'm glad he enjoyed the party. He's a good kid *and* from what I hear, he also gives pretty good advice!"

"Yeah, I don't think I'll trade him just yet," Omar says while laughing. "Sometimes he's a little hard headed, but the good thing is, that his heart is in the right place. So you said you're tired, am I keeping you up?"

"No, it's just been a long Monday. So what are you up to?"

"Just thinking about you…"

"Oh, really? And what exactly were you thinking?"

"Well, since you asked, I was wondering what you have on. So, now you can tell me."

I look down at my t-shirt and see *Michael* tipping his hat, knees bent while standing on his toes with his white shirt blowing in the air and smile. "My black lace bra and black sheer thong."

"Mmmm, is that all?" he asks.

"Yep, not a stitch more," I say smiling.

"Black lace, huh?"

"No, not black lace, *Chantilly* lace."

"Damn woman! Don't tell me that your toes are painted too?"

I glance down at my ashy feet and see that a little of the white polish from my two week old French pedicure is beginning to chip. "Oui monsieur."

"What color?"

"Fire engine red."

"Baby, you're killing me, black Chantilly lace, red toes *and* you're speaking French! Where are you?"

As I prop my feet up on the coffee table in the living room, I reach for my emery board and tell him, "I'm in the bedroom laying across the bed."

"Don't tell me you have candles lit too?"

"Only one," I tell him as I file down the chipped toe nail.

"Are you on your back or stomach?"

"My stomach, legs bent."

"Indulge me baby and pull out one of those lollipops that you have in the top drawer of your night table."

Surprised that he remembered the lollipops, I pick up the long pork chop bone that fortunately (for him) still has a little meat on it.

"Did you get it?"

"Yes, I'm unwrapping it now."

"Okay, now put the phone on speaker."

Obediently, I press the **SPEAKER** button on my phone.

"Okay, it's unwrapped and now I'm putting it in my mouth," I tell him while positioning the bone so that as soon as I lick it, I'll be able to bite the meat off. I see a little juice on the bone and lick it dry. Then I start gnawing lightly on the little bit of meat that's left.

"Oh yeah baby, *suck* that lollipop…Ouh, baby, you know you're turning me on with the way you're lovin' that lollipop! Damn, I wish I was there," he tells me as I hear him shift positions.

"Mmmm," I moan while digging in the container and exchanging the dry bone for a nice meaty one.

"Okay," he continues, "now suck it nice and sl-o-ow; just like the way you kissed me Friday night."

I lick the bone slower. "Is this slow enough for you?" I ask seductively.

"Yeah, and now I want you to suck it like it's the best, damn lollipop you've ever had."

I smile then continue to lick and suck the bone for another thirty seconds or so before receiving my next order.

"Okay, now wrap the lollipop back up then put it down. Now, I want you to tell me how that Chantilly lace feels."

"Okay," I tell him softly as I drop the bone in the white cardboard Chinese take-out container along with the other well-polished bones. Then I grab the clear polish and continue with my quick fix pedicure by putting a top coat of polish on my *almost-as-good-as-new* nail.

"So baby, how does it feel?"

"Mmmm…both soft and rough."

"Yeah, that's what I'm talkin' about," he mumbles through the phone. "Okay now, I want you to touch your skin underneath the lace."

"Mmmm," I moan into the speaker as I feel my skin under my white sports bra.

"Now tell me how that feels."

"Like buttered silk satin. Smooth and soft."

"Damn." He pauses for a few seconds before continuing. "Okay, now take the phone off the speaker and put the headset on. Now, close your eyes."

Smiling, I take the speaker off and place the headset on as I close my eyes.

"Okay, now listen closely because from this point on I'm going to whisper everything else… *Are you ready?"* he whispers.

"Almost," I whisper back.

I jump up from the couch, rush into my bedroom then quickly strip down to my underwear and lay across the bed.

"Are you ready?" Omar whispers.

"Yes, now I'm ready," I whisper back as I close my eyes and wait patiently for my next order.

Five

Today is the day I've been waiting for. My big presentation! This meeting will pretty much determine if I'm on track with DK*Urban* and even more so with my designs. I worked all day on Tuesday fine tuning the preview portion of the presentation and if I say so myself, it turned out pretty well.

As I get off the elevator and walk toward the office entrance, I see Zoe, the receptionist admiring a stunning floral arrangement. Hmm, I wouldn't be surprised if they're from one of the guys she met last weekend. My guess is the Wall Street trainee. I swear I'm not hatin', but that girl meets more men than any woman I know, with the exception of probably Halle! Of course it doesn't hurt that Zoe's parents are in the entertainment industry and are forever sending her comps to every imaginable venue known to man. Her dad is the lead singer in a popular rock band and her mom is a renowned actress. I'm dying to tell someone who they are but Zoe slapped me with a verbal gag order in a desperate attempt to keep her parents identity a secret. Personally, I think pinkie swearing would have sufficed, but that's Zoe for you. Though I can't say that I blame her and truth be told, I actually admire her for several reasons, but mainly because Zoe never uses her *celebrity-by-default* status to gain any special treatment, not even to avoid standing in ridiculously long lines. She's proud of her parents' success, but is fiercely independent and very determined to make it on her own merit.

"Good morning Zoe. What a gorgeous arrangement! Who's the lucky guy?"

"You are!"

"Uh duh, I've been busy, but I think I would remember if I sent you flowers." I said with a poker face.

"Ha ha, no I mean the flowers are for you. Now *you tell me*, who's the lucky guy?"

"Hmmm maybe from a client, is there a card?"

Zoe hands me the card, which was nestled artistically in the middle of the exotic mix of white pink and green hydrangeas, calla lilies, roses, freesia and water lilies. I open the card while still admiring how nicely the flowers complement one another.

Cydney, To new beginnings…O.

Smiling, I put the card back in the envelope, pick up the small square vase then take it into my office. Feeling Zoe's eyes beginning to take root in my back, I continue to walk away without turning around. "Do I have any messages?"

"Yes, Constance from *Essence Magazine* just called and she'd like to set up an appointment to see the line. Do you want me to get her on the line for you?"

"Great! Yes, thanks Zoe. Any other messages?"

"They're on your desk. So, aren't you going to tell me who the flowers are from?"

"No-oo," I sing, "I'm not telling you because you probably already looked at the card and now you're just trying to figure out whose initial it is!"

I close the door while burying my nose in the fragrant bouquet. Since Omar has come back, he has really made an effort to pick up from where he left off. We haven't done much, but the little time that we have spent together has been very revealing. I especially appreciate that Omar wanted me to meet his brother, Brendon. To me, that was major. This time together is exactly what we both needed to make sure that nothing has changed between us and that we're both on the same page, romantically and able to pick up from where we were, B.O.D. (Before Omar's Disappearance).

As I enjoy the lingering scent, I place the vase on the corner of my desk then sit down while looking through my messages. Hmm, nothing urgent and certainly nothing that can't wait until I finish my presentation for Federated Stores. Meanwhile, I can't wait to pitch our new division's concept to them. This is major for DK, the company, as well as for me, especially since they have put their trust in me to present this solo. And hell, why wouldn't they, since the concept of the division was mine along with all of the designs! The concept in two words is *urban chic*. The designs are divided into four groups, which for the premier line translates into 32 pieces. Although, in all fairness, as much as I hate to, I really have to give Kyle, my assistant, some of the credit because his input gave me a fresh perspective, which is extremely helpful when putting a line together. Or anything for that matter. Now, if only I could trust him.

"**Beep, beep**." The intercom button stops flashing as I press it.

"Yes Zoe?" I ask while checking my make-up in the gold star-shaped mirror on my desk, a gift from the sample hands in my old division when Donna accepted my DK*Urban* division pitch.

"Constance is in a meeting so I left a message that you were returning her call. And the lobby called and said that the Federated gang is on their way up. Do you want me to take them into the conference room?"

"Yes, thank you. I'll be right in. Can you also let Gretchen and Kyle know? Oh, and can you ask Kyle to find out what they would like for refreshments? Thanks Zoe!"

I glance at my watch and it's 10:45 a.m. One of my messages is that three revised samples for one of today's groups will be delivered by courier and will be here by 11:30, at the latest. Unfortunately, in this industry, I've learned not to hold my breath unless it's something *you* can control. But if the samples aren't here by then, it won't be the end of the world, since I still have the original samples, but of course, it's ideal to show the revised or final samples.

Our usual client format typically begins with semi-healthy refreshments followed by our VP and Director of Sales, Gretchen Kingsley discussing and reviewing the clients previous season and their store's performance level and sales in addition to chatting about color trends. Once they finish, then I will perform my magic, which probably won't be until 12 or 12:15 which will give Kyle plenty of time to check the revised samples and place them with the originals. I take a couple of deep breaths and then head toward the conference room.

As I enter the long, impressive room, Gretchen is already there talking to Federated's VP of Merchandising. In addition to the VPM there are seven buyers present plus the company's new Fashion Director, Babette Wintour, slight resemblance, but no relation to Anna. I greet each one individually, starting with Babette who is petite but dynamic. I met each of the buyers several months ago when we first introduced the new division.

While talking to one of the buyers, our company's server rolls in a cart with mini croissants, whole wheat muffins, two egg white omelets, coffee, tea, milk and three berry protein smoothies. Just as I look at my watch and see that it's 11:30, Kyle comes in and whispers that the revised samples have arrived and are in their proper grouping. I smile and thank him as I nod to Gretchen so that she can start the review portion of the meeting. Then excuse myself so that I can check the samples firsthand. As I walk into the reception area, I stop midway, dead in my tracks! *Wow, this is a nice surprise! But wait, did we make plans last night that I forgot? Well, plans or no plans, it's good to see him. And just the fact that he's here, tells me that he's stepping up to the plate and trying to get back to where we were. B.O.D.*

"Hey you, what brings you here? Oh and thank you for the flowers; they're beautiful. That was very thoughtful!"

Omar smiles and leans in to kiss me on my cheek.

"Hello gorgeous! Good, you got them. Glad you like them. Zoe is staring at Omar and me like she's at the last live taping of *All My Children!* "I took a few days off to take care of some business and just stopped by hoping that maybe we could have lunch."

"I would love to but I'm just about to start my presentation …unless you don't mind waiting until I finish," I tell him as I look at the clock on the wall, "My VP is doing her portion now and my segment should begin in about 15 minutes."

The phone rings and our attentive one-woman audience is forced to take an intermission break to answer the phone. After a few uh-huhs and one right away, Zoe hangs up and asks me if Kyle can help Tasha, one of the company models carry several garment bags downstairs to a waiting car. She has a plane to catch and she needs help *A sap!*

"Kyle can't help, he's in the meeting taking notes. Where's Eddie?"

Zoe shrugs her shoulders.

"Um, I can help her," Omar offers. "I have the muscle and looks like the time since you're about to start your presentation."

"No, that's okay, Zoe can find Eddie."

"No, really, it's cool, I can do it."

"You really don't mind?"

"No, it's fine."

"Okay. Thanks! Zoe, where's Tasha?"

"She's across the hall in the DK reception area. I'll call and tell her that "O" will meet her in front of the elevators," she says while winking.

I ignore her. "Thanks again Omar. I'll wait for you here and when you come back up I'll take you to the lounge where you'll be more comfortable. Now, you're sure you don't mind waiting 'til I finish my presentation?"

"No, it's cool," Omar said as he turned toward the door leading to the elevators. He stops then turns back to me and says, "And just for the record, waiting forty five minutes or even longer is nothing if I'm waiting for someone that I'm into. And I'm sure by now, it's pretty clear that I'm into you."

I smile while trying not to blush, especially in front of our little one-woman audience. I stand still while I watch *my boo* walk toward Tasha while my mind immediately plays a scene of innocent prey walking straight into a lion's den. As I blink I see Tasha smiling like a big, hungry lioness getting ready to eat her last meal. If that hussy was any more obvious her ass would be wearing a sign! I wish you could see her checking my boo out from the top of his smooth, clean-shaven head down to his black Kenneth Cole leather covered toes. Unfriggin'believable! I swear that girl's like a damn piranha in Prada! And unfortunately, she's drop dead gorgeous. Tall with a beautiful, Selma-like olive complexion and alluring, brown almond shaped eyes, which collectively give her this air of confidence that has been fed time and time again by countless men drooling over her exotic look.

Omar says hello, presses the elevator button then picks up the garment bags. The elevator opens just as Tasha begins to speak. We can hear her voice as the doors close. I look at Zoe as she cocks her head while raising her eyebrow then looking away with an expression that clearly reads, *dumb move!* Then she looks me square in the eye and says, "*She's* why I meet all my male friends downstairs!"

"Oh, please, Zoe, what do you think she's going to do, attack the daggone man in the elevator?" I ask sarcastically as I nonchalantly walk slowly over to the window and look down at the waiting car. Luckily, we're only on the 8th floor so we have a pretty good view of people on the street. As soon as Tasha emerges from the buildings entrance, Zoe distracts me.

"Cydney, it's about that time, should I call to have the rolling racks sent in?"

I look down at my watch. "Yes, thanks, Zoe. I've got about seven minutes before my segment so can you also make sure that the Polaroid camera is taken in as well. Oh and diet cokes, ginger ale and more bottled water. Thanks Zoe, you're the best!" I turn back to the window and my heart stops as my entire body freezes. I can't friggin' believe my eyes! I see Omar getting into the car, well, the bottom half of him. His ass got in so fast that all I can see is his right pant leg and black boot. Nano-seconds after his foot is in, the driver slams the door then jumps in the car and speeds away faster than friggin' Andretti in the *Indy 500*!

Wh..what the hell is going on??? Why in the world would Omar get into the car with Tasha? What could she have possibly said to him in that elevator to make him leave with her? What the hell is going on? He knows I'm waiting for him. What about our lunch and our so called new beginning? This is craaazzy! Hell, I'm still on cloud nine from the flowers he sent me just, what was it, thirty minutes ago? Not to mention him coming here to surprise me for lunch!! From that to this? Maybe this is a dream or nightmare… And if this is a nightmare, dream whatever, just pleeeease let me wake up NOW! Ring phone ring so I can wake the hell up and know that none of this really happened!

Brrrrng, brrrrrng! "Whew, thank God!" I say loudly with a huge sigh of relief!

"Cydney, wah WAH w a h they're wah for Wah you, C-Y-D!" I hear in the background. I turn toward the noise and to my disappointment Zoe is sitting at the reception desk staring at me with her mouth moving in s-l-o-w motion.

"A-r-e y-o-u o-k C-y-d?, did you hear me?"

Damn this shit is real, I'm awake! "Uh no, I'm sorry Zoe, what did you say?"

"Gretchen just called and they're ready for you."

"Oh, okay, thanks." I turn toward the window one last time, my heart hoping like crazy that I see Omar re-entering the building even though my eyes saw otherwise. No matter what direction I look, there's no sign of him; just a bunch of speeding yellow taxi's and hundreds of over-worked people in all shapes and sizes walking rapidly up and down Fashion Avenue.

"Cyd, Omar is cool. I like him! Should I take him to the lounge when he comes back up?" Zoe asks.

I can't bring myself to tell her what I just saw, let alone respond to her question as to where she should take his triflin' butt when and if he returns. So, I just walk right by her avoiding all eye contact. I head to the conference room and mumble, "*No, if you see him, just tell his golden, two-timin' ass that he can go straight to hell!*"

As I enter the room, all eyes turn to me, which makes me slightly uneasy, especially since my mind is clearly elsewhere. No matter how hard I try, I can't get that damn image of Omar getting in the car with that hussy ass Tasha out of my head! It's all I can see and all I can think of. But right now I'm just glad as hell that I memorized my part of the presentation and that all the groups are already set up. Once I see that everyone has a copy of the line sheets complete with fabric swatches in front of them, I clear my throat hoping that audible words if any, come out.

"Hell…hello and thank you again for taking time out of your busy schedules to come to New York to view DK*Urban's* premier launching of our Urban*Chic* line."

Why would he do something like that? This was supposed to be our new beginning…and what was that …" I'm into you" crap about? I feel so stupid for even thinking for one second that we had something special!

"You have the line sheets and swatches in front of you but before we review them, I think it is important for you to know the concept of the line which is very simple…"

Damnit! It took me months to accept and deal with never seeing him again after his first disappearing act and almost as long to finally be able to put some closure on it. And if it hadn't been for my mother always saying, "If it was meant to be, it will be," I'd probably still be agonizing over him leaving New York the way he did.

"Urban*Chic* is Urban with several touches of chic and/or couture detailing. We all know that Urban is here to stay which is why it is fast becoming an industry staple…"

Maybe he's back and Zoe already took him to the lounge…and if he is, I don't know if I should hug his ass or just slap him! Probably both…

"Adding a twist or a new element to a new or existing staple that has proven its value to you in dollars will only increase your sales, possibly even double your profit. This line provides that twist, the couture element that Urban needs. Ladies, this is a no-brainer and a must-have for each of your stores. Before we show you the line I want to suggest a buying strategy that I believe will give you the maximum potential and sales from the line."

It's killing me not knowing if Omar came back or if it was even him in the car…maybe it wasn't! But if he wasn't, then where is he? He has to be back; there's no way he would leave just like that, not again! I need to wrap this up so I can find out for sure if he's in the lounge.

"For our premier line, we have four groups and we believe that in order to make a statement for maximum sales that you purchase a minimum of two groups per store. By adding the Urban*Chic* groups to your buy-list you will be leaders in the market along with all the other stores that also carry the line."

I have to find out if he's here. I'm almost done so maybe Kyle can show the samples and close the segment. Hell, everyone in the company knows that he wants more responsibility, so fine, he can have it. I don't want to leave but I need to know if Omar's back. Not knowing is driving me crazy and making it more and more difficult for me to focus…And everyone knows that her highness is the queen of perfection, so, this not being able to focus thing could possibly be a problem…

"Damn, but what if he's not here? This was supposed to be our new beginning. And I don't even wanna think that we aren't going to have the mind-blowing, toe-curling, headboard bangin', who's-your-daddy sex that I've been waiting for and fantas …."

Wh.. why is everyone looking like I have three friggin' heads? Were the quantities that I suggested too much? I just told your daddy to buy two groups minimum for the headboard… Daddy? Headboard? Oh shit! Please tell me that I didn't say that aloud! Damn, damn and damn!!!!

I hear Gretchen's voice, and there's no way in hell that I want to hear what she's saying…

"…Cydney, it's clear that you have something else on your mind so Kyle will take over while you take the time to clear your uh, shall I say, thoughts and whatever else that you need to do."

I turn to look at Kyle who looks like a friggin' baby deer caught between a pair of bright ass headlights as he slowly gets up and walks toward me. I can't get out of here fast enough. And I refuse to look at Gretchen… I hear her highness' voice but my head refuses to turn in that direction. I start to leave and once I'm at the door, I turn back to thank everyone but nothing comes out so I just force a half smile and leave.

As soon as I get into the corridor, I let my guard down and immediately feel weak before collapsing against the soft, suede covered wall for some much needed support. After taking a few minutes to compose myself and regain control of my breathing, I try not to think about what appears to be my first career faux pas and fingers crossed, my last.

Once I get it together, I walk toward the reception area where Zoe is chatting with a salesman. He hands her some materials then leaves. Zoe looks up as she hears me approaching.

"Cyd, that was quick! How'd it go?"

"Good," I lie, "Kyle is actually finishing up as we speak. Got anything? Any messages for me?" I ask, probably sounding like some love-struck teenager waiting for that infamous call to be asked to the school prom. Well, this is not the prom and all I want to hear right now is that Omar is waiting in the company lounge or at the *very* least, that he called.

"Just these two," she tells me while handing the messages to me. I snatch them, not meaning to and quickly read them only to have my heart take a dive. Nada, zilch, nothing, not one word from Omar…not one.

Six

"Whoa, hold up! Cydney Michelle, *headboard bangin', who's your daddy?* Dang gurl, I never knew you had it like that!"

"Do we really need to have this conversation? Don't you think that yesterday was embarrassing enough? And, for the last time, it was a stupid *fantasy*! Robyn, how many times do I have to tell you that I dreamt that whenever Omar and I first make love, that it would not only be extremely passionate but *beyond* incredible and like nothing I've ever experienced. And for whatever reason that stupid fantasy took a life of its own yesterday after Omar's disappearance. And unfortunately for me, that little *dream-turned-fantasy* malformed into a friggin' nightmare when *it* decided yesterday to go public in front of a live audience. With *my boss* front row and smack dab in the center!!"

"Uh-h I don't know, Cyd. It didn't sound so *little* to me, you little vixen you!" Robyn laughed. "But seriously, gurl, don't beat yourself up; everyone fantasizes about incredible sex! Including your gurl Gretchen! Now, all dreams and fantasies aside, gurl please tell me that you didn't really walk out on your *own* presentation for a division *you* created over a damn *man*?"

"You do know that you have a special gift, don't you? That special gift of always making things sound so much worse than what they really are! Listening to you, makes it sound like I'm one of *those MMCF* women that would put her job in jeopardy," I tell Robyn as I press the speaker button and hook my cordless phone to the top of my low-rise Gap jeans.

"You weren't before, but you have to admit, in this case you did put *Mister-I-just-waltzed-back-into-your-life*, before your J-O-B or in your case your C-A-R-E-E-R!"

"Robyn, the man disappeared, one minute he was with me and the next minute he was gone!" I explain while opening my closet doors. "*That's* what you call C-O-N-C-E-R-N so please don't even go there with the *my-man-comes-first* crap!!"

"Disappeared? Did you say disappeared? Gurl, that man didn't disappear, his ass LEFT with your company's model, and a gorgeous model at that!"

"You don't have to remind me, I was there, remember?"

"Damn right I remember that's why I'm telling you to F-O-R-G-E-T his golden brown playa ass!"

I knew I shouldn't have told Robyn what happened. At this point I don't even know what to think anymore. But I can't argue with her about my needing to put Omar out of my mind, which is what I'm trying to do. I hate it when she's right, even though I shouldn't because usually what she tells me is something that I already know but just need to hear someone say. Robyn is a good friend and always has been. And my girl, bottom line, calls it the way she sees it! She might be a tad rough around the edges, but her intentions are always good. I start pulling clothes out of the closet while making mental notes of possible coordinating accessories.

"Look, I hear what you're saying. It's just that I'm tired of feeling this emptiness, you know, like there's something missing from my life. And when Omar came back, I kinda hoped that the emptiness would be filled. I mean I really wanted us to work. But now this whole Tasha thing happened just when it seemed as though we were getting back on track. Now, it looks like I'm back to square one. And Robyn, just for the record, since it seems as though your memory is short, *playa* is not at all what *we* got from Omar when we all first met."

"Start-up playa, undercover playa, I-*don't-look-like-a-player* playa, gurl, I'm just calling it the way I see it *now, today and in the present!* And playa or no playa, you got to move on! What your ass really needs is a damn distraction. And I know exactly the distraction you need to take your mind off ole *brown eyes*. Throw some clothes on; I'm coming over to get you!"

"Excuse me?"

"Look, Cyd, the last time something like this happened you refused to get out of bed and Shaye and I had to come over and literally knock the damn door in and drag your depressed ass out of that high-thread-count Egyptian cotton pit! So, get dressed, I'll be there in twenty minutes!"

"Thanks Robyn, but I'm okay this time," I tell her taking a deep breath before continuing. "It's obvious I had a slight relapse yesterday, but that was then. I realize now that I can't let my emotions control me like I did back then, or for that matter, like I did yesterday. And girl, it's not to say that I won't lose it again, because I just might. And it's not to say that I'm not hurting, because I am. And it's *definitely* not to say that I don't want to strangle his brown ass, because I do. I really, really do! But Robyn, if I've learned nothing else, I've learned that I have to pull the lessons from my life experiences and apply them to the present. And another thing that I've learned is that if this is who he really is, then it's better that I find out now than later. Besides, if it's meant to be, it will be. And believe it or not, for once, I'm actually okay with that."

"Well, damn who dropped your ass off at Dr. Phil's boot camp?"

"Ha, ha. No girl, it wasn't boot camp; this is the *we-meet-once-a-month-book-crap* in action," I tell her in a rather impressive, if I do say so myself, Robyn impersonation.

"Touche!" she says laughing. "Well, whatever it was, good for you. I just thought a fun distraction would do your ass some good."

"And you're absolutely right which is why *my ass* is packing as we speak!"

"Packing? Where to now, *Deepuck's* retreat?"

"Oh, you're on a roll tonight! No, Florida. Remember I told you Milanya's thing was coming up? Well, it's this weekend."

"Oh, okay, cool. Now that's what I call good timing!"

"Yep, you can say that again. She called last week to make sure that I was still coming and girl, after the day I had yesterday, getting out of New York is *exactly* the distraction that my butt needs! Plus you *know* anything Anya has her hand in is going to be worth traveling for. She and Que planned the whole weekend from beginning to end starting with their guests' choice of an airport limo pick up service or complimentary car rental and ending with a VIP outdoor R&B concert!"

"Remind me again why I'm not going."

"Uh…because she's *my* old college roommate and not yours. Oh and FYI, the man's name is *Deepak NOT Deepuck!*"

"What-evver O.J…. By the way, there was a part missing from your story."

"Whaaat?" I ask impatiently ready to hang up.

"Uh, the end! You never did tell me what Gretchen said when you went in earlier today."

"That's because her highness wasn't there. She left for Europe at 6:30 this morning. And left a note on my desk saying we'll meet when she returns next Tuesday," I tell her while reading the printed shoe descriptions on my neatly stacked shoe boxes. *Hmm, if I just limit my outfits to two or three base colors then I will only need two pairs of shoes, three at the most, plus of course the ones that I'll wear on the plane.*

"Was this a scheduled trip?"

"Yeah, she was originally flying on the same flight as Donna but at the last minute, Donna decided to take her private jet along with her daughter."

"Well, did Lyle say anything or did he go too?"

"KYLE!" I yell into the phone while juggling four shoeboxes in my arms, "His name is Kyle for the umpteenth time and no, he didn't go; he was in the office. His take was that the buyers really liked the samples and that they wanted to first discuss it amongst themselves before calling Gretchen with an order."

"Kyle, Lyle, whatever. Just keep me posted!!"

"Yeah, I'll know something when Gretchie gets back… Okay, Rob, I need to finish packing so I'll call you when I get back from Orlando."

"Okay. Just try not to think about anything that happened and have some fun. By the time you return I'm pretty sure I'll have some stories for you from my online dating chronicles."

"Good luck with that," I tell her while smiling, "and don't hurt *nobody*!"

We hang up as I lay the open shoe boxes on the floor. As I sit on the edge of the bed trying to decide which shoes to take, my mind drifts to Omar and everything that happened yesterday.

Why can't men just be open and up front with their intentions and with what they want? If they want to date several women at once, then just say it! I think everyone deserves to know what they're getting into when they meet someone new.

Maybe we need a law to mandate that all men must come into their next relationship with papers! Papers along the line of, *Relationship Resume*s and *Letters of Recommendation*, or in most cases, *Condemnation Summaries* from all of their exes! And all of them must be *NOTORIZED!* Yeah, and the exes could permanently attach or clip the resume, L.O.R.'s or C.S.'s to their ex-boyfriend's coat or shirt sleeves like moms do with their children's mittens!!! "I LOVE IT!" I yell and laugh while falling back on my bed as I picture men everywhere walking around city streets, malls, restaurants, bars etc. flapping like little penguins with envelopes attached to the bottom of their sleeves! Flap, flap, flap, FLAP, FLAP, flap, FLAP, flap…flap!

Seven

Thank God I packed everything in my carry-on so now I don't have to deal with that whole baggage claim scene. Going through that intense scrutiny at the security check is enough drama for one day.

It's 9:30 Wednesday night and my flight just landed at the Orlando International Airport. Fortunately, I got a complimentary upgrade to first class, so I was the second one off the plane and was able to make it to the passenger pick-up area in record time, even with a quick pit-stop to the bathroom.

As soon as I walk outside in the balmy 78-degree weather, I see Milanya's metallic army green Range Rover. She waves at me to make sure that I see her. Milanya looks like an exotic princess from a faraway land. Her mom is Black and American Indian and her dad is Italian. Suffice it to say, the girl is gorgeous!

Milanya and her daughters' father, Quentin, have been together for eight years. Milanya had hoped that she and Que would marry several years after they first met, but Quentin's first marriage ended so badly that he swore that he would never *ever* get married again. Que was playing professional basketball, initially in Italy, then in the States when his three year marriage ended at the height of his career. It was widely reported that his wife couldn't deal with the groupies and the "alleged" affairs so she filed for divorce. And according to the tabloids, she took his butt to the cleaners then hung his ass out to dry. Que and his ex have a son, Jax, who's ten and as cute as he can be. He looks a lot like his dad who, not surprisingly, is quite handsome standing at about 6'5" and bald by choice — which I might add, on him, looks extremely attractive. Milanya and Que's girls, Kai and Nico, are six and four and both are the spitting image of their mother, beautiful and exotic princesses-in-training.

"Hey girl," I yell as Milanya gets out of her army truck to greet me.

"Hey Cyd, I'm so glad you're here," she beams as we hug. "For a minute, I thought you were going to try to surprise me by bringing Jordyn with you. You know, how you always like to surprise everyone!" she says while hopping her 5'6" shapely 127-pound body back into the driver's seat just as the airport traffic cop's car slowly passes us. I throw my bags in the back then jump into the passenger's seat.

"No, unfortunately my sister couldn't make it. Remember, her husband had a business trip in Cincinnati but at the last minute it was rescheduled. And he, rather *they* wanted to take advantage of the extra days to spend time together."

"Well, I'm sorry Jordyn couldn't make it because I know how you hoped that this weekend would help bring the two of you back to the way you used to be."

Milanya weaves in and out of the airport traffic and onto I-528 like a seasoned NASCAR driver.

"Yeah, it would have been nice especially since our priorities have us on different schedules in different cities. But thanks anyway and I really appreciate you extending the invitation to her. But girl enough of Jordyn and me! I can't even begin to tell you how much I am sooooo looking forward to this weekend! *If you only knew!* So, tell me who all is coming?"

"I know, me too, it should be a lot of fun! We invited about fifteen friends in the area and three couples from out of town who are also staying at the house. There's Liza and Jon, David and his new girlfriend and you remember Kenya and Yousef. They met us in New York last year?"

"Yes, I remember, we all went to *Tao* for dinner."

"Exactly! And Cyd, you're going to *love* Liza and her husband, Jon. He left his six figure job at Disney to follow his dream of being a stand-up comedian. Needless to say, Liza wasn't too thrilled about it, but she's coming around….slowly. Oh and Que's friend, Ty came in this morning from Italy. And by the way, Que put *him* in the guest house so, if it's okay, you'll be our first guest to stay in the pool house since we had it renovated. *Cecil Hayes* did the interior. I think I told you, she's the one that did Wesley's house here in Florida."

"Yeah, I remember seeing her work in *Architectural Digest.* And girl, please, don't be ridiculous, the pool house will be fine. In fact, I can't wait to stay in it. Hey, and if the mood hits me, girl, I may even take a little midnight dip! So, what's the game plan for tomorrow?"

"Well, I thought the three of us would have breakfast first then you and I can run a few errands."

"Oh good. Que is joining us for breakfast?"

"No, Ty is, Que has to work."

Eight

I open my eyes and am surrounded by hues of cocoa and seafoam with white accents and splashes of mango. It's Thursday morning and I'm in Milanya and Que's pool house which is reminiscent of a beautiful Caribbean villa. I notice various textures throughout the pool quarters, which seem to mimic similar textures outside as I look through the white framed French doors.

I'm still in bed, which, surprisingly, is an incredibly comfortable, sleep sofa sandwiched between a pair of white, stacked vintage Louis Vuitton suitcases and a white patent antique shoe trunk, each multi-purposing as end tables.

On the LV suitcase table, there is a weathered white wicker basket filled with all kinds of goodies, from copies of this month's *O Magazine* and *Elle Decor* magazines, along with bottled water to my favorite Jo Malone scented candle and Olay make-up removal wipes. Milanya even put a *Bose* docking station on the table for my iPod. That girl thinks of everything and definitely has my vote for the hostess with the *mostess!*

Directly across from the sleep sofa and table is a beautiful white and taupe-ish stone fireplace. And above it are three very large sepia tone photos of the girls on the beach in white wooden frames which are embellished with varying sizes of starfish.

The French doors lead out to a cozy sitting area which is about twenty yards from the pool. As I look out the double doors, I see Nico and Kai running toward the entrance with their shoulder-length pony tails bobbing up and down. As soon as they reach the doors, they knock then enter before I can even get a chance to tell them to come in.

"WAKE UP, Auntie Cyd, wake up!" yells Nico as she runs over to hug me.

"Hi Auntie Cyd," Kai joins in as she jumps on the sofa bed and hugs me too.

I smile while struggling to sit up so that I can hug my adorable godchildren. "Hi, sweeties, how are you? I snuck in your room last night to say hi but you guys were fast asleep!"

"You could have woken us up," Nico said.

Just then, Giselle, the girls' au pair, knocks on the door and I motion for her to come in. Giselle became the girls' French au pair by default. Milanya had her heart set on hiring an Italian au pair so she could help the girls with their Italian, but the wait list for one was a year. Que suggested that they go with Giselle; one, because she was available and two, so the girls could also learn to speak French.

"This way," he reasoned, "when we travel to Europe the girls will be tri-lingual. Needless to say, Milanya agreed.

"Bonjour mademoiselle Cydney."

"Bonjour Giselle. Comment allez-vous?"

"Tres bien, merci. Kai et Nico avez- vous donné le message de votre mere à Tante Cyd?"

"Oh, Mommy said she'll be ready in forty minutes," they both say in unison.

"Now, come on girls, you said hello. Now we need to let Auntie Cyd get dressed."

The girls jump down from the bed and start running toward the door.

"SEE YA LATER GATOR," yells Nico.

"BYE AUNTIE CYD," Kai yells with her sister.

"IN AWHILE CROCODILES!" I yell back.

They leave and I check my phone to see what time it is and realize that I never turned it back on when the plane landed. As soon as I hit the **ON** button, it beeps as the message screen pops up showing that I have two messages. As I hit the voicemail button while pulling together some clothes, I'm secretly hoping that one of the calls is from Omar even though I promised myself not to think about him while I'm here.

"Hi Cyd, it's Shaye! One of Jackson's friends saw your photo and wants to meet you! Call and let me know if you're interested!"

To save this message press 9, to delete press 7. **BEEP**.

I smile as I press 9. **BEEP**.

"Hey girl, it's Robyn. Having fun yet? If you get a minute, call me. I got a hit from my profile on NoLosers.com, gurl, this dude's name is Chauncey! What Black guy's name is freakin' Chauncey? Hell, for that matter, what White guy's name is Chauncey? And who's his damn mother, freakin' Chauncella? Gurl, I am not feelin' this…. I don't think I'm gonna go. How will that shit sound, Robyn and Chauncey? Oh hell no! So call me and let me know what you think. I shouldn't go, right? Ok, have fun. Call me!"

To save this message press 9, to delete press 7. **BEEP.**

Laughing, I press 7 then jump into the shower.

Nine

During the ride to the restaurant, Milanya gives me the low-down on Ty, who's following us in a rental car. Que and Ty (which by the way, is short for Tyson, *not* Tyrone) played in the NBA together; Ty was a rookie when Que was one of the top players in the league. During that time in their careers they not only played with and against one another but also with and against Michael Jordan, *my* all-time favorite (MJ has been my favorite since I was a young girl when I watched all of the games with my dad. Whomever he rooted for was the team or person I rooted for! And now, as an adult and still loving basketball, MJ is *still* my all-time favorite!). Ty played in the NBA for about seven seasons and now coaches basketball in Italy where he's been living for the past three years. That's all I know about Ty. Milanya doesn't offer any personal information about him and I don't ask.

We pull into the restaurant's parking lot and as we head in, Milanya introduces us. Ty is fine. Not pretty, Rick Fox fine or gorgeous, Boris Ko fine but that type of fine that can't be defined by looks but by the way a person carries himself with a certain commanding presence that cannot and *will not* be ignored. He's a beautiful Morris Chestnut brown, 6'3" with an athletic build and deep, dark brown eyes that as Robyn would say, not only speak to you but, baby, say *your* name! Although, I have to admit as fine as he is, it's really his *smooth-as-velvet* voice that pretty much got me at hello *and* unexpectedly now, has me in slight state of confusion. I'm not sure if this is a physical or romantic connection. Or, maybe even something else. All I know is that when our eyes first met, there was something there. I don't quite know the words to describe what that something was but whatever *it* was, I'm pretty sure he felt *it* too. My first thought was *hmm, this could be kinda nice* but then that "nice" wore off real fast, almost quicker than it came. Maybe I just need to re-focus. I didn't come down here to meet anyone, platonic, romantic or otherwise. Too much has happened in the last few days and although I swore that I wouldn't think about Omar, it's hard to think of anyone or anything else. Besides, my head is not ready for any more drama. And this weekend is supposed to be about hanging out and having fun with my girl, her family and friends, the way we always do. Period.

But just for the record, as far as Mr. Ty goes, I wasn't reading more into something than what's there. Although, I know women who do that all the time. Woman meets Man, (or in some cases, Woman meets Woman) then there is an attraction of some sort and within nano seconds of meeting that person the woman attaches her first name to the man's last name first, on paper, then out loud to hear how it sounds. Then soon after, she envisions walking down the aisle in her Vera Wang dress. Followed by finding the perfect home in a good school district for the 2.5 kids she *hopes* they're going to have! Puh-leez. And the poor guy (or gal) barely said *boo*! Well, *this* isn't that but *what* it is exactly, I'm still not sure but I do know, it *ain't* that!

I just need to shift my butt into *going with the flow* mode. Hmmm, or maybe just hook Ty up with Robyn. She's always been a sucker for men who challenge her and Ty, being a former NBA player, seems like he could easily give a woman or two a run for their money. But then on the other hand, knowing Robyn she could and probably would just as easily turn the tables on him and sop his brown ass up in some gravy and tear his butt up like a homemade buttermilk biscuit! And then smile, while licking those lips and say, "Mmmm ummm good!"

The hostess seats us and takes our order. Fortunately for our stomachs, we all knew what we wanted before we even sat down. Milanya sits next to Ty who is sitting across from me. Completely shunning any semblance of small talk, we somehow get on the somewhat controversial subject of Black athletes dating and/or marrying White women.

"Shouldn't people, athletes included, date and marry whomever they choose regardless of color?" Ty asks.

"Well, personally I don't have any issues with Black people dating White people or Blue people either for that matter. But I will tell you what bothers me in the same way chalk screeching across a blackboard does and that's the people, athletes included, that only date *exclusively* outside of their race. Personally, I think those people have some serious, deep-rooted issues that I'm pretty sure stems from their childhood. And if that's the case and it probably is, then they need to *run, not walk* to the nearest therapist!"

Ty laughs as the waitress returns with a basket full of sweet potato and buttermilk biscuits along with strawberry jam and whipped pecan toasted butter. I help myself to a sweet potato biscuit and pecan butter while Ty slowly reaches for the buttermilk biscuit. For a minute the way he hesitated, I thought for sure he was going to ask the waitress to bring him a bowl of gravy! Sop! Sop!

"I agree with a lot of what you're saying, Cyd," Milanya begins as the waitress returns with our coffee and teas, "but my take has always been that *some* of the players seem like they believe that White women are some type of reward or prize once they reach the professional level."

Milanya takes a sip of her latte. "It seems like a lot of them think that now that they have a few dollars, that that puts them on a level which makes them too good to deal with Black women, which to me sends the negative message that they believe that White women are better. And because of that belief, they also think that being with a White woman, in turn, makes *them* look better, which some athletes feel goes hand-in-hand with their new level of success and celebrity status."

"I hear what you're saying but keep in mind, Anya, that most Black women don't take any crap, from their men," I tell her, "and from what I've heard from several of my Black male friends, is that White women are a lot easier to deal with because they pretty much go with the flow with few or none of the interrogational sessions we Black women have *allegedly* been known not only to have, but have initiated." Milanya shoots a *girlfriend-puh-leeze* look to me.

"Look, all I'm sayin' is… that it might be more about men not wanting to be interrogated about their actions and less about White women being *supposedly* better," I tell her.

Ty looks a little stunned at Milanya's comments, I'm sure because of her biracial background, but what Ty doesn't realize is that although she doesn't look like it, Milanya has always considered herself 100% Black.

Not to disregard her father or grandparents but Milanya has just identified more with her mother's struggles from day one and has pretty much taken them over vicariously. Her mother, as a girl had dated a boy who later became a professional football player and then, a year later, dumped her for a White woman after they had been together for eleven, long years!

However, with that said, Milanya's Italian roots are equally important to her, just as the language itself is.

A language which she has spoken fluently since the age of five and is now teaching to both of her girls. She even has plans to open an Italian restaurant once Kai and Nico are a little older. And from a fashion stand point, there's no one who supports the Italian fashion designers the way that girl does!!! Armani, Prada, Dolce & Gabbana, Gucci and countless others are all well represented in that girl's closet. But I digress, bottom line as far as mindset and self-identity go, the girl is all B-L-A-C-K!

The waitress brings our food which looks as good as it smells and we don't waste any time digging in. As Ty swallows a forkful of pancakes, I notice a small drip of maple syrup seductively rolling down the corner of his perfectly shaped mouth. He slowly catches it with the tip of his tongue before talking. *Mmmm!*

"Just let me say that, I had and still have friends in the league that date White women as well as some that have dated and married Black women. And well, as far as myself, I pretty much just go with the flow. So, ladies, let me just state here and now for the proverbial record that I, Tyson James Banks think *all* women are beautiful no matter what color they are…present company included!"

Milanya and I look at each other with a half-smile and half-smirk. That's pretty much all we could muster after Ty's little *don't-blame-my-ass* soliloquy.

So after hearing Ty's *love-all-women-of-the-rainbow* speech, I'm now even more convinced that he is one with the ladies which would without a doubt give Robyn the challenge that her crazy butt thrives on. Two problems though, one, Robyn's not here; I am and two, I *still* don't know *jack* about Ty's personal life!

Ten

Initially, I just thought this was another room until I saw the big, humongous citrus tree in the center and then looked up and saw the beautiful, open, moon lit sky.

Everyone who's staying at the house arrived earlier this afternoon and now we're all going out for a night on the town. Most of us are waiting in the atrium, which is located in the center of the house just off the foyer. It's my favorite room in the house because although it has four walls, one of which is stacked stone, it's actually *outside.* Outside in the sense that it doesn't have a roof, but as atriums go, the only way to enter is through the interior of the house. Milanya's inspiration for the design of the atrium was the lobby of an exclusive Turks and Caicos hotel in which she and Que stayed in several years ago. Milanya loved the hotel's lobby so much that she flew back to the island with her mother and shot what would be the equivalent of six rolls of film on her digital camera to show the design consultant who assisted her with the atrium's interior.

While on the island, she also asked Leighton, the head bartender at the hotel, to show her how to make two of his most requested drinks (personally, I think it was Milanya who did most of the requesting). He did and now, she can make them both, blindfolded. Tonight, she pre-mixed several pitchers of each which she has set up on a long, Asian ancestor table (which she had weather-proofed once she and the consultant decided to put it in the atrium). Meanwhile, Liza is multi-purposing the table as a bar while playing both barmaid and the ever-loving, supportive wife. She's serving us Leighton's delicious pomegranate mojitos and kiwi coladas while hubby Jon tells us about his comedic debut in New York where he recently opened for Wanda Sykes.

Jon is actually pretty funny in a *Chris Rock meets Bernie Mac* kinda way and I'm actually looking forward to seeing him perform the next time he's in New York. And who knows, maybe I can even get Robyn to bring ole Chauncey!

In the meantime, Que is trying and has been for the past ten minutes to get everybody downstairs and out the door. At this point, most of us are in the atrium and David and his girlfriend are the only ones who have not come down yet. And now, Milanya just slipped into the back, probably to give last minute instructions to Giselle for the girls.

Jon's been telling various stories which have segued into an entire comedy routine for the last fifteen minutes and for the *entire* time, although I was laughing, my feet were and still are killing me. That's what I get for trying to wear a 9 ½ when I'm really a size 10. The pain is insane! And unfortunately, this is the only pair that I brought to go with this outfit in my successful and desperate attempt to pack lightly. Now, I only have one outfit for each day, so even if I did have time to change, I would be short one outfit. I guess I'm definitely S-O-L!

Yousef and Jon both have rental cars, plus Milanya's army truck and Que's Sport Bentley, so any two or three should be enough for the nine of us. I'm not counting Ty because when he was at the house earlier, he told us that he had a 6:30 meeting so he and possibly several of Que's other friends will meet us later. Once Milanya returns, Que heads to the front door and gestures for us to follow (he must have gotten my telepathic message, either that or he can see how miserable I am in these torture chambers encasing my feet), just as David and his girlfriend, Ikea (yes, like the store) come downstairs.

"Sorry about that guys," David says flatly.

Ikea follows behind David while adjusting her loud, clanging, low-slung chain belt. Que nods as he opens the door and we all start heading out.

"Ooo, Cydney those are some bad ass shoes!" Ikea shrieks.

"Thanks!!" I say while checking out her feet, which I'm sure had to be at least size 10 1/2 if not 11!

Then under my breath added, "Glad you like them, do you wanna switch?"

Eleven

As we all walk out the door, all of our mouths drop. Wow! Smack dab in the middle of the driveway is a larger-than-life gold, stretch hummer which could easily be on a JFK runway prepping for take-off! Que and Milanya always do things in style and it looks like tonight is no exception.

"Way to go bro-tha-a," Jon says proudly while admiring our golden chariot.

"Hot damn, Que. You always do things first class, man, always." Yousef grins while hi-fiving Que.

The rest of us are speechless but eager and ready to jump in and get this party started. The chauffer opens one of the limo's six doors and the ladies go in first, followed by the men. The interior is so big; it looks like a small New York nightclub. Just as I get both feet in, my mind immediately goes into APM (Automatic Perusal Mode) and instantaneously reveals front to back, door-to-door carpet throughout, fiber optic lighting, padded cream leather couches (not seating mind you but *couches*), four flat screen televisions, two of which are large screen complete with AV plug ins, an on-screen laser karaoke set-up, a twenty foot split mahogany bar with matching low stools, two sun-roofs and a banging, stereo surround sound system. Que must've had them pre-program the system's iPod because as soon as we step in, it starts, spitting out oldies from back in the day.

While Que's taking care of the music, Yousef is happily playing bartender, making drinks for everyone. The music sounds so good and the acoustics are so unbelievable that for a minute I wonder as I glance over to the bar if somehow *Dru Hill* slipped in the limo without being seen. Once Yousef makes sure everyone has a drink, he motions for Que to lower the volume while he tries to get everyone's attention.

"Before we go any further, I just want to take time out now to make a toast to our hosts. Everyone please raise your glasses. Here's to Que and Milanya for inviting all of us into your beautiful house for the weekend and making us feel at home. For those of you that don't know, Que and I go way back and Kenya and I consider ourselves blessed to have Que, Milanya and their two beautiful daughters in our lives. And I'm sure I speak for everyone when I say thank you to you both. We're all looking forward to what we know will be a wonderful weekend. Love you guys!"

After everyone says a few "Here ye, Here ye's" and takes a sip of the their drink of choice, Que does a man-to-man, hand/arm gesture to Yousef, (that I assume from the expression on his face translates to *thank you* in some sort of top secret man code) and then pumps up the music as we talk, drink and laugh throughout the rest of the ride to the restaurant. We're having so much fun, I would be just as content staying in the limo, *with my shoes off* and just ride through the city for the rest of the night.

Just as Kenya attempts to point out the song choices for the laser karaoke, our golden chariot turns onto International Drive, then slowly follows the long, illuminated driveway leading to the restaurant. Milanya moves toward the front of the limo and gets everyone's attention.

"Okay, everyone, we're here! Que and I just want to welcome you to the *Texas de Brazil Steakhouse!* We love this restaurant, which is why we wanted to share it with you. So, before we go in I just want to give you a quick overview; for starters, they have an unbelievable *fifty* item salad menu with everything that you could possibly imagine plus more and for you cheese lovers, Liz and David, they have delicious right-out-of-the-oven baked Brazilian cheese bread. *Texas de Brazil* is known for their delicious grilled to perfection meat and since none of us are vegetarians, we can all take advantage of and enjoy their sizzling Angus beef, pork, chicken and Brazilian sausage, all of which are grilled to your specifications over a roaring, open, flame grill. And for the seafood lovers, Cyd and Kenya, they also have cold-water lobster and a succulent Brazilian shrimp cocktail. As for sides, you really can't go wrong, but Que and I especially love the garlic mashed potatoes and the sweet fried bananas.

And Yousef, if we have time after dinner, they have a great cigar room where they offer hand-rolled Cubans rolled by Miguel, the restaurant's on-site cigar specialist. Then for those of us who aren't into cigars, my personal after dinner pleasure is the new glass Martini bar. So, let's keep this party going and go break some bread!"

Twelve

The chauffer opens the door as we all climb out of the limo, most *still* salivating from Milanya's mouthwatering overview. As we enter the dimly lit restaurant we are immediately greeted by Sonja who leads us toward the back to a private dining room. Milanya asked the couples not to sit next to one another and for us to mix it up by alternating man, woman, man, woman. Milanya loves doing this when some of her and Que's guests don't know one another so that they (we) can talk to someone that they (we) might not have had the opportunity to converse with otherwise. Just as we finish Anya's little *boy-girl-man-woman* seating arrangement, Ty walks in.

"Hey, hey, hey how's everyone?"

"Glad you could make it man," Que says.

The rest of us smile and greet him as he takes the only seat available which just happens to be between Milanya and me. Now, with him on my right, I'm happily sandwiched between Ty and Jon.

The room is tastefully decorated with an obvious Spanish influence, including the small bar at the end of the room. Our dining table is a large rectangular, rustic oak table with chunky, ornately carved legs adorned with over-sized antique bronze nail heads.

We have two waiters, a bartender plus Sonja, the private room coordinator. As I continue to look around the room, I notice that the artwork on the reddish venetian plastered walls is also Spanish with an impressionist touch. Shortly after we are settled in our seats, a few of the men get up and gather at the bar just as Mario, the executive chef walks in and directly over to Que.

"Welcome Quentin! How are you? I see you brought a few friends with you. But where is your beautiful Milanya?"

"Hola Mario, I'm here," Anya says smiling as she gets up and walks toward Mario, "It's good to see you!"

Mario bows as a British commoner would for the Queen of England then gently kisses Milanya's hand while smiling from ear to ear. Que wastes no time breaking that little scene up as he begins introducing Mario to each of us.

"It's a pleasure to have you all here, and if there is anything at all you need or want, please feel free to let me, Sonja or any of my staff know." Mario then motions to the bartender. "Eduardo, *Caipirinha's* for everyone!"

Thirteen

Before our drinks are served, compliments of Mario, Que tells us that *Caipirinha* (pronounced kai-pur-reen-yah), is a popular Brazilian drink as well as the restaurant's signature cocktail.

"And don't let its appearance fool you," Milanya adds, "it may look like a mojito but the taste is somewhat different because there isn't any mint or rum. Instead of rum it's made with a Brazilian product called cachaça (pronounced ka-sha-za)."

I'd be willing to bet that Milanya not only *has* the recipe but probably pulled a *Martha Stewart* and already pre-mixed shook and chilled several pitchers for tomorrow's barbeque. Even though I know Anya says the taste is different, I'm eager to try one because it still looks like and in my mind will still taste somewhat like a mojito. However, *one* is the operative word since I am *already* at my drink limit for the night but being the ever so appreciative guest that I am, I would never want to insult Mario so after one Caipirinha, I am done, kaput, FINITO!!!

Meanwhile, Ty walks back over to the table from the bar and sits down then smiles at me thinking *no telling what* and then I smile back thinking *damn, your ass is fine!* The waiters are standing at each end of the table like tall, *Banderas* toy soldiers waiting for us to put our menus down so that they can come over and take our orders. Once the menus are down and all the orders are taken, Milanya hands David a small pack of red mini envelopes and asks him to take one and then pass the rest around the table. Once we all have an envelope she explains what they are.

"All of your envelopes have a card inside with a question on it. Please do not share your question with anyone until it's your turn to read and answer your question. Cydney and her friend do this at their monthly ETF gatherings in New York and the questions….."

"What's an ETF?" Ikea interrupts.

I jump in before giving Anya a chance to answer, "It's an acronym for *Every Third Friday* which is when we meet," I tell her.

"Right, so as I was saying," Milanya continues, "the questions, which topics range from sex to politics, are a great tool in helping everyone to get to know one another. When I was in New York, Cyd took me to one of the ETF gatherings that she and her friend Marcus hosted. It was a lot of fun so I thought it would be a good way for us to start the weekend. Sooo, it looks like everyone has an envelope. Please open them, and when it's your turn, read your question aloud and answer it."

We all open our red envelopes and silently read our questions.

"Before we start, other than the one written on your card, are there any questions?" asks Milanya.

"Yes, does it matter if we tell the truth or not?"

"Cyd, why don't you answer that?"

I smile at Milanya, then answer Ikea. "Yes, the whole point is to get to know one another and if we don't tell the truth then that will defeat the purpose."

"Okay cool, let's do it!!"

"Alright, so I'll go first," Milanya says as she begins to read her question.

"What's the best gift you've given?"

"Hmm, one of the most memorable things that jumps out at me was last Christmas Eve when Que and I took the girls to Orlando Memorial Hospital to deliver Christmas gifts to terminally ill and post-surgery children whose stay extended over the holidays.

It was important to Que and me to instill a sense of *it's better to give than to receive* in the girls at an early age and we felt what better time to teach this than at Christmas. It's ironic because my intent was focused on the girls and their experience but just seeing the looks on the children's faces after the girls gave them the gifts, it not only affected Kai and Nico, it affected me as well. In fact, it was life-altering."

"But you've always given generously to charities," Kenya comments.

"Yes but my community contributions and charity donations have always been in the form of a check or clothes donations to Goodwill or local homeless shelters. But now, after seeing the indescribable joy we gave these children, up close and personal, Que and I have made it a point to contribute regularly to the orphanage with Kai and Nico. The smiles on those little faces and in their hearts was worth much more than anything I presently own or could ever buy. And truth be told, as wonderful as it was for those children it was twenty times as wonderful for us as a family!"

Jon shakes his head and says, "Damn girl, what's next — excerpts from Will Smith's movie, *Seven Pounds*?"

Everyone laughs except Ikea who I presume didn't see the movie.

"Anya, thank you for that, it was very nice" I tell her.

"Yes, I agree! I think it's great that you and Que are instilling traits of sharing and giving in the girls so early in their lives," adds Liza, "And I'm sure Kai and Nico saw how much it meant to those children."

"Thanks, guys. Yes, in fact Kai and Nico can't stop talking about the toys that they want to give to the children this Christmas! So, yes, it was a great experience, that not only taught the family an important lesson but one that will now become part of our holiday tradition. Ok, who's next, Ty, Yousef?"

"I'll go," Yousef says as he pulls out his question.

"If you could have dinner or spend an evening with anyone, who would it be?"

"Hell, that's easy, my man Barack Obama! No matter how you look at it, no matter how you feel about him and no matter what your views are, the same as his or different from his, this prez is going down in history and not only because of the obvious, but aside from his many achievements, my man has transcended color and party barriers and not too many presidents can put *that* on their political resume! It would definitely be an honor to sit down and have dinner with that brotha."

The waiters bring our salads, which look incredible. A third waiter rolls a cart filled with additional veggies, fruits, nuts and any other topping that you could possibly imagine for our salads. There's so much to choose from that it's almost impossible for me to decide what I want. As we all eye the toppings and make our selections from the cart, Milanya announces that we can probably squeeze in two more questions before our dinner is served.

"Ok, Ty," she said. "Why don't you read yours?"

Smiling as he finishes chewing, Ty reads his question.

" What was your most embarrassing moment?"

"Well, coincidently it happened at Que's and Milanya's, say probably about a year or so ago."

Que shakes his head and gulps the last of his drink. The waiter quickly takes the empty glass and walks over to Eduardo for a prompt refill.

"Que and I had gone to the Orlando/Cleveland game then afterwards for a couple of drinks. Later, I drove back to the guest house while Que went to the main house. As I drove up the gravel driveway I saw this gigantic rodent at the door trying to get into the damn house. Let me tell y'all, this thing's front legs were pushing the front door and look, I'm not gonna lie; I straight out freaked cause I had never seen anything that looked like that thing! So, I immediately call Que at the house from *inside* the car and Milanya answers the phone and I tell her that, THERE'S SOME SORT OF LONG-TAILED MONSTER TRYING TO GET INTO THE GUEST HOUSE. TELL QUE TO BRING A GUN!

So, she calmly asks '*Well, what is it?*'

I yell, I DON'T KNOW, JUST TELL QUE TO BRING A KNIFE, GUN ANYTHING, NOW!

So, approximately three minutes later, Milanya comes *casually strolling* over to my car in her bare feet carrying a damn BROOM! Hey and not one of those big, heavy-duty janitorial brooms but a regular, scrawny ass kitchen broom and of course, my man Que was nowhere to be found."

Everyone looks at Que who's just sitting there smiling as Ty recounts the incident blow by blow.

"So, Milanya comes over with her *girlfriend* who, can I add, was carrying nothing, not even a damn stick!

Meanwhile, my ass is *still* sitting in the car sweating like a big pig in wool! So, I point at the alien rodent through the cracked window where the thing was *still* trying to push the damn door open."

I glance over at Anya who's smiling as Ty continues.

"Then her non-broom-carrying girlfriend said, *Maybe it's hungry and looking for food* and proceeds to walk over to this alien rodent, with no food, no bait no *nothing* and picks it up like it's some puppy and starts walking toward my car while stroking that thing. The crazy girl starts talking to it like it was a freakin' newborn! And as if that wasn't bad enough, her friend approaches my car and, **BAM!** The damn thing lunges at me while I'm trying to roll the window up and its face and nose hits the window. I jump back just in case it comes through the window and tries to bite me and as soon as I jump, Milanya's friend starts hee-hawing. No, wait, let me rephrase that: the girl was howling! So, now I'm pissed because that shit wasn't funny and to make it worse, Milanya joins her friend's howling session and starts laughing with her. So, at some point in between howls, Milanya manages to tell me that the damn thing that I have been sweating like a wool-clad pig for and was ready to shoot, was actually Nico's life-like RUBBER TYRANNOSAURUS!!"

Everyone at the table bursts out laughing with the exception of Que who just shakes his head. And Eduardo who tried his best to act like he wasn't listening, joins in on the laughter! The waiters, seemingly on cue, return to clear the salad plates while Eduardo, downgrades his laugh to a grin, and refills several of the empty glasses.

"Now, *that* was some funny shit but yo man, the damn thing never moved for what, twenty minutes and you mean to tell us that you couldn't tell that the alien rodent wasn't real?" Yousef asks.

"Look man, number one, I had been drinking, and two, it was pitch black. So, to answer your question, HELL NO I couldn't tell, especially after seeing every imaginable bug and insect *inside* the house. So, how in the hell was I supposed to know what was *outside* the house?"

David jumps in, "Now that we know that *little Dino* wasn't real, how did he get to the door?"

In a matter of seconds our little *get-to-know-one-another* session seemed to turn into *20 Questions from Hell* and I was really beginning to feel a little sorry for Ty sitting in the proverbial hot seat. And don't get me wrong, when Anya first told me about the joke, I thought it *was* funny as hell and the way it was set up and played out, to me was just a tad short of brilliant. Something that I totally would have done! But in Ty's defense, he really couldn't see much in the dark, and if I remember correctly, Anya's friend Leslie had even turned the outside light off intentionally so that Ty wouldn't be able to tell that *little Dino* was really rubber.

Milanya quickly answers David, "First of all, it was a rubber *stegosaurus* and my friend, Leslie put it there as a practical joke since Ty made a special point of commenting about the bugs and asking me to buy spray for the insects and spiders inside the guest house. She thought it would be funny and I, well, went along with it. And at the time, it was funny but to tell you the truth I really didn't expect Ty to have reacted so uh…well, for lack of a better word, as, uh, *dramatically* as he did!

I honestly thought that Ty would be able to tell that it wasn't real especially with the one million and three humps on its back, but all kidding aside, Ty has really been a good sport about it, so thank you Ty for that! Well, I think we have time for just one more and Cyd I know Ty's a tough act to follow but why don't you go ahead and read yours!"

"Gee thanks Anya. Great intro," I say facetiously. Okay…"

"What book, movie or person has made a significant impact on your life?"

"Actually, it's three books but it was the first one, *The Celestine Prophecy* that really got me on my spiritual path, which in turn has made an impact in every aspect of my life. I guess you can say that it has pretty much transformed me."

"Well, who's the author, Dolly Lamo?" *my-mother-named-me-after-a-store,* asks while smirking like a mindless chimp.

I'm not sure if this is just a poor attempt of Ikea's to be funny or if she's just trying to impress somebody. Whichever, I opt to give her the benefit of the doubt and simply answer her with a straight face. "Hmm, maybe one could guess that but no, Ikea, the Da-lai La-ma isn't the author, James Redfield is."

"I actually have the book and tried to read it but just couldn't get into it. I think I got through the first three chapters then gave up!" Liza says semi apologetically.

"I've spoken to several people who have said the same thing, but for me, it was the exact opposite because the book *hooked me* from the first few pages."

"Without giving it away, what is *The Celestine Prophecy* about?" Kenya asks curiously.

"Well, in a sentence*, The Celestine Prophecy* is a parable that offers nine insights into life."

"Isn't that the one with the companion workbook that you, Devin and Will have been meeting monthly for the last five or six years to discuss?" Milanya asks just as Sonja returns to the private dining room and announces that our dinner is ready.

"Yes that's the one, but Anya this is actually our *ninth year* working with the companion workbook."

"Damn girl, what is it, the sequel to *War and Peace*?" Jon jokes as everyone laughs.

"Yeah well, you would think so; for as long as it's taking us, it very well could be! But I must admit, it really has been an incredible journey. And I can't lie, initially, I did find it extremely challenging but well worth it because that leg of my journey not only turned a simple book discussion into an *once-in-a-lifetime* experience, it actually exposed me to extraordinary experiences that I never knew were possible. *Metaphysically* speaking, that is."

Silence. The entire table except Milanya and Que is staring at me in complete *I-can-hear-a-pin-drop* silence. Most, I would assume are staring with a sense of legitimate curiosity and partial amazement, then several including Ikea, Yousef and Eduardo, are looking at me with what seems to be a genuine concern about the rumors of strange beings on Earth!

Just then the waiters roll in the carts with our food, which is not a minute too soon, because one, I am absolutely famished but more importantly, I'm hoping the food will distract anyone from asking me questions at which point I might have to defend or authenticate my earthling status! Meanwhile, the food looks absolutely delicious and pleasingly reeks of that well-seasoned, flame grilled aroma. Knowing that we're hungry, Sonja pitches in and helps the waiters serve the food. While our dinner is being placed on the table, Ty looks at me and smiles, probably thinking, she *looks* like an earthling. I smile back wanting to say, Really Ty? A million plus humps, in the millennium?

Fourteen

"I don't know how much more this world can take.
Yes we truly need more love for each other.
Lord it's me, it's your son
trying to take a stand for peace, like your other one.
Send us your love
cause we need each other……"

Before we can even see the stage, the gentle night air is filled with the smooth, soulful voice and music of Kem as he sings his song, *Each Other.*

Que has total access to all of Disney's parks including Pleasure Island, which is where Kem and Maxwell are both performing this evening.

Immediately upon our arrival at the concert site, we are promptly ushered to the reserved section directly in front of the stage. We take up three tables with the help of several of Que's friends who were already waiting at the entrance. Milanya dropped her *musical chair* fixation and left it up to us as to who was going to sit next to whom. Actually, I think it was Que who dropped it, but either way, Ty sat next to me and all of the couples sat together.

Kem's music is great to begin with, but tonight it's on a whole 'nother level, levitating us to a special place way above the clouds. It sounds like music that one would hear in heaven. He has one more song and then, although no one has confirmed it, Maxwell is going to join him for a *one-time-only* duet before he begins his set. If it's true, this will definitely be an unforgettable night, even more so than it already is.

Ty leans into me and whispers in my ear. "Remember what you said earlier at dinner about being transformed?"

His warm breath against my skin feels good, damn good, like a warm fire on a cold winter night. *Mmmmm*…"Uh…huh."

Just then the waiter comes and stands next to Que while taking everyone's drink order.

"Hey guys, what are you drinking?" Que asks Ty and me.

"I'll have a glass of pomegranate *iced* tea," I said.

Ty glances at me as he tells the waiter that he wants a Caipirinha, then leans back in to me, shoulder to shoulder and asks intriguingly, "So tell me, in what way did that book transform you?"

Kem begins his last song as everyone stands up and begins swaying to the music. As I sway closer to Ty, I whisper, "Actually, in several ways but mostly by realizing that it's not all about me, that it's about *all of us*, as one."

Ty looks at me with a twinkle in his eyes and smiles.

It's your voice in my ear
It's your perfume in the air
It's your smile and your laugh
It's the greatest feelin' that I've ever had
I'm into you girl…..

Fifteen

Milanya and Que could not have ordered a better day for the barbeque. It's got to be at least 85 hot, friggin' degrees, but fortunately for us their house is on the lake making the heat bearable and surprisingly, quite enjoyable. Just about everyone has begun to come out onto the deck where Que is manning the grill. Other than the ribs, burgers, steaks, chicken and shrimp that are on the grill, Milanya had a lot of the food catered from *Plate of Soul* and from what I hear, they're the best soul food caterers in Orlando.

As much as Milanya loves to cook, there is no way that woman *could or would* have a barbeque without making a few of her family's special dishes. Lucky for me, they just happen to be all of my favorites. She made her grandmother's *put-my-foot-in-'em* collard greens, her very own *make-you-wanna-holla* mac and cheese, and both her aunt's Key West key lime and Southern Carolina pecan pies. *Plate of Soul* provided the crab cakes, eight spice southern fried chicken, fried coconut shrimp, sautéed cabbage, tossed salad, string bean and seafood salad, potato and pasta salads, homemade rolls, cornbread, peach cobbler and rum cake. Thankfully *P.O.S.* also provided three servers to help set up the food, serve and clean.

Damn, I've gained ten pounds just *looking* at all this food! I might as well just duct tape a couple of chicken legs and smear a couple of slices of pie all around my hips! Oh and FYI, my friend pre-mixed not one, not two but three pitchers each of, raspberry mojitos, mango coladas *and* surprise, Caipirinahs!! That's right, my girl pre-mixed, set-up and beautifully placed each one on top of large, freshly cut, green palm leaves on the *I-betcha-it's authentic* Tiki bar. And if that isn't *Martha-esque* enough, she poured each of the cocktails into large decorative glass jars complete with *flavor-color* coordinated lids and the cutest brass nametags on small little chains around the neck of each jar!

Que, with a little help from his better half set up the deck with areas for playing cards and eating. They have a cozy, small corner lounge with about twenty yards of white mosquito netting swaggered over three large, long, chunky bamboo poles. Also, in the lounge area is the *I-betcha-it's-authentic* Tiki bar which has a thatched straw roof and Brad, one of the cuter bartenders from Pleasure Island.

By now most of the women have migrated to the kitchen and are talking about how great everything looks. Then Lady Ikea decides to elaborate on *something else* that she thinks looks good.

"…and ummm, mmm how beautiful is that fine, scrumptious ass, Ty?!"

OMG! I cannot believe that this hussy is going on and on about this man! What about David? Remember him? Meanwhile this girl is carrying on and on about what a great body Ty has and talking about how smooth and beautiful his complexion is and any and everything else her little hoochie behind can think of. This girl is just too, too much! Puh-leeze let David walk in and hear her talk about this man who her butt just met. That may sound catty, but look, I just met him too and you don't hear me going on and on about him non-stop the way she is, at least not out loud to people, *especially* when there's a chance, a very good chance, that my man can walk in at any given minute!

Humph, well, apparently Lady Ikea isn't the only one thinking about how good Ty looks because once Ikea put it out there, several others joined in on her little *love-thy-fine-Ty*-fest by happily adding their own unsolicited, complimentary two cents.

"Where is he anyway? What time did he say he was coming, Cyd?" Milanya asks while pouring several bags of ice into a huge hammered copper ice bucket.

Before I can even open my mouth, Ikea jumps in and says that she saw him drive off about an hour or so ago. Almost as soon as she said it, we see Ty's rental car through the window as he pulls up to the house. As we all peer out the window, it appears as if there is someone in the car with him.

"Who's that?" asks Liza, squinting through the window. We all squint but all we can see is a shadow. Then, suddenly, almost as if he could feel all of our eyes, Ty glances up toward the window and we quickly turn to the right like precision cadets in our final drill formation. We waste no time changing the subject to last night when just a few minutes later, we hear Ty talking to the guys. Ty and *the shadow* must have gone directly to the deck from the car. Not too long after that, Ty and his *shadow* come into the kitchen.

"Hello ladies. How's everyone?" Ty asked.

We all smile *Mona Lisa* like and say hello like little well-trained parrots.

"I'd like to introduce all of you to my friend, Calle. First, this is Milanya, our host and Que's wife, Milanya this is Calle."

While the rest of us are still in *Mona Lisa* mode, Milanya says hello to Ty and walks over to them and extends her hand to Calle. "Hello Calle, it's nice meeting you. Welcome to our home."

Anya is smooth. Not that I would expect anything less but considering our discussion at breakfast on Thursday, I thought that she might be just a *little* taken aback when they walked in. But then again, she's always been able to keep her feelings in check and maintain her cool demeanor, so why would I think that she would be flustered now? So what if Calle is White.

"Hello Calle, I'm Cydney." The introduction continues until, of course, they get to Lady Ikea.

"So Ty, wassup, is Lily a *friend* friend or your *gurl* friend?" she grills with a *straight-as-a-pin* face.

Uh unh, oh no she didn't! Hey, I gotta admit, there really *are* times when you just gotta loo-ve Ikea, hoochie butt and all!

Smiling and seemingly prepared for inquisition with not even a bead of sweat in sight, Ty calmly holds his *don't-try-to-put-my-ass-on-the-spot* smile then responds.

"Not that it should matter to you or anyone else but since you asked, Calle, *not* Lily is *my* friend. Now," he continues while he turns his attention back to our hostess, "woman, do not tell me …that that's your *make-ya-wanna-slap-your-momma* collards that I smell!"

Damn. That boy's good! And I thought *Denzel's* ass was smooth!

Milanya laughs, obviously flattered that Ty recognized her dish by its aroma, while totally being oblivious to his proficiency in the art of segueing and tells him, "Nooo Ty, that's my *put-my-foot-in-'em* collards that you smell!!"

Everybody laughs except Calle who has a smile on her face but something tells me that *girlfriend's* smile has absolutely nothing to do with Milanya's foot-slappin' collards! Ms. Calle's eyes, fixated on Ty, clearly reading, *Is that all you think of me as, a mere friend?* Fortunately for Ty, or depending on how you look at it, maybe, fortunately for Calle — Kai and Nico run into the kitchen with three of their little friends.

"Mommy can we have some hamburgers?" asks Kai.

"And some hot dogs too," adds Nico.

Milanya bends down to wipe a crumb from the corner of Nico's mouth with her moist thumb, then kisses both girls on the top of their heads.

"Yes, sweet-peas, Daddy has some for you out on the grill but everyone has to eat vegetables with their hamburgers and hot dogs! Understood?"

"Yes, Mommy," both girls say in unison.

"Yes Ms. 'Lanya," Jayla, Kai's little friend says while the other two nod.

"Dove Giselle è?" Anya asked the girls.

"Lei è in bagno che!" Kai answers her mom.

My Italian is a bit rusty to say the least but it sounds like Giselle might be in the bathroom so Milanya and I start to take the girls and their friends out to prepare their plates just as Que announces that the food is ready. Giselle meets us out on the deck and helps Milanya and me fix plates for the children. Once they're served and eating, Milanya checks everything one more time before letting the servers take over. Once everything meets her approval, we join the buffet line, fill our plates then FINALLY sit down and eat!

After everyone eats, eats and eats, people pretty much spread out and do their own thing. Most jump in the pool, probably not only to cool off but to work off some of those deliciously earned calories. Some play cards and everybody else hangs out at the Tiki bar. About a half hour after we inhaled the food, Que announces that he's taking the boat out and if anyone wants to go, he'll be leaving in about twenty minutes. So, those who are playing Spades and want to go, call last game. Those who are wet and want to go, dry off. And whoever is sitting at the bar and wants to go, finish their drink before ordering one last round (at least for now).

Sixteen

Jax (Que's son) flew in this morning and he and his friend, Julius are helping Que get the boat ready for our late afternoon ride. For a minute Anya and Que didn't think that Jax was going to make it, but fortunately, at the eleventh hour, his mom decided to let him come. Julius is the son of Que's friend Ed, who lives directly across the lake. Ed has borrowed the boat on several or more occasions and Julius has helped Ed prep the boat every time they've taken it out.

I think Ed is the only one that Que has let drive the boat and *definitely* the only one to borrow it! Milanya told me that Ed's wife died last year from breast cancer so I believe that might have a little something to do with Que loaning the boat to him. Although, only a few people have seen it, Que definitely has a soft, sensitive side to him, which is one of the many things that attracted Milanya to him. And it's mostly that sensitivity that has helped strengthen his bond with Jax, especially during his divorce from Jax's mom. It was during that difficult time that Que recognized just how important bonding between a father and son is, especially in times of crises. Knowing that, Que probably thought that being on the boat might be a great way for Julius and Ed to bond while they both try to heal from their difficult loss.

I can see the boat from the deck and it looks big! Not big *Diddy* big but big enough to hold about eight to ten people comfortably. Que already told everyone that he's taking the boat out again later, so whoever wants to go that didn't make the afternoon ride, can go in the evening.

Milanya decides to stay and continue her role as hostess so, of course I offer to stay to help her but she insists that I go on the boat and enjoy myself. Sorry to admit it, but she did not have to tell me twice! She knows that I've wanted to get on the boat ever since she told me about it.

Meanwhile, Calle finally dropped the little smiling act and is now standing by Ty (like *Tammy Wynette* stood by hers) while playing Spades with David, Kenya and Liza. A few of us start heading to the boat after Liza motions to Jon to go ahead. Then quickly adds that she'll be there as soon as she and Liza finish the hand or as she *really* put it, "*….as soon as they finish whupping David and Ty's butts!*"

Meanwhile, everyone is admiring the boat while claiming a seat. Ikea sits down right in between Ty and David. *Tammy Wynette* of course, sits on the other side of Ty. Once we're all situated, Que starts the boat and we head out into the beautiful pristine lake. Que has the music pumping while I take it all in. I *love* it!

As the sun shines, the soft wet wind blows on us while we're enveloped in a cocoon of the feel-good, soulful, music of *Jill Scott* blasting from Harman & Kardon. It's a perfect day and I am so into this…that is until the boat police pull us over to tell us to lower the music.

According to *Starsky*, it was louder than regulation volume. *Regulation volume?* Is that a boat or water police term? Whichever it is, it's new to me. And Que seems to be okay with it — that is, until *Starsky* asks for his registration and ownership papers. Then Que does what Que does in these situations; he gives Hutch's boy the infamous Que look that says, *I really don't think you want to f--k with me!*

Now, Que would never say that and no words were actually spoken, but then again, they didn't have to, because S*tarsky* immediately said, "Hey wait, aren't you, don't tell me…. Quentin James? I know you! You used to play for the Chicago Bulls. I'm sorry to have bothered you Mr. James. You and your friends enjoy the rest of the day." And poof, just like that *Starsky* sped off as quickly as he appeared.

Que wasted no time blasting the music *above* regulation volume and then accelerating almost twice as fast in the opposite direction creating a huge eighteen foot spray of picture-worthy waterworks!

Butler Lake runs along the back of about 20 exclusive estates, mostly all belonging to professional athletes, CEO's and other top level executives. The party continues while I'm still slowly taking in this incredible moment and enjoying the jaw-dropping real estate.

Que reduces the speed as he points out Shaq, Tiger, Ken Griffey Jr. and Wesley Snipes' homes. Their three million plus estates are somewhat bigger than Milanya and Que's 6200 square foot house and from what I can see, they're worth every penny. When Que points out Shaq's compound, Ikea quickly asks if we could swing by to meet him. Que made the mistake earlier of mentioning that he had been to Shaq's house on several occasions.

"Isn't Shaq at his west coast ho…?" I remind Que.

"Yes," he responds before I could even finish saying *home*." I know that he appreciated my quick response because he winks while smiling like he just got the lead in a Crest white strips commercial.

Que goes on with the tour while *"I Will Always Love You"* plays in the background. Now, I really love Whitney but I think my girl's rendition is right up there with the Queen of Pop! As soon as the song started, Liza asks Que who's singing vocals. He told her Shirley Murdock with Roger and the Zapp band.

As we continue the "Orlando Rich and Famous" tour along Windermere's premier lake, we see one of the Orlando Magic players in the back of his house. Que tells us his name but since I'm not that familiar with the Magic team, I forgot (And no, it wasn't LeBron James!) From the boat it looks like he's having his own cookout with a loaded grill and a few friends chillin' on his huge ass deck. Ne-Yo is blasting through the small but powerful speakers. As we ride by, he glances up at the boat and sees Que and waves for us to join them. Que waves back and does a different man to man gesture that I assume says thanks but no thanks since he steered the boat in the opposite direction. As the boat turns away it looks like Ikea is about to jump in the damn water and I guess, dog paddle her way over there, solo, without Que, David or any of us! David looks pissed as hell and immediately shoots Ikea a quick *woman don't-even-think-about-it* look. And sadly, I'm pretty sure David's look was the *only* reason her crazy butt didn't!

When we get back to the house, the servers have cleared and cleaned mostly everything with the exception of a few snacks, fresh fruit and dessert, including a delectable champagne sorbet topped with fresh kiwi and mango shavings that I might add, is beyond heavenly!

Most of us dance to the music of one of Orlando's best kept secrets, deejay *Bebop Sol (he* dropped the u, not me*)* He and Que became friends a couple of years ago when they met at a Disney function and now Bebop deejays for Que whenever Que asks. It's great publicity for Bebop, especially among Orlando's and Windermere's elite. Plus he loves Que and Milanya's parties, so it's pretty much a win-win situation for everyone.

Those not dancing sat in the deck's lounge area and started discussing some pretty intense topics, which seem to be mostly sex and relationship oriented questions. After a question or two, it is apparent that the topics are getting to be a little too personal for Ty because once the second question, *"If men just want sex, then why don't they just ask?"* is read, my man gets up and tells his girl, Calle, that he's ready to go! Puh-leeze, if his telling her, "Let's go" doesn't ring any bells for her, then I don't know what will. I have to admit, even though, a lot of women bring this type of behavior on themselves, I still feel a little sorry for Calle. I believe the biggest mistake most of us make is not taking the time to get to know the person we're with before having sex. Not that I'm an expert on the subject because Lord *knows*, I am the first to admit that I've made some mistakes, but I also pulled lessons from each and every one of them and tried to apply them to other life challenges going forward.

As great and as fun as this day has been, I'm exhausted and so ready to go to bed. Most of the guests left by 1:30 a.m. and now the remaining eleven or twelve of us are singing karaoke, dancing and enjoying the last of Anya's specialty drinks! It's about 3 a.m. and although I am a bona fied night person, at this point I can hardly keep my eyes open so I'm just going to give in and take my sleepy butt down to bed and call it a night. When I reach the pool house and am about to open the door, I hear footsteps from behind, coming toward me through the night's blackness. I turn quickly, and can only see a melon-colored shirt. It didn't take long before realized it was Ty!

Seventeen

Did you know that there are fifty different flavors of waffles? Well, this was news to me but I guess if you go to a four star restaurant that specializes in waffles, you should expect a large variety or at least you shouldn't be surprised by it.

Yousef and Kenya are treating all of us to brunch at *Waldo's Gourmet Waffles* to thank Que and Milanya for their wonderful hospitality as well as to say goodbye to everyone. The restaurant is very nice and looks nothing like *Roscoe's Chicken & Waffles* in L.A. — not that *Roscoe's* isn't nice, *Waldo's* is just slightly more upscale. Actually, a *lot* more upscale. Overall, the brunch was great … but then again, what wouldn't be great about sweet potato pecan waffles? Plus there aren't too many people that I know who wouldn't want to at least *try* red velvet waffles. But it wasn't just the delicious food that made it great; it was what Kenya asked all of us to do during brunch that made it special. Kenya borrowed a page out of my book and asked us to go around the table and say our own personal thank you to Que and Milanya. And I must say that gesture alone pretty much set the tone for our last day together, not only as a group but in marking the beginning of new friendships formed while sharing a commonality. And at the risk of sounding slightly more sentimental than usual, I have to say that it was very touching to hear the warmth and raw emotion in everyone's voice. Listening to each of the stories further confirmed exactly how much Que and Milanya inherently care not only for their friends but for those who are less fortunate as well.

"Excuse me," Kenya says loudly enough for us to hear over all of our voices. "We want to thank everyone for sharing your stories and appreciation for Milanya and Quentin. However, during our speeches, Ty had to leave to take a business call and therefore missed his turn. So now, that he's back and if it's okay with everyone Yousef and I would like for Ty to share his story with everyone at this time. Ty?"

"Thanks Kenya," Ty says as he stands. "Since I'm meeting most of you for the first time, you probably aren't aware of my long history with these two. Hmm, I see that a couple of you shifted and repositioned yourselves in your seats when I mentioned the word *long*."

The guilty ones laugh while the rest of us smile.

"Not to worry, it's not that looong of a history but I'll try my best to keep it as short as possible."

"This should be good," Jon whispers to me.

"When I first met Que, I was a rookie playing for the Milwaukee Bucks and he was playing with Chicago and MJ. Our first meeting was on a Friday night and it was a home game and the Bucks were playing the *forever winning* Bulls. The clock was down to six seconds and we were tied, 88-88. MJ had sprained his ankle and was struggling but was still very much in the game. And as luck would have it, a couple of my teammates were out, which to my delight had me in the game although time was quickly running out. Then Michael, of course being *Michael* shoots a one-handed two pointer as we all watch in slow motion. The ball trickles in and leaves me in perfect position for the rebound. After grabbing the ball, I faked left then dribbled down half court until I had a clear shot with just two and a half seconds left on the clock. With my arms bent and in *all net* position for the three point shot, Que comes up from behind and knocks the ball out of my hands just as the damn buzzer rings! I yell *FOUL* and the ref signals the play *GOOD* and there you have it, the Bulls won. Man, talk about being mad. I was so pissed that one of my teammates had to pull me back because he could see that I was about to deck Que. That entire night on through the next time our teams played, I was talking mad smack about Que."

All the guys laugh except for Que who just shakes his head.

"Apparently Que heard about all the things I was saying from his teammates and minutes before our next game against one another, he came to the entrance of the locker room and told the security guard that he needed to see me. Usually that's not allowed but somehow Que got around it. I came out and there we were face to face."

Ty pauses and looks at Que and asks, "Que man, you remember what you said?"

Que smiles and says, "Not really but I'm sure you're going to tell us." Everyone laughs.

"That I am, that I am," he confirms before continuing. "So Que looks at me and said, *I hear that you've been talking smack about me.* I looked at him and said, *Uh, okay and?* Que told me that he was glad that I admitted it but then wanted to know why I was talking about him. And honestly, I was glad he asked so that I could finally tell him to his face. It's actually kind of funny because I remember the conversation like it was yesterday. My exact words were, *Yo man, I had the perfect shot to win the game and an even better chance to make the sports headlines and because of you, that opportunity was taken away from me.* Que shook his head then asked me if I really believed that it was his fault? *Yeah, I do*, I told him. Then he laughed and said, *Well, let me school you, young blood. A good player isn't given points, a good player earns his points. That, my man separates the good players from the lucky players. Now, I know you will say that you didn't have time to do this but when positioning yourself to shoot, you have to not only focus on the basket but on everyone around you. At least, that's what good players do. That's what you call good use of peripheral vision so don't blame me; blame yourself for not watching your back. Now, hopefully today I will see a new and improved player on the floor, one that I will be proud to play against.* Then Que walked away and it was at that moment, that I knew I had a friend in Quentin James and I was right because we've been friends ever since. And the bonus was that several years later when Que met Milanya, I gained a sister and a friend in his significant other, for life. Sis, you've been there for me almost as much and as long as Que and I thank you both for a wonderful weekend and an even better friendship! Love you both."

The brunch ends on a final high first, with Ty's story then with Que thanking all of us for coming as he toasted Milanya for putting together a perfect weekend, one, which he said all of us are likely to remember for the rest of our lives.

When we get back to the house, we all gather in the front foyer to bid our final goodbyes. Giselle and the girls are standing on either side of the intricately etched double front glass doors and are strategically positioned next to several large black baskets which are perched on a pair of black marble pedestals. Both baskets have Milanya and Que's monogram, MJQ painted on them in a beautiful lime green. Leave it to Milanya to have friggin' straw baskets monogrammed. They're filled with beautifully wrapped gifts each with a one inch lime grosgrain ribbon on top with letters that spell *Friends for life!* Unfriggin'believable! As we all hug and say our goodbyes and "have-a-safe-trips" to one another, the girls start to hand out our parting gifts, giving strict instructions for us not to open them until we get home.

Milanya wants to drive me to the airport but I tell her that it isn't necessary and to stay home and get some rest. Plus Ty already offered to give me a ride last night once we realized that our flights were departing within thirty minutes of one another. Ty and I are the last ones to physically leave the house.

As Milanya and I hug, I thank her for everything and tell her that I'll text her as soon as I land and will call her on Monday. Ty gives Que the bro-to-bro hug and they say whatever men say to show appreciation while still maintaining their manly bro-hood status. The only thing left now, is for them to beat their hairy ass chests and yell out some primal chant!

My flight lands at LaGuardia at exactly six pm. As I walk outside into the pick-up/taxi area, I'm surprised at how much I missed New York, especially since it feels so good to leave the five or six times a year that I do. Just as I'm about to get in the taxi line, my cell phone rings and automatically I look at the caller I.D. and see **PRIVATE** displayed.

I press **TALK**, "Hello."

"I'm to your right, in black, *all* black."

Without thinking, I immediately turn to my right and see a chauffeur standing next to a sleek, black limousine nodding. At moi? I turn around to see who he's nodding at, but there's no one behind me. When I turn back, the chauffeur's stare intensifies as he nods seemingly for the last time. I step out of the taxi line and slowly walk toward him. Once within earshot, he asks, in a deep baritone voice, "Ms. Rochon?"

"Yes," I answer curiously while wondering if Barry White was somehow reincarnated and if so, why no one told me. Smiling, the chauffer hands me a white envelope with **"Ms. Cydney Rochon"** typed on it as he opens the limousine door. Intrigued and somewhat relieved to at least see my name, I return his smile while taking the envelope as my mind goes a hundred miles an hour, swirling with a triage consisting of who, what and why's. The chauffer extends his arm and points to my carry-on bag while politely motioning for me to get in the limo. I hesitate momentarily but then go ahead and climb in. *Barry* then closes the door and places my bag in the limo's trunk. I sink back into the plush leather seat and pick up the remote and turn the radio on to *98.7 KYSS FM*. And as soon as I do, the smooth, sexy male host's voice flows seductively through the surround sound speakers. I slowly open the envelope while *Dallas* welcomes his listeners to his show.

"Good evening folks. My name is Dallas Knight and welcome to a special Sunday edition of The Dallas Knight Show.

Our first segment is called Where Do We Go From Here? And for those of you who are not familiar with the segment, this is where we talk about love, sex and relationships. Tonight's topic is "How to Move On." So many of us have been in a relationship when suddenly our partner or lover decides to just pick up and leave. So tonight we're going to delve into how one moves on while keeping their heart intact. If you have been left behind by someone or if you have an opinion on how to pick up the pieces then pick up the phone and let us hear from you…."

I close my eyes and allow my mind and whatever residual worries I have to drift off into the night as we merge slowly into the airport traffic.

Eighteen

"Funky Tom, fun-ky! Show us some funk!!"

"Oh, so it's *funk* you want? Then by all means, let me pull out my funk," Tom says playfully while quickly looking through the racks of hanging fabric samples in *Innovative Wool's* showroom.

Kyle and I are at one of our fabric appointments looking for something basic but with a cool, funky edge. Even though the fall line for DK*Urban* is complete, I never stop looking for something new and different to either add to an existing line or use as inspiration for future lines. It's imperative for me to stay on top of my game because the *last* thing I want is for a *Kimora* or *Ralph* to one up me!

Tom pulls out a little over a dozen fabric samples and spreads them out on the table in front of us. Kyle and I review and pour over Tom's selection, then choose four collectively.

"Great, I'll get fabric cards for these. And Cydney, now that I have a better idea of what you're looking for," Tom says while eying the group of samples we selected, "tell me, would graffiti painted wool with a silk blend, fall into the funk category that you're referring to?"

"Now you're talkin', Tom. That's *exactly* the type of funk I'm looking for! Now *please* tell me that you have sample yardage."

"Not yet, but we will tomorrow and as soon as we get it, I'll bring it by your office. It's actually being Fed-ex'd as we speak."

"Perfect. Tom, I'm lovin' this whole graffiti concept and can't wait to see it. But if we want to use DK*U* artwork for a custom graffiti design, can we?

"I don't see why not, but let me talk to our textile designer as well as John, the president, to see what that will entail aside from of course, the obvious additional cost. Meanwhile, I'll get these fabrics on information cards and I'll be right back."

"Thanks, Tom."

When Tom returns and gives us the fabric cards, Kyle and I rush to our next and last appointment for the day. The appointment is with *Design Trenz*, which is probably the industry's leading source as far as trend forecasting services go. DT's showroom is absolutely *fantasy-comes-to-life* amazing! If you didn't know where you were, you would *swear* that you were on a *Steven Spielberg* movie set! This season as you walk in, it's like entering a real live forest. Imagine being surrounded by life-like, floor to ceiling petrified trees with real grass and simulated dirt along the perimeter of an actual rock pathway. Continuing through the showroom, to the four rooms that the design team created. Each room has a theme inspired by that season's trends which were previewed months in advance. In addition to the overall theme design, each room has huge colorful storyboards comprised of sketches, fabric swatches, accessories, photos and trims providing a multi-dimensional visual overview of the trend for that particular room.

Forecasting services pretty much dictate what styles and trends the designers will use as a spring board for their lines each season. However, some designers, including me, view the trends and internalize the information and/or looks, then choose a different direction or a different route for a similar destination.

Once again, *Design Trenz* has exceeded my expectations after having explored all four rooms in the seventy minutes that we've been here and yet again, I'm leaving with a notebook full of ideas and sketches laced with enough inspiration to stuff, bottle and sell!

As I enter our office, surprisingly there is no one at the reception desk. Knowing Zoe and the way that girl shops, she's probably in the sample closet filling up a shopping bag! Meanwhile, I'm having mixed feelings about being back in the office; glad on one hand to be back so that I can hopefully tie up a few loose ends but sad, because this is where I last saw Omar. I still haven't told Zoe what happened, so now I have to deal with her constantly asking about him and going on with how much she likes him, which quite frankly, is the last damn thing I need. For now though, I need to concentrate on these loose ends before her majesty returns on Wednesday.

Considering the circumstances, I think it would be in my ass's best interest to be *at least* two steps ahead of her highness just in case the presentation blunder comes up. I do know one thing for sure; Gretchen is going to absolutely *love* the graffiti concept so much so that her royal butt will forget that I was even at the presentation, let alone walked out on it! Her majesty's focus will be right where it should be, on the big, fat order that I am 99.9% sure that Federated is going to place.

While I'm reviewing my, as Robyn calls it, *all-my-shit-to-do* list, Zoe barges into my office and is visibly startled when she sees me.

"Oops! I didn't know that you and Kyle were back from your appointments. I must've been in the sample sale room when you came back," she says somewhat taken aback.

"Yep, I'm back but Kyle went to a doctor's appointment after we left *Design Trenz."*

"You don't even have to tell me, I already know; their showroom was fabulous, as always, right?"

"Zoe, it was unbelievable. It was like walking into Jurassic Park! Kyle didn't want to leave." I tell her as I notice several messages in her hand. I point to them and ask, "Are those for me?"

"Oh yeah, that's actually why I came to your office, I was going to put them on your desk," she explains while handing me the square pieces of paper.

I quickly look at them and ask, "Is this all?"

"Oh yeah I almost forgot, Gretchen called and won't be back in the office 'til Monday. She decided to fly to Milan for a quick shopping trip. Oh — and right after you and Kyle left for your appointments, a man stopped by and asked for you but he wouldn't give me his name."

"Probably a fabric salesman."

"No, I don't think so."

"Did he ask for me by name?" I ask curiously as I hear ringing in the background.

"Actually he did, excuse me Cydney, that's my intercom," she says and darts out of my office.

I take the messages and look through them while wondering who that man could have been especially since Zoe said he wasn't a sales man.

Nineteen

"A *heffa could go gray waitin' for your ass …"*

As I fumble with my keys and rush to open my apartment door, I can hear a voice coming from inside.

"*…c'mon gurl pick up! You know you're home ….C'mon Cyd…"*

Once inside, I recognize the voice and quickly hook my purse strap around the arm of my slightly worn pony skin chair while rushing to pick up the phone and finally freeing my feet from these tight ass Miu Miu's.

"Hey Rob," I said slightly out of breath, putting the phone to my ear.

"Gurl, are you screening again?"

"Not yet. I just walked in. What's going on?" I ask as I plop down on my *a-little-too-distressed-leather-I'll-never-buy-online-again* sofa.

"Just wanted to make sure you're still going to James' birthday thing tonight at the *Water Street Lounge*. If you want I can swing by and pick you up."

"Oh shoot, I totally forgot it was tonight! What time are you going?"

"Around 8 o'clock. C'mon Cyd get it together and let's go. I know James wants you there and you *know* I wanna hear more 'bout Florida and that Tyrone guy!"

"Okay, okay, I'll go. Eight should give me enough time," I tell her while being hypnotically summoned by the flashing red button on my phone's base.

"Oh and miz *I can't-remember-a-damn-name-to-save-my-life* Ty's name is TYSON NOT TYRONE! Girl, what is it with you and names?"

"Tyrell, Tyrese, Ty-bo whatever the hell his name is! Gurl, I just want to hear about his fine Hershey chocolate ass!"

"C'mon Robyn, Tae-bo??? Hershey chocolate? Girl, I can't with you! Just call me when you're leaving!"

"Okay, later!" she tells me while laughing then quickly adds, "Bring your camera."

After I hang up the phone I notice the gifts that Nico and Kai handed out to all of the house guests as we were leaving for the airport. When I got home Sunday evening I put the gifts on the side table with every intention of opening them while sipping my tea but somehow must've gotten sidetracked when I decided to unpack and take a long bath instead of my usual ten minute shower.

Anya wrapped the gifts so nicely that I don't even want to open them. Okay, well that thought didn't last long, since I immediately start to untie the magenta and lime ribbon while pressing **PLAY** on my phone's base to listen to my messages but more so to stop that friggin' mini strobe light from flashing!

BEEP

"Hey Cyd, it's Devin. Will and I can't make it this Sunday, can we change it to the second or third Sunday? We have an appointment to look at an office space. I'll explain later when we talk."

Hmm, since when did they start looking at office spaces?…..

BEEP

"Cyd, it's Shaye. Look, I have a styling gig in Philly but let's plan to get together Thursday night when I get back. Jackson and his friend want to take us out to dinner."

Sure, why not? After all, a girl's gotta eat! Wait a minute, Shaye hasn't even told me one thing about this guy.

BEEP

"Baby, it's your mother. Now, are you sure you can't go to Connecticut with your sister and me? I know you're busy with work and that you just got back from Florida, but if you can, we wish you would come with us. Well, try sweetheart, it's not often that Jordyn has free time, Love you! Oh and your father sends his love. Bye honey."

I wish I could go with mom and Jordyn but I can't. Maybe the three of us can plan something next month….

BEEP

"Hey Cydney, it's Ty. Looks like I'll be in New York sooner than I thought. I actually have several meetings this week, two on Thursday and one Friday morning. If you're schedule permits, I'd like to get together with you Thursday and Friday evenings, as well as all day Saturday and Sunday. My flight doesn't leave til Monday morning. I know it's last minute but I just got the call and well, let's just say, it's a pretty good opportunity. Anyway, hope you can squeeze some time in for me. Call or text me and let me know if you're free. I'll be staying at the *Muse* on West 46th. Looking forward to seeing you!"

Wow, Ty's coming to New York....this should prove to be interesting! He did say that he would be coming sometime in the future but I didn't think it was going to be this soon!!

BEEP

"Hi sweetie! Listen Que and I are taking the girls to the new Disney flick tonight so let's try to talk tomorrow, okay? Love you!"

BEEP BEEP BEEP

While listening to my messages, I opened the gifts that Anya and Que gave all of us and let me tell you, my girl didn't miss a beat. I have thought it and have even joked about it but now I'm thoroughly convinced that that girl stays up nights just to think of new and creative things to do. And always in the biggest and most imaginative way possible! I honestly don't know where she finds the time to do all that she does with a partner, two children *and* all of her charity work. Inside the gift box and bag were mementos from the weekend which included a CD comprised of songs from the initial limo ride to some of the songs Que mixed at the barbeque. Then there were two group photos of all of us taken after the concert, one with Maxwell standing next to moi and another photo taken at *Texas de Brazil* which was in a frame engraved with the words, "*Good Times, Good Friends.*" Then of course, there was a small stainless shaker and a mini bottle of cachaça with a recipe card for Caipirinha's. And last but not least, a small tin of rum cake from *Plate of Soul* as well as a jar of Que's secret eleven spice steak sauce! And surprise, surprise, all the packaging was color coordinated in the black, lime and magenta palette. All I can do is shake my head and think, Lady Martha has some serious competition!

I put all the memento's on the ottoman with the exception of the photo with Maxwell! (I just need to figure out how to *photoshop* this bad boy so it'll just be the two of us in the shot!) While getting up to jump in the shower I notice a small envelope on the floor.

Dear Cydney,

Thank you for coming down and making a good time great!

The weekend would not have been the same

without you or your help!

Love, Anya & Que

P.S. We hope you enjoyed the limousine ride home, it was the least we could do!

Smiling, I put the card back into the envelope then turn the radio on to listen to my new best friend, Dallas Knight, before getting into the shower. As I get undressed, Dallas' voice travels through to the bathroom.

"....If you're just tuning in, this is Dallas Knight and you are listening to our request segment of the Dallas Knight Show. We just received a call from a caller who would like to remain anonymous and requested that I sing this particular song for a special friend named Sidney. So, Sidney this one is for you."

First time I looked into your eyes
I saw heaven, oh heaven in your eyes
It should have been you all the time
I'll do anything and everything to please you
You know how much I need you
You're always, always on my mind.....

Twenty

Robyn and I just arrived at James' birthday gathering and are sitting in front of the open, metal-rimmed glass doors which frame the riverfront magnificently at the *Water Street Lounge.* Both the lounge and restaurant reveal a tasteful ambience although surprisingly, they are dissimilar style-wise. There are several areas of the restaurant that are actually situated directly under the Brooklyn Bridge which is only visible through the partial glass roof and angled skylights, unlike the neighboring *River Café* where the bridge is visible from all of the restaurant's windows. For the last several years James has had his birthday soirees at venues that have jaw-dropping views and tonight he has disappointed no one.

"So what happened? Did you guys do it?"

"Hello, my name is Cydney Rochon and you are?"

"GURL, WHAT THE HELL IS WRONG WITH YOU? I know who you are!"

"Well, you sure as hell aren't acting like it by asking me if I slept with a guy just two damn days after meeting him!"

"Oh, hussy, puh-leeze, can you blame me? Who would have thought that your butt would have been suckin' face in the middle of crowded ass *Lula Mae's* either, but your ass did! So how in the hell am I supposed to know what your butt is gonna do next?"

"Robyn please, not *that* again! Gir-rl let it go already!"

Talk about running something into the ground. Robyn not only runs stuff into the ground, that girl digs a ditch, buries it, then places a daggone marker on top! Please, enough already!

When I ran into Omar at *Lula Mae's* that night, we both knew that it was on. Or at least, we both hoped it would be. B.F.D. (before the first disappearance), we had already gone on five or six *kiss-less* dates (not for lack of him trying) and at that point, we had already developed feelings for one another. So, to say that I was eager to pick up from where we left off would definitely be an understatement! And of course I never told Robyn, or anyone for that matter, about my little *six date no-kiss, pecks only rule.* And don't get me wrong, I enjoy kissing as much as anybody but I'm not going to kiss a man *just* for the sake of kissing. Men will know, when I kiss them, it's because I have developed *real* feelings for them. So, if I feel that way about kissing before the sixth date then I'm *definitely* not going to sleep with a man on day two of meeting him! It may seem drastic to some but this is my way of protecting my heart from being hurt as it has so many times in the past. It was after my last long-term relationship that I decided to do things differently in order to get different results and believe it or not, it actually works. The players and wannabes don't stick around but the guys that are genuine do! Not surprisingly, Robyn and I have different views when it comes to sex. And I'm sure if I told her about my *six date no kiss* rule she would probably tell me that I've been looking at too many reruns of that TV show *Girlfriends,* in which Tracee Ellis Ross's character, Joan, practices a three month no-sex rule. Hey, Joan has her rule and I have mine and mine is just that, *mine.*

As I continue telling Robyn about Ty and my Florida vacation, I notice James over in the corner with Chris Rock and Steve Harvey. I would love to be a fly on *that* wall! Meanwhile, this is the first time I've seen James since we were at *Lula Mae's*, the same night Omar and I reconnected. Seeing him this evening brings back memories of that night as well as certain *stored away* emotions that I'm not really prepared for. I've made a point of not talking about Omar to anyone, especially not to Robyn, even though a day doesn't go by that I don't think about him or envision the day that I will hopefully see him again. *And* get some damn answers!

Robyn sees that I'm slightly distracted and quickly draws me back into the conversation.

"Ok, so if you two didn't do it then why did Almond Hershey come down to the pool house? What did he want?" she persists like a relentless prosecutor in a *whodunit* murder trial.

"Obviously he wasn't coming to see me because at that point he didn't even know that I was back at the pool house."

"Then where the hell was he going?" the prosecutor continues to cross examine.

"It's not rocket science Robyn, he was going back to the deck to see if the party was still going on and while en route saw me going into the pool house and stopped to talk."

"Well, so what did you two talk about? Hmm…and did you invite him in?"

"Robyn, it was nothing," I snapped, ready for this inquisition to end! "First he asked if there was anything to drink inside and when I told him yes, he asked if I was up to company. And that was it, nothing super juicy."

"What do you mean by juicy? He came in didn't he? C'mon Cydney, I feel like I'm pulling teeth out of a freak in' mouthful of quik-dry cement, one by one!"

I smiled on the inside and thought, *GOOD*!

"Can you just tell me blow by blow what happened so I don't have to keep asking you a million and one freakin' questions?" she begged like a *New York-subway-pan-handler-at-the-start-of-her-shift.*

"Girl, I don't know what you want me to tell you. He came in. We opened up a bottle of *Gewürztraminer* and then he asked me the usual *trying-to-get-to-know-you* questions. *What do I do, how did I meet Milanya, do I have a boyfriend etc.* Then before I could answer him, he leaned in to kiss me, once…then twice and before we knew it, one thing led to another and well, we ended up making *incredible* love, first on the floor, then the couch then… well, let's just say, I was *very* satisfied!"

Robyn's mouth flies open and has yet to close! While she's digesting and vicariously reliving my little rendezvous, I'm enjoying another sip of my *Ruby Red Cosmo with Champagne.* They gave all of James' guests a choice of two drinks as we entered the party. Robyn guzzled hers before we even sat down. Finally, Robyn's mouth closes although it's not long before she re-opens it.

"Shut up! Guurrl I can't believe this! Really?" she shrieks with her tongue wagging back and forth.

I take another sip then look at her and smile devilishly.

"No Robyn, I'm just kidding! I just threw your ass a bone since you keep begging for something to chew on!"

Robyn looks disappointed as hell as she rolls those big ole eyes of hers.

"Sorry girl but all we did was talk. Oh, but he did ask me if I had a boyfriend, now *that* part was true!"

"Whoopty damn doo."

"Girl don't be….," as I'm talking Robyn's eyes drift. Although, I'm sure she's still listening, it now appears that *she*'s the one who's distracted. I turn to pinpoint the target of her attention but as I do she turns back to me.

"Well, little miz playa-magnet it seems as if you might have another admirer in the midst."

"Huh?"

"That man over there," she nodded in the same proximity of her *distraction.*

I turn to check out my admirer and see a tall, nicely built man standing next to a large potted palm tree. Unfortunately, the plants' leaves are blocking the man's face so all I can really see is his black sports jacket and torn jeans. I shrug my shoulders as I turn back around and take another sip of my yummy Cosmo.

"Gurl, he's been watching you from the moment our cute asses walked in the damn door," she tells me. I turn back around to take another look and when I do, *poof!,* he's gone, disappeared into thin air and nowhere to be found.

Now I'm curious. "What did he look like?" I ask as I grab a small handful of nuts.

"Like that hot ass, Rock, but bald. Okay, enough about plant man! Moving along, okay, so finish telling me what *really* happened with you and Ty."

"Robyn, there is no *me* and Ty."

"Whatever, what did you tell him when he asked if you had a boyfriend?"

"Uhhh…the *truth.*"

"Okay, so damn, did you two at least kiss?" she asks now getting even more frustrated with *any* and *all* letters, syllables, words *and* sentences exiting my mouth.

"No, but I kinda think that he wanted to. I got the feeling that he was waiting for *me* to make the first move. My guess is that he didn't want to come off like a player. After all, he did come to the barbeque with Calle!"

"Oh yeah, *lil miss Calla Lily*. But just tell me, did you *wanna* kiss him?"

I pause while trying to figure out how I can put a halt to this girl's ridiculous ass questions and finally end this damn inquisition! Because the last time I checked, no one called me up to a witness stand. And don't get me wrong, I love Robyn, that's my girl but she does not need to know *every damn thing*! I'm sorry but there are some things I just want to keep to myself and not have to worry about them being thrown back in my face when I least expect it. So, instead of answering her million and one questions I'm stepping down from the witness stand and am turning the table on Robyn's *inquisitive-I-should-have-been-a-damn-lawyer* ass and question *her* about *her* friggin' love life!

"Look girl, enough about me, what happened with you and whatshisname, uh, is it Chauncey? Did you guys ever go out again?" Without any warning, Robyn's expression immediately changed from that of a probing prosecutor to a *surprise* defendant.

"Uh, yes…we did. And at first everything was cool, especially once I found out that he wasn't the nerd that I initially had him pegged out to be."

"Hey, some nerds are kinda cool, but what do you mean *at first?* What happened?"

"We went out on about three dates and had a good time until one night, when we came back to his apartment."

"Don't tell me. You did it and it was horrible?"

"No but we were about to until —"

"Until what?" I interrupt, "a girlfriend showed up? Or worse, a *boyfriend*?"

"No, gurl…"

"Rob *please* don't tell me the guy had on *Manx*!"

Laughing she says, "No he didn't but remember that guy I went out with that did? Gurl, then he had the nerve to ask me to help him take the freakin' thing off! Now Cydney you *know*, if Robyn doesn't wear *Spanx* then I damn sure don't wanna a man that wears *Manx!*"

"Girl, I'm with you on that one," I tell her while laughing. "Okay, so now tell me, what happened with Chauncey?"

"Gurl, I went to the bathroom and did what I always do, I looked in his medicine cabinet. Ma told me a long time ago that a woman can always find out what kind of man she's dealing with by looking into a man's medicine cabinet."

"And what did you find detective Caruso? A box of teeny weeny condoms?"

"No but I'm sure he had some! Gurl, I found an *open* as in *I have been using it* box of *ExTenze* in there!"

"Shut up!"

"Gurl, if I'm lying, I'm flying! That's the last thing I need is a man with a little …." Robyn stops as James approaches us and reaches out to hug her.

"Happy birthday, birthday man," Robyn tells him as they hug.

"Yes, Sir James, happy birthday!" I chime in as he slips out of Robyn's embrace and slides over to kiss me on the cheek.

"Thank you both. Lookin' good ladies, lookin' good," he tells us while eyeballing us up and down. "I'm glad you could make it, but I don't see any plates, I hope you both had something to eat."

"No, actually we were just about to get something," I fibbed.

"Okay, so, yeah, definitely help yourselves. I'm paying for *my guests* to eat, not the servers so please eat up."

"I heard *that*," Robyn says laughing. "This is a really nice turnout, James," she tells him as she looks around the room. "I know most of the people here but I don't ever remember seeing your bald-headed friend in the black jacket and blue jeans at any of your other parties. Who is he?"

"Who? Oh, the tall brotha by the plant? Yeah, I saw him earlier, but he must've come with somebody. Hell if I know who, though. Actually it's funny that you mention him 'cause Chris made a joke about him and the plant sharing roots," he says, laughing.

Robyn laughs, gifting James with a brief, courtesy *birthday* laugh, "I was just curious."

Twenty One

The week flew by. I can't believe that it's Thursday already. Thank God everything has gone pretty smoothly, work-wise. And thank goodness I was able to finish everything on my *all-my-shit-to-do* list, which makes me more than ready for Queenie's ass when she returns to work next week. Tom and the *Innovative Wool's* designer rushed to make sure that I had several two yard cuts (of fabric) using the graffiti artwork I gave him and the sample cuts could not have turned out better. In fact, they turned out so well that I gave the sample hands sketches of new designs to sew up for my meeting with her royal highness on Monday.

Now that everything at work is under control, I can focus on Ty and his visit this weekend. He called about an hour ago when he checked into the hotel and asked me to meet him there at 6:30. The plan is to decide what we'll do once I get to the hotel. Although, I did *casually* mention the Knicks game when we spoke. So the seed is planted. But considering that we're playing the Lakers and unless K.B. is out, that may be an unrealistic option.

While I gather my things for my mani-pedi appointment, Kyle sashays into my office like he's auditioning for ANTM (America's Next Top Model).

"Cyd-ney, do you want to keep these samples here or in Gretchen's private conference room?"

"Definitely here, in the sample closet," I tell him as I get up and start walking toward the door. "Thanks, Kyle, you're the best. Now I'm outta here. Oh and tomorrow… I'm only here in the morning and I know you won't be in until the afternoon so have a great weekend and I'll see you on Monday!"

"Ok-ay, thanks. You too," he says in his usual syrupy voice.

Zoe is returning from a late lunch just as I'm walking out the door. Rushing to her desk she grabs several messages from her message pad and hands them to me.

"Nothing urgent, oh…that Dwayne guy stopped by again asking for you but before I could intercom you, his cell phone rang, then he left."

"Who?"

"You know, that salesman who stopped by before and wouldn't leave his name."

"Sooo, then how do you know his name?"

"I don't, I just called him Dwayne because I think he looks like the Rock and that's the Rock's real name!"

Wait a minute, what the hell? This is the second person who said a stranger looked like the Rock! First Robyn and now

Zoe… "Zoe, by chance do you remember what the guy was wearing?"

"Actually I do, he had on a nice black sports jacket and blue jeans, why?"

"Just trying to figure out who it could be." *What is going on? Who the hell is this man?*

Twenty Two

It's been about a year since I've been to the *Muse* hotel and as I walk into the lobby area with its elegant metallic leather, silk velvet and marble furnishings in the lobby's living room, it definitely brings back good memories. Unfortunately, I'll have to save *that* story for another time. Meanwhile, I called Ty to tell him that I'm downstairs and he's on his way down. I smile at the handsome man behind the desk as I walk by him and sit down on one of the many sofas. I open my satchel and quickly reapply my lipstick while sucking on an *Altoid.* I had just started to people-watch when the elevator door opens across the other side of the lobby. Several people emerge before I see him. *Damn! Still fine!* Ty proudly shows off his perfect *camera-ready* smile as soon as he spots me and then walks toward me in s l o w m o t i o n while everyone else in the lobby freezes. Seconds later, I realize he wasn't really walking in slow-mo however in my mind he *definitely* was!

As I stand up to greet him I do a little *Kyle sashay* into those long, strong, chocolate arms... which, coincidently remind me a lot of Omar's. His arms were in fact, one of the first things that I noticed about him. And loved. I smile like a teenager with a crush as we embrace and hold one another. He feels good, as my body instantly conforms with his. Hmm, I don't want to but I better let go before he gets the wrong ass idea. And knowing him, he would!

As I start my release, Ty whispers in my ear, "mmmm…you smell good!"

I want to say, *mmmm….and you feel good* but I just smile and mutter "Thank you."

"Are you hungry?" he asked.

"Actually I had a late lunch, you?"

"I'm good. *Actually* I had a *big* lunch," he says while rubbing his taut, *LL Cool J-ain't-got-nothin'-on-me* stomach. Not that his sweater is tight but it sure as hell is fitting his torso seductively as it falls smoothly along the top of his well-worked out pecks on down to those amazing LL abs. While touching his stomach, I could clearly see the six pack definition but most of the high definition I remembered from when he gave Kai and Nico diving lessons in Orlando. And believe me that was a visual that I could not and most likely will never forget.

"It's good seeing you," I tell him.

"Ditto and thanks again for making time for me."

"I'm glad you asked me to. Sooo have you thought about what you want to do?"

"Well, since you asked," he says, reaching in and pulling something out his back pocket, "I thought maybe we could use these."

"Yesss!! You got the tickets!, We're go-ing to the gaamee!" I sing, in an *Alicia-ish*, kinda way.

While we're in the taxi headed for Madison Square Garden, I ask Ty about his meetings. Ty's been very successful coaching in Italy and is now in the process of trying to get some of the NBA players to come to Europe for a series of fantasy games in conjunction with his Italian team. His meeting was with a couple of NBA execs, and according to Ty they seem to be a lot more than just interested. Ty talks a good game but something tells me that the fantasy games are just a means to something else, to something bigger.

"That's great Ty, so what's the next step?"

"I have to put together some footage of the team along with a detailed outline including Italian sponsorship and a few other things and that's pretty much the gist of it. But enough about me and my meetings, now that I have you face-to-face, Cydney, there's something I'm curious about."

I look at him while thinking, *Curious about what? My age? What do I like to do for fun? What happened with my last relationship? Wha….*

"What about the other two?"

"Wh..what other two?" I ask having absolutely no idea what two he's referring to.

He sees the look on my face then laughs. "Sorry, I know that came out of left field but it's been something that I've been thinking about ever since we were in Florida."

"Okaaay," I say still waiting for him to tell me what the hell he's curious about.

"Remember at the restaurant when we were doing that ETF question thing and you mentioned that there were three books that made an impact on your life. You mentioned *The Celestine Prophecy* but you never mentioned the other two books."

"Oh," I say, feeling somewhat embarrassed that I allowed my mind to think that Ty's *curiosity* was more personal. Recovering quickly, I tell him, "Oh, those books. They were, *Embraced by the Light* and *Mutant Message Down Under.*" I even managed to say it with a smile. As soon as the words left my mouth and before Ty had a chance to respond, our taxi pulls up in front of Madison Square Garden. Ty pays the driver and we jump out and disappear into the large crowd of Knicks fans.

Twenty Three

Puh-leeze tell me something exciting!" she pleads. I can hear her bated breath through the phone in what I'm sure is sheer anticipation for something, *anything* to feed that overly voracious and vicarious appetite of hers!

"Robyn, *once again*, there really isn't a whole lot to tell, Ty got us Knicks tickets right on the floor and of course, the seats were incredible. In fact, if we had been any closer Ty could have suited up and gone on the floor and played with the team! Lord knows they could've used the help. Oh, I do have a little something to quench your thirst and feed that vicarious appetite of yours! Girl, guess who was sitting *directly* behind us?"

"Who? D.Pak?"

"No smart ass, Gayle King!"

"Get out!! Was she with her BFF?"

"No, she was with her children, Kirby and Will who are quite mature and actually very entertaining. Rob, it was like we were with old friends."

"So, what did you *old friends* talk about?"

"Initially background stuff until Gayle asked about Ty's playing days then at that point her son must've asked Ty at *least* a million and two questions about M.J. and the Bulls. Then later when Ty went to the bathroom, Gayle first asked about Ty and if we were a couple then she wanted to know what industry I was in. She seemed very interested when I told her that I was a designer, especially when I told her about DK*Urban* and how I came about developing it. She even asked me to bring a few of my samples to *O Magazine*'s fashion editor."

"Damn, gurl, that's great. Did she give you her number?"

"Yep, we exchanged cards. She's really down-to-earth. I like her a lot. Ty thought she was cool too. Listening to them talk you would have thought they'd known one another for years. It was obvious that she's a huge basketball fan and you know Ty loved and appreciated that…"

"Sounds like you all had a good time. Good for you. So after the five of you held hands and swayed back and forth singing the first chorus of *Kumbaya,* tell me, did *anything* juicy happen with you and Hershey? *Anydamnthing?"*

Does it ever end? I swear that girl's like that friggin' energizer bunny. She just goes on and on just like that stupid ass rabbit! "Not really, after the game we went back to the hotel bar, talked over a drink and then I jumped in a taxi and headed back to Brooklyn. Then, early tomorrow we're going shopping, and later meeting one of Ty's friends for dinner."

"That sounds like a couple thing, so does that mean that there are some sparks?" she asks in a seemingly last ditch effort for something to chew on.

"No Robyn, no couple, no sparks, just two newly acquainted friends getting to know one another," I say with my voice dripping with allusions of being fed up with her never-ending, prosecution-style questioning. 'Sorry *Wendy Gossip-Queen Williams*, I have nothing else, juicy or otherwise to report. Now, I gotta go."

"Wait, wait!"

"What now, *Wendy*?"

Her tone now less aggressive, "Did Hershey mention his friend? Did you meet him? Cute, single, rich? All of the above?"

"Nope, have not met him and all I know is that he's an entertainment lawyer and if I remember correctly, Ty said that he just started seeing someone."

"Damn! Why are all the good ones taken?"

"Can't tell you, Rob. Now I really do have to go..."

"Well, try to find out what you can and call me when you get home. Call me."

"Good-bye, Robyn!!" I tell her while pulling a dress out of my closet for tomorrow.

Twenty Four

As I cross the street on Lexington Avenue, I see Ty waiting in front of Bloomingdale's. As soon as he sees me, he reveals his camera ready smile.

"You look nice," he tells me when I approach him.

"Thanks. So do you," I reciprocate as he kisses me on the cheek. "Looks like we hit the jackpot. Not only is it a gorgeous day, Bloomies is having one of their friends and family sales, so whatever we buy will be less 20%."

"Hey, that works for me. Let's go check it out," he says while holding the heavy glass door open.

"So, we're looking for a black leather blazer for those cool nights in Italy, right?"

"Si."

"Okay, have you given any thought to how much you want to spend?"

"No, not really, why?"

"So you can buy it for the price that you're comfortable with. Whenever I want something, I always think of how much I want to pay before I look for it. Then incredibly, when I find it, it's that price," I tell him as we walk through the handbag area. "Sooo all that to say, what you think is what you get. Or as Devin and Will would put it, *Our thoughts initiate the process to our reality*."

Ty stops and looks at me as if all of a sudden I started speaking in Swahili then quickly, as if retracting the look, laughs and says, "You know, Cydney, a year ago I probably would have thought that you were several cans short of a six pack but what you just said actually makes sense. Not to mention that I don't have a damn thing to lose by being open to something that in the long run will ultimately help me, so I'm game. Now, what do you say, we go find that leather jacket!"

"Uhhh, aren't you forgetting something?"

He looks at me blankly.

"Umm, like how much you want to pay for the jacket?"

"Oh yeah, hmmm, $300 is what I *want* to spend but we both know that a nice one is going to cost a lot more than that."

"Not necessarily *unless, of course* you really don't think you're going to find one for that price. Just stay focused on the $300 and believe that we will find it. Okay, now we know what we're looking for and how much you want to pay so let's go do this!" I tell him as we head down the escalator into the men's department.

Twenty Five

This is Ty's last night in town and surprisingly, I'm already beginning to miss him. We've had a really good time and I'm pretty sure that it's going to be hard for me to say good-bye. Actually, I think it's going to be hard for both of us.

We're sitting down at the restaurant's bar, where we're meeting Ty's friend for dinner. We're a little early so Ty suggested that we have a drink so we can finish our conversation before his friend arrives. Ty is checking out the wine list as I admire the cozy, family-owned restaurant. Just as I glance out the window I notice a man staring inside, more specifically, staring at us! Ty can see that I'm preoccupied and quickly puts the wine list down.

"What's wrong?"

"Uh, it's probably nothing; it just looks like someone is watching us through the window."

Ty immediately turns toward the window and surprise, surprise, there's no one's there. "It was probably just someone who wanted to see what the inside of the restaurant looks like," he reasons.

"Yeah, that's probably what it was," I say hoping Ty is right, although I didn't really think he was.

We came directly from the hotel to the restaurant but before that, we stopped in Barnes & Noble so that Ty could check out some of the books we had talked about. When we got to the section where all the books were, Ty's eyes lit up like Kai and Nico's the day I took them to *Dylan's Candy Store!* Ty couldn't believe that there were so many books with the same similar message. After looking through several of the books he concluded that if everyone was saying the same thing, there had to be some validity to their content. Ty had at least eight books in his basket but I whittled his selection down to the three that I felt would best help him get started on his newfound journey. Interestingly enough, one of the three books was appropriately titled, *Your Journey, Your Purpose* which also happens to be one of my favorite books. I told Ty in addition, it was the focus of our group's homework assignment for this month.

Several hours later in the restaurant, Ty's curiosity not only continued, it grew.

"When we were in the bookstore and you said that all the pieces were coming together and starting to make sense, were you referring to your journey or purpose?"

"My purpose."

"How's it coming?"

"This month's assignment focuses primarily on our parents; noting what they stand for, what's important to them, what they instilled into their children etcetera. It also zeroes in on the reader with questions regarding who we are and what our interests and strengths are. So, once I answered all the questions, it was like finding the last piece to a mysterious puzzle. And with each answer, more and more made sense."

"That's really cool. You must be excited. Can I assume that the mystery is solved?"

"Not quite, but since all the pieces are there, I would like to think soon. Now, the fun part begins—interpreting the completed puzzle and relating it to my purpose. Then, hopefully tomorrow during our meeting it will all make sense and I will live happily ever after, although *now* with purpose."

Ty is noticeably intrigued but just as he's about to speak, a tall and distinguished man approaches him from behind.

"Tyson, how are you my man?"

His voice is smooth and sexy like Terrence Howard's. Well, his voice may be Terrence's but his face is *all* Idris Elba with sprinkles of salt and pepper. Ty stands up, smiling cheek to cheek as he and his friend exchange a shoulder to shoulder man hug.

"Tony, wassup man? It's good seeing you! Let me introduce you to my friend. Cydney, this is Tony, Tony, Cydney."

I stand and extend my arm to shake Tony's hand but instead of extending his, he smiles and opens both arms for a full embrace.

"Hello Cydney, any friend of Tyson's is a friend of mine!"

As we break from our embrace, I glance toward the entrance and surprisingly, see my "NBF" (new best friend), Gayle! She looks over in our direction then smiles and walks over. As she approaches us, I prepare to greet and introduce her, just as Tony turns and sees her.

"Oh good, you found us," he tells her, grinning like a boy with the latest *X Box* game! "Let me introduce you," he said stealing my line as my "NBF" eases effortlessly into his open arm. Gayle, smiles warmly at Ty and me.

"Hello Ty and Miss Cydney! Well, this is a pleasant surprise! I had no idea that I was going to see the two of you this evening."

Ty greets her first, and then she and I hug as confusion swirls around in my head while Tony stands there as if someone just snatched his new *X Box*. He looks dumbfounded and completely mystified.

"Wa -wait a minute, you three know each other?" he manages to stammer.

"Yeah, man, Gayle and her children sat behind Cyd and me at the Knicks game the other night," Ty answers, laughing at, I'm sure, the look on Tony's face.

"So obviously you two know one another as well! Ty deduces."

"Yes, yes, we do, Gayle is the new friend that I told you about. Damn, man this is a small world."

While we're laughing, the hostess comes over and shows us to our booth. As we're being seated, I notice Tony checking out Ty's attire.

"Nice jacket, man."

Smiling, Ty looks at me and winks, "Thanks man, I just got it."

Twenty Six

"So, tell me wassup? Is Hershey's friend with someone or not?"

I smile as I think about how confused Ty and I must've looked last night when Tony introduced Gayle to us.

"Rob, you're not going to believe this, not only is he with someone, but that someone is *Gayle King!* You should have seen Ty's and my faces when she walked over to us, well, so we thought, but ended up joining *Tony!*" I tell her as I turn the volume up on the phone's speaker.

"Shut the hell up!!!"

"I know, we couldn't believe it either," I tell her while carefully pulling one of my porcelain serving plates down from the kitchen shelf.

"It sure is a small damn world! Well, so much for wanting to know more about Ty's *now* unavailable friend. So, once you and Ty got over the *it's-a-small-world* shock, how was dinner? Anything else happen?"

"Dinner was a good time squared. Gayle and Tony both told stories that had us laughing all through dinner, which needless to say, was delicious! And girl, that key lime pie was so good I thought my butt had died and gone to pie heaven! So yeah, the four of us got along quite well and all in all we had a great time."

"Okay, so with which course did all of you break out and start singing the Kumbaya remix?"

"Hmmm, sounds like Robbie Poo is jealous."

"No I'm not!"

"Okay, then, don't be a hater. We can't help it if we got along."

"Yeah, yeah whatever. So tell me what happened with Hershey? Anything?"

"No, Ty and I actually left Gayle and Tony at the restaurant then headed back to the *Muse* for one last drink and to say our good-bye's. And then I went home."

I really want to tell Rob about the man in the window but decide not to since she would probably just make it worse by asking another million and one questions. Questions that, right now, I can't answer!

"So, when did you come home? This morning?"

"No, Robyn."

"Well, did you at least go up to his room?"

"No, Robyn."

There is no way in hell that I'm going to tell her that I went up to his room. And then tell her that all we did was *talk!* She would swear on a stack of her daddy's bibles that I was lying. And I know she wouldn't believe that Ty and I talked mostly about Omar and me not hearing from him. I first told Ty about "O" in Florida, the night of the barbeque in the pool house. I think the wine we had got to me because before I knew it, I was telling Ty *everything,* even the embarrassing toe-curling sex comment during my big Federated presentation. Clearly, the wine was in full effect. It was all good though because Ty is a great listener, and has proven to be a really good friend. In fact, the more I was with him, the more comfortable I was opening up to him. Obviously, men understand men better than women so when you think about it, it makes sense that Ty would be the ideal person to talk to about Omar, more so than my female friends especially *Ms. Gotta-know-everydamnthing!*

"Don't try to tell me that you guys didn't kiss this time! Sooooo, tell me did you lock lips?"

Sooooo, tell me did you pass the bar? "Just a peck."

"That's it? Just a little peck?"

"That's what friends do, Robyn, P-E-C-K!!"

"Whatever! You two are hopeless. So, what are you doing today? Do you wanna go to *Two Steps Down* for brunch?"

"I can't, remember, it's the first Sunday of the month and Dev and Willie are on their way over as we speak. In fact, I just finished baking something for our meeting."

"Yummm, what did you bake?"

"I baked a loaf of sweet potato nut bread for Dev and me."

"What, no bread for little Willie?"

"Nope. I have fruit and nuts for him. Remember, Will only eats organic and natural foods."

"What's he doing, training to be a monk?"

"No girl, he's keeping his body in..." I begin to explain but am interrupted by my intercom's loud buzzer. I walk over to the intercom. "Robyn, I'm sorry, let me call you back later, they're here."

"Okay, tell them I said hey and gurl, save me some of that bread!"

"Okay, talk to you later," I tell her as I buzz Dev and Willie in.

Twenty Seven

In between chomps of sweet potato nut bread, Devin somehow, manages to spew out a sentence. "So last but not least…. Cyd, what, if anything were you…. able to pull from the exercise?" Devin asks while munching on a piece of bread.

"Nothing definitive. I answered the questions and all the pieces of the puzzle are there but I still haven't gotten a clear picture."

"Maybe it'll be clearer if you read your parent summary out loud," Will suggests.

"Well, I guess it's worth a try if you think it's going to help. Okay, here goes;

Like my father, a highly respected professor at Columbia University, I also, enjoy sharing my knowledge and wisdom with others, especially that which is spiritually oriented. And like my mother, I'm someone my friends and family come to for advice – advice that I've been told is not only helpful but on point. Creativity plays a large part of who I am as it does for my mother. Challenges, for both me and my mother are an integral component of our spirituality because of its correlation to growth."

"Good, good so now take a moment and silently review your summary noting the key points or trigger words in your head and see what, if anything comes to you."

"Okay." *...teacher, good listener, challenges, spiritual growth, creative, communicate, advice, inspire others, counsel...*

As I continue going over the trigger words in my head, the only thing I'm getting, is a friggin' headache. I'm probably trying too hard but one thing I do know, is that it *definitely* doesn't help with Devin and Will staring at me!

"Nope, nada, nothing," I tell them.

"Okay, well don't worry it, this is something that shouldn't be forced. I'm sure when the time is right it'll come to you," Will reasons.

"Yeah, you're close though," Devin adds.

"Thanks guys, I'm sure you're right. I just need to be patient and not try so hard."

"Exactly. Okay Cyd, we have an appointment so thanks again for the fruit and nuts," Will says as he heads to the door while juggling a *Granny Smith.*

Devin follows as he shoves another piece of nut bread in his mouth.

"No problem. And as soon as something comes to me, you two will be the first to know," I tell them as they walk out.

While locking the door, I'm wondering what kind of appointment they have.

As I take their empty glasses and plates into the kitchen I remember that Devin mentioned that he and Willie were starting to generate some interest from a good number of people in their life coach consulting company. As I wash the glasses I'm envisioning Will and Devin with clients and I think about how differently I believe they would handle clients compared to how I think I would. Their approach, my guess, would be the total opposite of my approach… "Oh my God! That's it! Yesssss! I got it!"

Twenty Eight

Surprisingly, I'm not nervous, although I probably should think about how all this is going to play out. Because the last thing I want is to appear pitiful or even worse, desperate! I mean, what do you say to someone when all the signs and I mean *all* the signs, point to that person not wanting to have anything to do with you?

I'm on my way to Omar's apartment to *finally* find out what the hell happened that day he left my office with one of the company's models. Last night when Ty and I were saying goodbye, he suggested that I man up (or in my case, woman up) and go talk to Omar face-to-face to hear his side of the story. This way, he said, even if it's something I don't want to hear, I'll at least have some answers and be able to move on from there. With or without him. So now, I'm marching my butt over to his apartment to confront his ass, once and for all.

The timing worked out perfectly with Will and Devin leaving early for their "appointment." If they hadn't, I probably would have changed my mind or made an excuse or two for not going. Speaking of the dynamic duo, I have to call them to share my new revelation with them. But that's going to have to wait because right now, I need to get over to Omar's for some long, over-due answers and this is not the time to get sidetracked. Besides, it's probably best if I let my revelation marinate some before sharing it with Will and Devin.

Meanwhile, this is my first time going over to Omar's apartment since he moved back to New York and all I can say is thank goodness for GPS! Omar's apartment building is tucked in between a small group of trees on a nice quiet street. Fortunately, there is a parking space right in front of his building seemingly just waiting for me. I rehearse my opening line several times before getting out of the car. As I march up the concrete walkway, a large man brushes past me, obviously preoccupied because he doesn't look up at all, not even when his shoulder blatantly grazes mine. I glance back at him expecting a grunt, nod or *some* form of an apology but instead his rude ass just jumps into his black sedan and hastily drives off.

As I approach the entrance of the apartment building my hands start sweating and I begin to get an uncomfortable feeling in the pit of my stomach. Meanwhile, my mind is filled with a million and one *what-ifs*; *What if he's not alone or even worse, what if he doesn't want to see me or maybe both?* I'm really not up for rejection. After contemplating various outcomes, none of them good, I head back to my car. While opening the car door, I rethink the situation and once more, change my mind then return to the building's entrance. I immediately press Omar's intercom before I chicken out, again. There's no answer. I ring it several more times just as a couple of kids run out of the building. I move quickly putting my foot in the door leaving just enough room to slip in. I don't see an elevator so I take the stairs up to the third floor. When I come out of the stairwell and turn the corner, I notice that the end apartment's door is partially open. As I check the apartments for #3G I soon realize that it's the end apartment. While walking… **BOOM!!!** I jump at the loud noise coming from behind me, ignoring every instinct to drop to the ground. *What the hell?* Suddenly three teenagers emerge from another entrance of a stairwell opposite of me. It appears that the practical joker of the three slammed the door in a failed attempt to scare the other two who were in front of him. Little does he know that it was *me* who he scared half to death! Laughing, the trio disappeared into apartment #3B.

Now that my *heart* is back in my chest, I continue toward #3G. *Why would he leave his door open? Maybe he was rushing out and forgot something and went back to get it?* Well, whatever the reason, rushing or not, I need some answers! Knowing that closure is imminent, a rush of adrenaline kicks in and my pace quickens. As soon as I get to the door, a dreadful stench greets me at the entrance. I knock cautiously as the cracked door opens further and the odor strengthens. Covering my nose with my hand, I cautiously kick the door open.

"Oh my God! OOOOMAAR!!!!"

Twenty Nine

"Ok wait, slow down, you're talking a million damn words a minute! So wait, why did you go over there in the first place? Don't tell me that his no good, two-timin' playa ass *finally* called you?"

"No Robyn, he didn't call," I start to tell her while pacing back and forth on my living room rug. "I went over there because I wanted closure," I tell her while trying to talk slower, "so I decided to confront him. I wanted…no, I *needed* to know once and for all why he left with…*her!*"

"Cydney, where is all this coming from? I thought you were over his *love'em and leave'em* ass! Okay, so wait, first things first. I need you to start from the very beginning, you drove over to his apartment and then what?"

"I rang his bell and no one answered. Then when someone came out of the building, I slipped in and went up to his apartment. His door was slightly opened so I knocked and went in. And Rob, I have never seen anything like it. The apartment was completely trashed! It literally looked like a tornado hit it. Girl, stuff was everywhere; garbage, loose papers, books and anything else you can imagine were all over the floor! His couch was turned upside down, chair legs were broken, laundry was everywhere from the front door through to the kitchen. Broken dishes, pots and pans on the floor, a broken lamp with the lamp shade smashed along with his stereo system completely destroyed, CD's all over the apartment floor…Robyn it was a mess, it looked like something straight out of a friggin' CSI episode!"

I can hear Robyn's breath accelerate through the phone.

"Wa..was there any blood?"

I'm beginning to feel queasy as I break out into a cold sweat. "Uh, I'm not sure, I didn't walk around so if there was blo…blood, I didn't see any."

"So, you're not even sure if he was in there?"

"No, but I don't think he was. I mean, I called, rather, I *screamed* his name but nothing."

"So you never even went past the living room?"

"No, I was too scared."

"Well, did you call the police?"

"No, when he didn't answer I just got out of there as quickly as I could."

"But what if he was in the bedroom hurt or maybe even dead?"

"Rob don't say that! That's the thought that keeps haunting me. But I really don't think he was there."

"But how can you be sure?"

"I'm not but I have to believe that he wasn't, uh…isn't."

"So what are you going to do, just pretend like nothing happened?"

"I don't know what I'm gonna do. Do you think I should call the police?"

"Did you touch anything?"

"No, the door was already open so no, I don't think so."

"Damn, I don't know, maybe you should call Black first, then call the police. Since he and Omar are friends, maybe he can help or even better, maybe he knows something."

"Yeah, you're right. I'll call him in a little bit cause girl I'm *still* shaking. And I'm driving myself crazy with a zillion who, why and what-ifs. I just can't imagine who would have trashed Omar's apartment like that. But for now, I just really need to try to calm down and believe that Omar's okay."

"Do you want me to come over?"

"Yes, I do, maybe for a little while if you don't mind. I could use a distraction from all of this, plus I need to get my head together to deal with Gretchen and our meeting tomorrow morning."

"Ok, I'm on my way. I'll stop by *Hop Kee's* and pick up some of those pork chops that we both like so much."

"Thanks Rob, but with everything that's going on, my stomach is acting up. So, the last thing on my mind is food."

"Well, I'll bring some anyway and they'll be there when you feel better. See you soon."

It didn't take Rob long to get here, and I'm glad she came because I really needed someone to help keep me calm. While she was here I called Black to tell him what happened. He went straight over to Omar's as soon as we got off the phone. He called back forty five minutes later and confirmed that the apartment had definitely been broken into but thankfully there was no sign of Omar *and* no visible blood stains in the apartment. The only thing he found were two large dead mice. Black didn't believe it was a robbery. He also didn't think that we should call the police or at least not until he spoke to Omar's mom to find out when was the last time she spoke to or saw "O".

My stomach was still a little upset after speaking to Black, but once I knew that Omar was not inside the apartment, I was, at least, finally able to calm down.

"*…in a city where Coca-Cola, United Parcel Service and Home Depot are the titans of industry, there appears to be new powerful forces on the block:…*"

I drank several cups of the ginger tea Robyn made for me while she was here. Shortly after Black called us back, she left so that I could try to get some much needed rest. As I'm in bed, nodding on and off, I realize the television is on. *That's funny I don't remember turning it on…Hmmm, Robyn must have turned it on.* I'm so out of it, I didn't even see her pick up the remote.

"The Mexican drug cartel's presence and ruthless tactics are largely unknown to most. Yet of the 195 U.S. cities where drug trafficking organizations are operating, federal law officials say Atlanta has emerged as the new Gateway to the troubled Southwest border…"

I try to stay awake to look at the 10 o'clock news but after the day I had, I'm so tired I can't keep my eyes open. I can barely stay awake to listen to the TV, let alone look at it. With my eyes closed, their lids too heavy to open, I feel around the bed for the remote to turn the TV off. During my blind search, I *feel* a couple of batteries, a book and my silk eye mask but no remote. As I slip the eye mask on and lay back, I remember that the timer on the TV is set so *hopefully* any minute now it will automatically turn off…

"In a recent development, a New Jersey man was held captive by Atlanta-based traffickers for allegedly owing over $250,000 to a Mexican cartel. The man was found chained to a wall in the basement of a Lilburn, Georgia home. According to Rodney Benson, the DEA's Atlanta chief, the man was blindfolded, gagged and badly beaten. Federal agents found the man alive but severely dehydrated. In a similar incident a Georgia man, was kidnapped earlier last month for non-payment of drug proceeds. When traffickers went to pick up what they thought to be a two million..."

CLICK

Thirty

"Good morning, Ms. Rochon."

"Good morning. And thanks again for squeezing me in. Will there be a long wait?" I ask while looking around the waiting room.

"No. The nurse will take you in momentarily then the doctor will come in shortly after."

"Great, thanks."

As I flip through this month's issue of *Architectural Digest* and see the perfect replacement rug for my foyer, the nurse calls me and takes me into the examining room. The doctor enters just as I finished changing into the gown.

"Hello Cydney, what brings you here today?"

"Hello doctor, I'm not feeling so hot. It's probably nothing but I'm just feeling drained and I feel a little nauseous. My stomach has been queasy but I haven't had any vomiting."

"How long has this been going on?"

"Since yesterday, uh well actually I had a slight stomach ache several days ago but mostly yesterday."

"Any dizziness, diarrhea?"

"Yes, if a spinning bed counts but no to the diarrhea, I'm happy to report."

"What have you eaten in the last three days that's not part of your usual diet?"

"Pork and fried calamari."

"Okay I'm going to have the nurse come in and examine you and we might as well do a complete physical since you're due for one. When you're done I'll talk to you in my office."

The doctor leaves and I lie down on the examining table. A few minutes later the nurse comes in, and after being prodded and probed, she hands me an empty cup. After the P.O.D (peeing on demand) thing, I got dressed then was routed to the doctor's office. When I enter, the office is empty. The box-shaped space is filled with a lot of interesting pieces of art from several genres. As I walk around and stop to admire one of the abstract pieces, the doctor enters.

"Well Cydney, in addition to your physical we have administered several tests, mostly routine and I'm happy to report that everything for the most part is normal…"

"What do you mean, *for the most part?*"

"Well, Cydney, congratulations! You, my dear, are pregnant!"

What? Congratu-what? I know this woman didn't just say that I'm pre, pregnant! I stop breathing. I look at the doctor with my mouth open waiting impatiently for the words that are whirling around in my head to hurry up and find their way out.

Knowing how absurd me being pregnant is, laughing, I tell her, "No way, nada…sorry but that's *totally* impossible! *These doctors and technicians really need to triple check tests before telling their patients false results. Humph, they probably gave someone else my test results, someone that's looking forward to having a baby and was just told that she's not pregnant when in fact she is! Well at least now, she'll have some good news coming.* Doctor, I don't think that you realize it but I'm celibate and have been for the last five years! This has to be a mistake!!"

"Well, these are the results right here in my hand and the test is positive which means that you *are* pregnant."

"Well, maybe the nurse or lab tech mislabeled or mixed up the cups of urine. I'm *sure* those results belong to one of your other patients."

Cydney, I'm sor…"

"Doctor," I cut her off, "you're not listening, there's no way in hell that I could be pregnant! I CAN'T BE PREGNANT, I just can't! THIS IS DEFINITELY A MISTAKE AND YOU NEED TO GET TO THE BOTTOM OF IT NOW! RIGHT NOW!!!!"

Thirty One

Walgreens must have a million and one pregnancy test kits. I stopped here after I asked the doctor if I could take another pregnancy test and she told me that they don't make mistakes then smugly handed me an *Uncommon Pregnancies* pamphlet. I wanted to slap her smug face with it! I'm sorry but *everyone* makes mistakes, know-it-all doctors included! That's okay, I'll take my own damn test which is precisely why I'm in the *pee-on-a-stick* aisle. There are several different brands so I just grab the two that I've seen advertised on TV, then head toward the check out.

As I pass the food section I also grab a quart of mint chocolate ice cream. I don't know why because I've always hated chocolate and mint together but for some reason now, it seems like it might actually be good. Go figure!

Once home, I can't get out of the car fast enough. I run into the bathroom with both tests. I pee on both sticks at the same time just so the urine is the same on both. Several minutes later the results are ready. I hear a drum roll silently in my head while sitting on the edge of the bed while taking a deep breath. I slowly peep at both of them…… P O S I T I V E….What the hell? Is this some type of conspiracy? My grip loosens as the sticks fall to the floor. I still can't believe it! How can I be pregnant *and* celibate at the same time? I fall back on my bed as tears slowly roll down my face.

It's been awhile since I've cried. Especially a cry of helplessness, fear *and* denial. And I mean deep, deep denial one that has me crawling into bed and rocking myself back and forth, knees clutched to my chest while wondering, how and why. How did this happen and why me? With no answers, I cry even more as I clutch my pillow tighter and tighter..

If I am pregnant and I do mean *if*, it couldn't happen at a worse time. Especially, since I haven't heard one word from Omar. I can't even begin to imagine raising his child without knowing where he is and why he left or at this point, if he's even still alive. But I also can't imagine having an abortion. Frankly, I don't think that I could go through with it. And if I did, I don't think that I could live with myself. Maybe when I was younger I would have considered it but now, I see life with a completely different set of eyes.

I just don't understand how or why this could be happening to me. If this did happen by some freak mishap then how in the hell am I going to explain to my friends and family that I'm pregnant by a man who up and left with a model from my job? How is that going to sound? I'll tell you, not good and leaving me to look like a complete fool! And, if it is true and I finally get the courage to tell my friends and family, my entire friggin' life is going to change drastically.

Sure, I make an okay salary but my entire lifestyle is centered around one person, me, not me plus one. I will have to cut back on just about everything, and I don't even want to begin thinking about researching schools! Wait, what the hell am I doing? I can't believe that I'm already thinking about schools! Hell, I'm still reeling from the pregnancy tests, all three of them! And here I am thinking about schooling when I haven't even confirmed or accepted being pregnant.

This is way too much for me to deal with right now. And I *still* need to mentally prepare for her majesty tomorrow. As I close my eyes, I tell myself that everything is going to be okay. "*Everything is going to be okay*, e*verything is going to be okay*," I whisper over and over until I finally fall asleep, damp pillow and all.

Thirty Two

Good morning, Zoe!"

"Good morning, Cydney. Gretchen is waiting for you in her office."

What? It's only 8:42. She usually doesn't get in til 9:30.

"How long has she been waiting?"

"She was already here when I got in at 8:25."

"Okay. Thanks, Zoe." I rush into my office, throw my stuff down, grab all of the Graffiti samples and high tail it down to Queenie's office.

As I enter, she's looking through a file.

"Welcome back, Gretchen, how was Europe?"

"Hello, Cydney. It was fine, thank you. Come in and have a seat," she says flatly while closing the file.

"Thanks. Should I call Kyle in or do you want to meet with me first?"

"I'll meet with Kyle later, right now I want you to fill me in with what's been going on while I was in Europe."

"Okay. Well, I found a *great* graffiti print fabric that I thought would be a perfect addition to the line so I had it custom designed for DK*Urban*, and asked the sample hands to make up a few samples." I tell her while showing her a small presentation board with my sketches along with the original graffiti design. Gretchen's expression is completely blank and not at all what I expected. Lord knows I've seen many faces of hers, but I'm not quite sure how to read this one. She should *love* this but instead she's looking at my mini board as if she's mentally dissecting it. One by one, piece by piece.

"You know, Cydney," she begins, then pauses for about five seconds. "I, I… It's not bad… and actually it could work. This is what the buyers ask for — something with that extra punch. Are those some of the samples that you have in your hand?"

"Yes," I tell her while holding up one of the samples. "I had some sample yardage made up so we could see how the print looks on a garment."

"Great, let's get Tasha in here so she can try them on."

"She's still on vacation, but I can have one of the other models try them on this afternoon."

"When is she…. never mind. I'll have Kyle schedule a fitting later. Okay, good. Now…I need to talk to you about the Federated presentation. Cydney, I'm sure I don't have to tell you from a financial viewpoint just how much Federated Stores means to this company. Federated buyers place orders for over 800 stores which are roughly in forty five states throughout the country and nailing the DK*Urban* presentation could very well translate into a twenty million dollar order, minimum! Just think about that for a moment, TWENTY MILLION DOLLARS!!!!

And single-handedly, within a mere fifteen minutes you showed them a very salable line while simultaneously compromising the integrity and professionalism of the company, which I might add, up until now has been flawless. But you alone, drastically reduced our chances of getting this or any other future Federated orders! I can't even begin to tell you how difficult it was for Kyle and me to pick up from your, your....mess! And I don't even want to *think* about how Donna is going to react now that she's back. I'm sure *now*, thanks to you *both* our butts are on the line.

Wah wah MILLION..Wah..integrity….my mind can no longer comprehend anything that Gretchen is saying. My head is in a complete fog. What the hell is happening? One minute I'm showing her the Graffiti concept which is what the buyers want and then the next minute, this! WTH?? I really thought that all this Federated mess was behind us and that we were moving forward! When I came in this morning I expected her to tell me that the Federated buyers loved everything and are ready to place a humongous order! Damn that Omar! He comes back, we reconnect and then his brown ass runs off with the first friggin' pretty face he sees and because of that now my ass is on the damn line! I cannot believe that I let this happen! Wah wah...WAH!

"Wah, wah …So Cydney, YOU'RE FIRED!!!!!"

Wait, wh…what? I know this wicked witch didn't just fire me! This cannot be happening, especially now when I might be pregnant!!! I'm numb and nothing and I mean nothing is making sense.

"Gretchen please, you cannot be serious! I know I messed up, but can't you re-schedule another meeting with Federated so I can do another presentation? After all, the urban division is my concept and I did design the entire line!"

"Oh, and let's not forget that you are *also* the one that almost destroyed it! Now, exactly what part of FIRED doesn't seem to be resonating? So yes, Cydney I am serious and no, we will *not* be rescheduling another presentation. You had your moment in the sun and you blew it and now we're going to try to recover from your verbal tsunami and move on, *without you.* And, as much as it pains me to do so, you've left me with no choice!! Now, that will be all," she tells me as she stands. "I will have Kyle pack your personal belongings and whatever it is you have here then make sure that they are sent to you. Now, if you don't mind, I have to fill Donna in on everything and hope to hell that firing you will save *my* ass from the chopping block."

This witch is really serious! "Look Gretchen, I know we haven't always seen eye to eye but don't you think that you are blowing this whole thing a little out of proportion?"

"And don't *you* think that your actions in the conference room were a *little* unprofessional and highly inappropriate?"

"C'mon Quee.." *Oops!*

"Queenie? *That* is what you were about to call me, isn't it?"

Damn that Kyle! I should have known better than to trust his two-faced butt!

"You didn't think I knew about your little pet names for me, now did you?"

I am sooo pissed that I can't even begin to try to defend myself! As it is, I'm using every ounce of strength not to grab the samples and wrap them around that wicked witch's neck! But at this point I realize that this witch's mind is made up and it doesn't matter what I say or try to do, so I just get up and head for the damn door before I say or do something that I will later regret.

"Gretchen, as much as I wish you would change your mind, it's obvious that your mind is made up so I won't waste my time by reminding you of all that I've contributed to the company and how much money I've made for DK. Up until this moment, my experience with the company has been good, and despite everything that has happened, I appreciate the opportunity that *Donna* has given me," I tell her while feeling like I just finished several rounds with *Laila Ali.* Then I grab the samples and walk out of her office. *Damn! Damn! Damn!*

Thirty Three

The *River Café* which is nestled under the Brooklyn Bridge has proven to be one of Brooklyn's premier restaurants with sweeping views of the New York skyline and the Statue of Liberty. And if you like lobster, they have the best on this side of the bridge.

"Sweetheart you look tired. Are you okay?"

"Hmmm, I'm okay mama. When is daddy coming home from the conference?"

"Tomorrow afternoon. Why don't you come over for dinner tomorrow evening or are you working late?"

"I'll call you but I should be able to make it."

"So, tell me honey, what happened with Federated? Did they place a large order?"

The waiter brings our appetizers – pear salad for my mother and the crab bisque for me.

Perfect timing. Now hopefully mama will focus on her salad and forget about work and that stupid Federated order. I really don't want to lie to my mother but if I have to I will, at least until I can wrap my head around what happened. Although, there is a part of me that wants to tell her about everything that happened earlier with that witch, but I'm still in my I-can't-believe-this-bullshit-happened-to-me mode.

"Mmmm these pears are sweet. How's your bisque?"

"Good, there seems to be a touch of coconut in it which normally I'm not a fan of but surprisingly it tastes good. Wanna taste?"

"No thanks, I'm enjoying my salad. So tell me, how big was the order?"

Damn! So much for perfect timing. "I don't know mama I'm not even sure they're going to place an order. I really didn't want to bring this up tonight but I met with Gretchen today and well…she hmm, kinda decided to let me go because of the whole presentation debacle."

My mother stops eating her salad and looks at me, initially in shock but seconds later a wave of maternal sympathy sweeps over her slightly wrinkled face.

"I'm sorry, baby. Are you okay?"

"Yeah, I'm okay. Money for now, isn't a major issue; thanks to *Mellody Hobson* and her emergency plan."

"Well, good baby, I'm glad you listened to her because she knows what she's talking about. Now, what about your resume?"

"Mama, you know how anal I am about keeping my resume up to date, so really all I have to do is get out there and start looking."

"Okay, well good honey. Now, I'm curious, did this happen as a result of that day dreaming blooper involving Omarion?"

My sister and her big ass mouth! Mama's cool and all, but I really didn't want her to know everything about that day, especially the headboard banging slip!

"Uh, yes mama, but his name is Omar."

"Okay, Omar then…Now look, sweetheart, you know that I don't judge anyone, especially not my girls. You are both grown and your father and I have raised you two to have good heads on your shoulders. So all I'm going to say are these two things: one, it is crucial to keep your personal life and your career life separate. Once the two are mixed or overlapped in some way, it spells nothing but trouble! And two, Cyd, as you know, *everything* happens for a reason and my experience has been, if we find ourselves in a situation that we have not consciously chosen then I see that as an opportunity to see and experience a new or different aspect of ourselves. An aspect or side of us that we would never have been privy to. So sweetheart, just pull the lesson from all this and move on with a light heart, an open mind and no regrets!"

I smile for the first time today and am so grateful for my mother and how she's always been there for me and Jordyn. In fact, I almost want to tell her about the baby…*almost!* But I need to know what's going on with Omar before I tell anyone, anything!

"Thanks mama, I really needed to hear that. You always know what to say to make me feel better."

Thirty Four

Before mama's *I'm-just-going-to-say-two-things* speech, being fired was not exactly on the top of my *things-to-talk-about* list. However, after her *exactly-what-I-needed-to-hear* speech I'm able to refocus and see the situation for what it really is, a challenge and an opportunity to explore myself in a new and different way. Okay, maybe those were mama's words but I really am ready to move on and embrace whatever's coming my way. For real. Especially with my little one on its way; I have to! So, starting tomorrow I'm going to make a few additions to my portfolio and put together a list of companies to send my resume to.

While preparing a fruit salad I see the message light on my phone blinking. With salad and organic tea in hand, I head into the living room.

BEEP

"Hi Cyd, it's Zoe. Look, Gretchen asked me to delete all your personal files on your computer and while I was deleting your emails I saw the one that your friend Robyn sent you with photos from "James' Birthday Thing." And there is one of you with a guy in the background standing near a palm tree. Cyd, I couldn't believe it, but that man is the same man that came to the office asking for you; Dwayne remember? Just thought you would want to know! Okay, call me!"

What? That's got to be the guy that Robyn said was staring at me when we first arrived at James' party! I remember I turned around to see him but the stupid tree was blocking his face…. Actually when she first emailed me the photos I remember that I was on my way to a meeting so I just looked at them quickly and don't recall seeing that particular photo. Robyn took most of the pictures that night and still has my camera. I need to call and ask her to forward the photos to my personal email so I can see once and for all who the hell this friggin' man is!

BEEP

"Cyd, it's me again, I forget to ask you what you want me to tell people when they call and ask for you? Okay, and when you get a chance, let's have lunch!!"

That's easy! Just tell them that I have moved on to bigger and better things!!

BEEP

"Uh..Hello, Cydney. It's Kyle. I heard what happened and I'm sor..sorry! Don't want to bo…bother you, but can you tell me where the graffiti samples are? I'll need them for a presentation next week. Thanks, and good luck!"

You have some damn nerve! Good luck with that!

BEEP

"Hey Cyd, it's Shaye. Jackson's friend told him that you two talked on the phone a couple nights ago. So, I'm just glad you guys finally connected! Call me and let know what you think."

Alex is great but right now I need to call Robyn and find out who this damn man is!

"CALL ROBYN" I demand as my voice activated wireless phone automatically dials her number. Within seconds her line rings and Rob answers.

"Hello."

"Hey girl, can you do me a favor and forward those photos from James' birthday to my home email?" I ask her while turning my laptop on.

"I emailed them to your job email, I thought you got them."

"I did but I'm at home and I need to look at them now."

"I'm actually on my way out, I have a date. Can't you just wait and look at them tomorrow at work?"

Now is not the time to tell Rob about Queenie letting me go, I'll tell her when I see her. But first, I need to figure out who the hell this man is! "Rob, this is important. I think the guy near the palm tree is the same man who came to my job asking for me. Remember, I told you that Zoe said a man came to the office several times? Well, this could be the same person according to Zoe, so can you just email it to me or you can bring me my camera, but either way I really need to find out who the hell this man is!"

"Ok, I'm not even gonna ask you how or why Zoe thinks it's the same man. Just give me a few minutes so that I can call Mr. Big and tell him that I'll be running a little late."

"Okay, thanks, Rob!" I tell her as I hang up and log into my email.

Wait, did she say Mr. Big? Nah, it can't be…..

Thirty Five

I just got the photos that Rob emailed me. Okay, let's see, here's Rob, James and me at the bar, oh yeah, and this is the one I took of Steve Harvey signing Robyn's copy of *Act like a Lady, Think like a Man,* Chris Rock, James and…"What the hell…? Oh my God!" I yell almost dropping my damn Earl Grey! "This is insane, IT *IS* HIM!"

The man in the background is not only the same man that came by my office looking for me but he's *also* the same friggin' man that brushed past me outside of Omar's apartment building! Even though his head was down and we never actually made eye contact, I could see enough of his face to remember his rude ass. This is CRAZY and there is no way in hell that these damn *sightings* are coincidences! Zoe saw him first at my job, then Robyn saw him at James' birthday party and then I saw him right outside of Omar's apartment! Okay, this is *beyond crazy!!* Who the hell is this man? I have looked and looked at the photo and he does not look even remotely familiar. I can't even begin to wrap my head around this insanity which means I am *definitely* going to need some help with this one. I just need to think of someone who I can trust and who's no stranger to situations like this.

I automatically start pacing back and forth hoping that it'll help me connect the dots. Lately, I've noticed that pacing helps me think. My theory is that the back and forth motion stimulates the brain thus the more I pace, the more active and alert my brain appears to be. The pacing also helps to alleviate my frequent bouts of nausea which is definitely an added bonus.

After a few minutes of pacing, I yell, "YES!" as I come up with the only person who I can think of to help get to the bottom of this insanity. I grab my things and run to the door However, when I open it, there's something in front of the door blocking the entrance! It's a covered basket in the middle of the doorway. I bend down to pick it up, and the damn thing moves! I instinctively jump. What the hell? I bend back down while carefully peeping under the basket's cover. I see a pair of little eyes. Holding my chest, I step back and slowly take the cover off. Ahhh, inside is the cutest puppy ever! I pick him up and find a note tied to his little collar.

Dear Cydney,

I don't know where else to begin except with sorry. I know that I have a lot of explaining to do and I'm ready to talk whenever you are. Along with my apology please accept this gift. I remember you saying you wanted a maltipoo puppy and that you wanted to name him Milo. So, here he is! I know he'll be in good, loving hands.

Omar.

OMG! Omar? He was here? While picking up the most adorable puppy on the planet, I quickly look down the hallway to see if I see Omar. Unfortunately, there is no sign of anyone, anywhere. I hug little Milo and take him into his new home.

I can't believe that Omar was here, right outside my door! Why didn't he knock? There are so many mixed emotions whirling around inside me that now that Omar's is here, I *really* don't know how I feel. I don't know if I should, hug, kick, smack or choke him! But the one thing I do know is that my butt better get some answers!

Looking down at my little cutie pie I can't help but smile. I can't believe that I finally have a puppy and that Omar remembered that I wanted one. However, I'm clueless as to what to do first. He's so little and vulnerable but is just as cute as he can be. I carry Milo over to the couch and spread his little blanket out. I pick up the phone and immediately dial Shaye, my newly appointed resident puppy expert with her two little yorkies.

Shaye picks up on the third ring. We talk for a few minutes before she rattles off a list of things that I will need along with her personal do's and don'ts for new mommies. As soon as we hang up, I pour some water in a small bowl and place it on the floor. And Milo wastes no time slurping it up. I look in the kitchen and get the box from *Costco* with the side already cut out then fold and place Milo's little blanket inside. Then I place the box next to the couch as a temporary bed for my new addition. Then I stuff my list in my pocket then grab my purse so I can go to *Puppies R Us* and buy a real bed, crate, dog clothes and food. I should also pick up a book on how to care for your puppy. I can alternate reading it with my *Your First Baby* book. Just as I walk toward the door, my intercom rings, I lean into the speaker and press **TALK**.

"Who is it?" I ask while pressing **LISTEN**

"Omar."

Thirty Six

I've been waiting for this day! And now it's *finally* here! I mean really, the nerve of him to come to *my* office to see *me* and then leave with a model from *my* company! Now, you *know* that was some bold ass nerve!

I can't lie; Omar looks *good*, a little tired but good, *real* good. And admittedly, it *was* really sweet of him to buy little Milo for me. But Milo or no Milo, I still need answers! I'm pissed and am trying my best to *stay* pissed but it's not going to be easy with Omar looking so good and then to have little Milo looking up at me with those cute little puppy eyes of his. *Don't get weak, Omar always looks good. Be STRONG, STAY MAD. HE OWES YOUR ASS AN EXPLANATION!*

That's right! And hell, he should be tired! My butt would be tired too, if I just returned from jetting off to an exotic island with a gorgeous friggin' model and am now back trying to make amends with the woman I reconnected with right before I left! Am I still bitter? Damn friggin' skippy I am and quite honestly I don't know one person on this earth who wouldn't be! Right now, all I want are answers and I just hope like hell that he has some.

While I'm in the kitchen pouring Omar a glass of juice there's an emotional tug of war whirling around inside of me, a dichotomy of sorts that I wasn't at all prepared for. Seeing him again face to face, post drama has surprisingly dissipated my anger and bitterness to a good degree, although there is still that part of me that wants to strangle his golden brown ass. However, as much as I would like to, I can't help that a small part of me is hoping that he looks me in the eyes while professing his undying love for me, pulling me close to his warm, rock hard, body as he kisses me until I'm weak in the knees, then picks me up, carries me into the bedroom and makes wild, passionate love to me! Just like in my fantasy dream. I know that sounds crazy given the situation, but we *still* have not *technically* made love. And frankly, my hormones are kicking in, so needless to say I'm more than ready!

As I re-enter the living room, Omar has turned on some music. *Joe* is crooning through the speakers.

"Girl, I just wanna…."

I walk over to the iPod and punch **PAUSE**.

"Look, all I want to know is why you left with the damn model?" I demand while handing him the glass of juice as I struggle with the growing urge to splash it in his face! "And where in the hell did you two go?" I'm on a roll and don't give him a chance to answer. "Did you go to Dubai with her? I still can't believe that you went from sending me flowers in the morning then surprising me just several hours later for lunch to leaving with the first pretty face you see without saying one word, not one word to me then or later! What the hell is wrong with…?"

"OKAY, okay you can stop right there, I can explain everything but first, baby you *need* to stop talking."

Don't you baby me! At least not until you start explaining! "Fine, go ahead. Please, by all means tell me. I'm all ears."

He takes a deep breath before gulping the last of the juice that I gave him.

"First off, I didn't leave with Tashana, Tashima or whatever the hell her name is. When we got off the elevator, her man was waiting in the lobby with a bunch of suitcases. Then the two of them got in the town car and drove off." *My heart is about to explode, Deep down I knew it! I knew Omar would not have left with Tasha! Sooo that means the man's leg that I saw get in the town car wasn't Omar's, it was Tasha's friend's!*

"So, wait! You're telling me that wasn't you that got into the car with Tasha?"

"Yes, eh no, it wasn't me. It was her boyfriend or whoever the hell was waiting for her in the lobby. So anyway…."

Yessss! My instincts were right!!

Omar continues, deaf to my hushed cheers, "I was going back to the building when these two guys came out of no damn where and before I knew what was happening, one of them pulled out a gun and shoved it in my back while the other one pushed me into a car. Then they blindfolded me and started questioning me about Brendon. It wasn't long before I realized that they were trying to use me to find Bren, who, by the way, is totally innocent."

WTH? Innocent of what? I think to myself but am too stunned to interrupt.

"Then they took me to what had to be a deserted building and drugged me with somethin' because it was several days before I felt strong enough to even try to get the hell outta there. Even now, some of the details are still somewhat sketchy."

Damn! Gun? Drugged? Escaped? This sounds like something straight out of a chapter in Alex Cross's dangerous ass life!

"At this point I had to get to my mom and little brother to make sure they were safe. I made a quick pit stop to my apartment to shower and grab a change of clothes before heading to the airport."

Okay wait, this is just too much drama not to interrupt!

"Wait a minute, this is unbelievable! Who are these men and why did they want Bren? And why didn't you call for help? I'm not sure what, but maybe I or somebody could have done something to help you."

"Cyd I'm getting to who they are, but just know there was no way in hell that I was going to involve you. I didn't want them to use you too, or even worse, harm you. I just hoped that they didn't follow me up to your floor earlier that morning when I came to take you to lunch. It was bad enough that they followed me to your building. So, there was no way I wanted you involved via phone or otherwise. Besides at that point I had no idea how far they would go to get what they wanted!"

"Okay, but if these men were following you before, weren't you afraid that they would follow you *after* you escaped? And maybe they wanted you to escape thinking that you would lead them to your brother."

"Yeah, but that was a chance that I had to take which is why at the last minute I decided not to drive and instead take the subway to the airport. Anyway, long story short, once I got to *LaGuardia* I took the next flight out then made the necessary arrangements to get my mom and brother somewhere safe. Then just a few days later I found out that that the police, DEA and FBI had been trailing them for a little over a year before gathering enough evidence to close in on their operation. And, seriously, the timing could not have been better for us 'cause Cyd, within three days, pardon my French, the fuckin' nightmare had finally came to a head. All their drug trafficking butts were sent to prison, including the assholes who held me captive."

"Wait, so these men were drug dealers? And how did Bren get mixed up with them?"

"No, these weren't your typical drug dealers. These men were part of a Mexican drug cartel here in the states and my brother's friend, who was doing a favor for someone ended up being at the wrong place at the wrong time. So when the police stopped the friend, Brendon was with him and the cops locked him up too. You know that damn guilty by association crap. Can I have some more juice?" he asks while handing me his empty glass.

"But if Brendon was in jail then why did they need you to help them find him?" I ask while walking into the kitchen.

"He wasn't in jail, he got out."

"How did he get out?" I yell while pouring the juice.

"The lawyer for the drug lord *literally* flashed a *Get Out of Jail* monopoly card in Brendon's face and told him that if he just did one pick-up for them in California, that they would make sure he was released. Eager to get out, my brother agreed. Then he disappeared. *With* the money."

Hmm, this disappearing thing must run in Omar's family.

I hand Omar the juice.

"Thanks." Omar takes a generous gulp then picks up from where he left off. "And so when Brendon never made it to the airport to make the pick-up in California, the cartel started looking for him. And when they couldn't find him, they came after me in New York figuring that by following me, I would lead them to Bren *and* the money. Now," he sighed deeply, "this is where it starts to get a little complicated…"

Starts to..? Are you kidding me? How much more complicated can it be? Either Omar is a great liar or his ass is lucky to be alive. I'll save my verdict for later.

"What the cartel didn't know was that their lawyer was following my brother on his own behalf as an undercover cop, or U.C. which is what Bren called him. The cartel had no idea of U.C.'s real identity. So, while U.C. was following my brother, he approached him right outside the police station. Bren's plan was to tell the cops everything that he knew but on his way to the police station he changed his mind at the last minute. That's when U.C. caught up with Bren and told him that he was in danger because he reneged on the California job. It was at that time that U.C. revealed his true identity as an undercover cop and assured Brendon that he would protect him and our mom. He also told Brendon that he had suspected that he was innocent from the beginning but needed to be 100% sure which is why he followed him to the police station. Anyway, this is longer than I wanted it to be but once again, long story short, he hid both my brother and mom at a secret location until the DEA finally closed in on the cartel. So, when U.C. told the cartel that my brother didn't get on the flight for the pick-up *and* disappeared with their money, several of them came to New York and followed me hoping to get to my brother. And while looking for me, can you believe that those assholes ransacked my damn apartment?"

"Uh, yeah I can, especially with everything that you've told me."

I'll tell him later that I went over there and saw firsthand what they did to his apartment. If I told him now and everything that he's telling me is true then he would just get upset thinking that I could have been in danger!

"So is everyone safe now?"

"Yes, everyone is fine. Hey, if not I wouldn't be here with you."

"Seriously though, someone could have gotten hurt or even killed! Well, I'm just glad that you and your family are all safe. And I appreciate you trying to protect me and keep me from being invol-" *Hey, wait a minute, the man with the black jacket who came up to my office looking for me, probably was part of the cartel and wasn't really looking for me but for Omar! He must have followed "O" up to my office when he came up to take me to lunch that day. It makes sense because he was watching me at James' party probably hoping to find Omar there and then later I saw him right outside of Omar's apartment…He's got to be the one who ransacked his apartment!!*

"Cyd… Cydney are you okay? "What's wrong?"

Damn, how can I make sure without telling Omar? "Uh, I'm okay. I'm just trying to digest everything….but I'm curious about something. Omar by chance, did one of the men who held you in the deserted building look like uh, the Rock?"

He looks at me like he just saw a friggin' ghost! "How in the hell did you know that?"

"Uh, I don't know, it's weird, that's just the face I pictured while you were telling me everything that happened." *OMG, he had just finished trashing Omar's apartment when I arrived! I could have been hurt! I think for now I should keep this to myself. Neither of us need any more drama. The most important thing right now is that everyone is safe.* "Look, I'm just glad that this whole nightmare is over and that you and your family are okay. And again, thank you for wanting to protect me and keep me out of harm's way."

He gets up and presses **PLAY** on the iPod then pulls me to him. "Woman, you may not know it yet but there's nothing I wouldn't do for you."

Girl I just wanna kiss and make up
We done been through a lot of things
How do you throw that away
You were the heart of me….

I blush as he gently lifts my chin up with his finger and kisses me. Milo barks then covers his left eye with his little paw as Omar holds my face and kisses me again, each time a little more passionately than before. *Mmmm…*

Thirty Seven

Eowwg, eowwg! *What the hell was that?* I quickly open my eyes and automatically look at the clock. It's three friggin' a.m.! A strange noise just woke me up. Eowwg! It sounds like it's coming from the living room. On impulse, I grab the hand-carved Buddha on my night table, quietly slip out of bed, and then tip toe through the room's blackness. Once in the foyer, I turn the light on and look around. Smiling with relief after looking down into the wire crate, I am visually reminded of my new little addition. The strange noise was my little Milo crying. I can't help but grin as I bend down to pick him up. It's our first night together, and it seems as though we *both* have some adjusting to do! I gently massage his curly back then kiss his little head. He looks so cute and vulnerable that I *almost* hate putting him back into the crate but the book that Omar gave me says that crates are crucial for house training; one, because the dogs will not relieve themselves in the same area where they sleep and eat and two, the crate provides the little ones with a place of their own, a place where they can feel safe. Milo can hardly keep his eyes open when I place him back on the small pillow inside of his small wire sanctuary. Once comfy, Milo immediately curls up next to his stuffed toy and falls back to sleep. I watch him for a few minutes before sneaking into the kitchen to get a glass of juice, then quietly tip-toe back into the bedroom.

Through the dark room, I feel my way back into the bed. I slide in between the sheets and begin to quiver when suddenly I feel something warm on my leg. As the *warmth* glides slowly around my thigh, I damn near drop the juice as *it* travels north then rests on top of my lace thong. I shudder slightly, while smiling as I hand him the glass.

Omar slides his hand away from my buttocks and takes the glass. "Is everything okay?" he asks while taking a sip before setting the juice on the night table.

"Uh huh, it was Milo. I think he's just a little scared," I whisper.

Omar slips his large hand back on top of my lace thong and begins to gently massage my butt before slowly lifting me on top of him while kissing me softly with his moist lips. First my upper, then the bottom and then both. Soon his tongue slides in. It feels warm as it slowly reacquaints itself with mine. Our tongues play with one another as his flirts with my tongue's perimeter before quickly pulling back, I'm sure, wanting mine to chase his. *Damn, this cannot be happening, not now*.... I'm trying not to get overly excited as Omar's hands ease slowly from the top of my lace-clad buttocks and then begin to travel seductively up my back. His skilled tongue continues to slow dance with mine as it unknowingly takes control of practically every single fiber within me. My heart is racing so fast that I can hear it. Omar's hand struggles slightly with the back of my bra before slowly unhooking it while the thumb on his other hand teasingly encircles the base of my nipple. Mmmm…I can *feel* his anticipation as I lie helpless in total submission. *Damn, no I can't, we can't….we have to stop. Damn, damn, DAMN!!! I have to tell him...* I take a deep breath and try to pull myself together.

"Uh, Omar please stop…, ca… can we talk for a minute?" I ask while feeling a waft of warm breath on my left breast followed by the tip of Omar's tongue on my firm nipple.

"Now?" he asks, unhappily recoiling his tongue.

Damn! "Uh, yeah, I'm sorry, I know my timing sucks," I tell him softly.

"*Sucks* is pretty accurate! I can say one thing for sure, your vocabulary is definitely on point," he tells me as he slowly and reluctantly rolls off of me and lies on his side. "And this can't wait?" he asks with a heavy sigh.

Damn, I wish! "No, no it really can't. I wanted to tell you earlier but we fell asleep while talking and then when Milo woke me up, well you know, things just kinda started," I tell him while touching his nice, flat, rock hard stomach.

He leans over and kisses me on my forehead while resting his hand on my thigh.

"Okay, baby, what is it that you want to tell me that can't wait? Is it that time of month?"

"Uh, no and please it'll be easier if you aren't touching me."

Omar sits up and slowly removes his hand from my thigh then crosses his arms. "Okay, so what is it?" he asks as his face quickly shifts from high frustration to pure, unadulterated agitation which is the last thing that I want, especially with everything that he's gone through. *Just tell him! He needs to know!!!*

"Omar, remember that night we went to the listening party, then came back to my apartment?"

"Yeah, we dropped Brendon off at his godmother's house in Queens then came back here and you made mango martinis, if I remember correctly."

"Right, an…and then later things got a little heated when we…"

"Yeah, then we, I stopped. And I agreed to wait until you were ready."

"Omar, I, we, at this point, it really doesn't matter…what I'm trying to tell you is th…that I'm preg….pregnant."

He glares at me for more than several seconds before speaking.

"Cyd, I…I don't know what to say because we *both* know that I couldn't be the father. So, do you wanna tell me who is?"

"YOU! You're the only person I've been with! Recently, that is."

"How in the hell could I be the father? Cydney, it DIDN'T EVEN GO IN! Not to mention, you had your damn thong on!"

"I know, I know, that's what I told the doctor," I tell him as I reach in the night table drawer and hand him the *Uncommon Pregnancies* pamphlet. "She said that I have what's called a *virgin pregnancy* which is basically conception without penetration and well, it's all here in the pamphlet. It explains everything in detail so there you have it, one long passionate night, two mango martinis and three pregnancy tests later and well, now I'm pregnant."

"Uh you forgot something."

"What?"

"How about ZERO penetration?"

"I know. I know it's hard to believe but it's all here in the pamphlet, look, *PREGNANCY IS POSSIBLE WITHOUT PENETRATION!*

Omar gets up and starts walking in circles. I don't think I've ever seen him this upset.

"Cydney, I don't give a damn what the doctor says, it just doesn't add up! First of all you're not even a virgin so I don't know what the hell the doctor is talking about! But regardless, virgin pregnancy or not, I still don't believe that *if* you are pregnant, that the baby you're carrying is mine! And I don't need some pamphlet to tell me that something happened when I know good and damn well that it didn't! Look, Cyd I'm sorry…I gotta get outta here," he tells me as he quickly puts his pants on then grabs his keys and storms out of the bedroom.

"I'M OUT, I'LL TALK TO YOU LATER," he yells, slamming the door as he leaves the apartment.

What the hell just happened?...I grab the first thing within reach which ironically, happens to be the box of condoms Omar bought and slam it against the wall. The moment I do, Milo starts barking. I'm so friggin' angry, I'm numb! How can he think for one minute that I would tell him that I'm carrying his baby if I wasn't? I can't believe this, what the hell just happened? I'm so pissed, I can't even friggin' cry!

Thirty Eight

The next morning I wake up in a cold sweat. In a matter of hours my life completely changed, spinning out of control and crumbling before my very own brown eyes. My baby was born and was sadly much more than I could handle. She (I had a girl) cried hour on hour, each and every day, all day and all night. Omar, unable to deal with being a father, left New York and returned to Atlanta. All my friends kept busy and no longer had time for me. The rumor was that they were tired of my constant complaining about how difficult motherhood was. They were *not* trying to hear it! Essentially, I was alone excluding my family but even they somewhat distanced themselves from me. And to add fuel to the fire, I still couldn't find a job. Before I had the baby and was showing, potential employers would take one look at my stomach and tell me that the job was filled or that the position begins in four months which was right around the time my baby was due.

It was an awful dream, or I guess it was more of a nightmare. All I know is that at the end of the nightmare /dream, I wanted to get an abortion but I couldn't because I was already in my second trimester. That's when I woke up, in a cold sweat.

Now, that I know that I was dreaming and that I'm actually still in my first trimester, the dreaded "A" word is floating around in my head. I look at my iPad on the night table and pause before reaching for it. I quickly access the A's in the business listings while still contemplating if this is something I can actually go through with. As much as I love children and want to be a mom, I also don't want to lose everyone I love and everything that I have worked so hard for.

As I reach for the phone, I notice that I have a message. *When did the phone ring?* I wonder while pressing **PLAY**.

BEEP

"Uh, Cyd, I'm still having a hard time with this whole baby thing. I don't know what you plan to do, if you're going to keep it or not but I really can't deal with this right now so I'm on my way to Atlanta for a few days. Uhh… I'll call you when I get back."

Are you friggin' kidding me? I can't believe that my damn nightmare is becoming a reality!

I pick up the phone and immediately start dialing Omar's number but stop midway and press **END** before slowly dialing the first listing.

"ABC Clinic, how can I help you?"

"Uh…yes, I… I would like an appointment. Um, today if possible."

"Well, let's see. It looks like we just got a cancellation, can you be here in forty minutes?"

"Yes, yes thank you! I'm on my way!"

As soon as we're disconnected, I press "3" on my phone's speed dial.

"Hello."

"Oh, good, you're home. Look I need you to go somewhere with me. Can you be ready in fifteen minutes?"

"Uh, I guess so…wassup? You sound kinda weird. And where in the hell are you taking me?"

"Just be ready, I'll tell you when I see you."

◊◊◊◊◊

"Okay, first of all, before I tell you anything, I just want you to know that today is not the day for drama," I begin to tell her before she even has a chance to get in the car, "because *right* now I need support without all your *over-the-top* comments and Robyn antics! Do you think you can do that for me?"

"Cydney, what the hell is going on? Are you on some type of medication? Cause gurl, your ass sure is actin' and soundin' like you are!"

"See, that's what I mean! Look, I'm a little on edge right now so, I just need you to listen without talking please. I'm nervous enough and don't need to get upset or be any more emotional than I already am."

I look over at Robyn and she's looking at me like any minute now I'll be pulling out *and* modeling the latest in strait jackets.

"Look, I know I'm acting a little out of the ordinary…"

"Out of the ordinary? More like some crazy person!"

"Excuse me, I have a good reason for it. Okay," I stop then take a deep breath and continue in a few decibels higher than a whisper, "here goes….Rob, I..I'm pregnant. *And*, I'm on my way to get an abortion."

"You're what? Gurl, I know you didn't say what I just think you said!"

"I know, I can't believe it either. I just found out several days ago. Oh and one more thing, Omar's back. And when I told him that I was pregnant, he didn't and still doesn't believe it's his baby."

I turn to look at Robyn and I can actually see her words prepping to make their exit but I quickly halt their departure.

"But that's a non-issue because we can always get a DNA test…"

"Or go on *Maury!*" she snuck in.

"I'll pretend that I didn't hear that! What's more of an issue, is that he doesn't *want* any children. But quite frankly, as much as I want them, I'm not prepared to raise a baby now, not by myself. Especially with Gretchen just firing me…"

As soon as I said it, it hit me that I hadn't told Robyn that I lost my job. There's a minute or two of silence. I glance over at Robyn and for the first time since I've known her, my *in-your-face-tell-it-the-way-she-sees-it* friend has surprisingly been rendered speechless. Robyn's mouth is partially open but nothing is coming out. This is a rare moment and the silence is music to my ears. A few seconds or so later, her mouth closes.

"Cydney, …I don't know what to say." I can tell by the look on her face that she has plenty of words. In fact, I can see the letters of the words trying to worm their way out from in between her full, but not too full, lips. But I think for my sake, she might be holding the words back. At least, that's what I'm hoping.

"Look Cyd, I'm not even gonna comment on the whole job/Gretchen thing. We can talk about her ass later. But first I wanna know if you're absolutely sure that the baby is Omar's and not Ty's?"

"Damn Robyn, not you too? YES, yes and yes. 100%" I tell her as I roll my eyes. *This girl doesn't give up!*

"Alright, alright, I just wanted to make sure. Okay, now I *know* how much you love kids, so are you sure that you want to do this? Cause gurl, you know, once it's done, it's done."

"Yeah. I'm pretty sure. I'll feel much better about having children when I'm more financially prepared." Robyn turns and looks out the window at the New York skyline as we drive along the FDR drive. Neither of us says anything for several minutes. I'm glad though that she's with me because for a minute I thought that I might regret telling her. And truth be told, I don't think I would have been able to go through with it if I was by myself. She turns and looks at me for five or ten seconds like she might be trying to assess my emotional state.

"I'm not trying to upset you but I have to ask you something…"

"What Robyn?" I ask as I exit off the FDR.

"What was the reason he gave you for leaving with that model?"

This is not the time to get into all that but I know if I don't tell her something that she will think even worse of Omar than she already does. And quite frankly, he's not looking so good as it is. To either one of us!

"He didn't leave with Tasha. The man's leg that I saw get in the car with her was actually Tasha's boyfriend's. And Omar didn't *voluntarily* leave; he was kidnapped at gunpoint just seconds after they drove off. Then he was drugged by two men who were part of a drug cartel looking for Omar's brother. Fortunately, several days later he was able to escape and fly down to Atlanta to check on his mother and brother. Then *finally*, when the men were caught and everyone was safe, he returned to New York."

"Ohhh, okay. And tell me, did *Batman and Robin* fly him back to Gotham City in their cute *little* black bat mobile? Oh, and let me guess, he couldn't call you because *the Joker* cut off all the phone lines in Atlanta?

Am I right? Gurl, c'mon and I'm the freakin' *Cat Woman!* Cydney Michelle Rochon puh-leeze tell me that you don't believe that crock of bull!"

"Well, *Cat Woman*, unlike some people, *I* look at the news. And *those of us that do,* know about the drug cartels and how they operate! Besides, why would he make something like that up? You know what; don't even bother to answer that. Oh, and FYI the man at James' party in the photos was one of the men that kidnapped him! Well, we're here. There's a parking lot two blocks down, so will you park the car while I go in? I can't be late for my appointment."

"Fine, what's the name of the clinic?"

"ABC Clinic. Suite 1301"

This is not at all what I expected an abortion facility to look like. Not that I've thought about it before but whatever preconceived image I would have had, this is not it. This is a posh office with not one but *two* flat screen televisions, *Bose* speakers mounted on the walls, zebra wood furniture, accented with colorful pillows and purple and yellow orchid filled vases. While I'm taking in the cheerful color scheme, I can't help but hear two young women laughing in the corner. They sound like a pair of hysterical hyenas. Can someone just tell me how they could laugh at a time like this? Especially given the grim circumstances. All of a sudden my entire head goes numb. I try to brace myself as the room begins to move.

"Hello, can I help you?"

I look around as the room begins to spin. All the colors in the room are now bleeding into one another while the hyenas get even louder.

"HELLO, MAY I HELP YOU?"

I see a woman across from me, her mouth is moving. She gets up and walks over to me.

"Are you all right? Here, why don't you sit down," she tells me as she pulls out a yellow chair, "What is your name?"

"Cyd…Cydney."

"Oh you must be the cancellation appointment. Cydney you feel warm. Let me get you some water."

While the receptionist is getting me water, the room slows down and the hyenas seem to have quieted down. *Where is Robyn?*

BEEP. I have a text. *That must be her, knowing that girl, she probably forgot what the suite number is…*I look at the phone screen and see that it's actually a text from Milanya.

Hi aunty Cyd, mommie said we culd send u a text. When r u comin back to vis it us ? We luv u!

Kai & Nic o"

As I look at my godchildren's text I can see their little faces, almost as clear as if they were right here in front of me. I see them struggling to press the correct buttons and then when finished, their excitement in sending it. I smile then quickly stop when I remember where I am and why.

As I imagine the future, I actually see my little boogala as a toddler playing with the girls and how happy the three of them are. This image alone makes me smile, tugging heavily on my heart strings. The receptionist hands me the water. Just as I begin to drink it, Robyn walks in. I get up and walk toward her.

"Let's get outta here. Rob, I…I can't go through with this!"

Thirty Nine

These last few weeks have been stressful. And *that's* putting it mildly! It's one thing to have to deal with Omar and him not wanting children, but then for him to verbally doubt my baby's, *our baby's* paternity — well, that's a whole 'nother thing. I can understand him maybe ***thinking*** it, especially under the unusual circumstances, but to come out and actually tell me to my face that the baby couldn't be his, was hurtful not to mention insulting. Then on top of that, I'm also dealing with the added stress of not working. And the sooner I find a job, the better because let's face it, the bigger I get, the harder it's going to be to find one.

I'm trying my best to stay optimistic that something will come through soon. For the past two and a half weeks, which to me seems more like two and a half months! I have been in and out of interviews practically every day. And *finally* today I got a call back for a second meeting which I'm hoping, fingers crossed, will lead to something. I met with the president of the sportswear division for Liz Claiborne and she asked me to come back because she had a few more questions that she wanted to run by me before making a final decision. And as encouraging as second interviews can be, I've learned not to uncork the Möet until I know for sure because I have definitely seen *and* personally experienced, how *anydamnthing* can happen in this industry.

As I get off the elevator, a young woman is thanking the receptionist. I hold the elevator door for her, then walk over to the oversized reception desk.

"Hello, Ms. Rochon. I'll let Abby know that you're here."

"Thank you," I tell her, impressed that she remembered my name which I'm hoping is a good sign.

The reception area is more modern than I expected (when Abby and I met last week, we met in one of the showrooms). The furniture is made of blond wood and is upholstered in a neutral palette with the room's accessories providing vibrant splashes of color. Most of the color is reflected in the larger than life photos of models in Liz Claiborne clothing which are hung throughout the reception area. Just as I get comfortable on the custom built sofa, Abby walks out in a red fitted Liz Claiborne suit.

"Hello Cydney, come on in," she tells me as I follow her into her office. Abby has been with LC for seven years and knows better than most who the LC customer is and exactly what that customer wants. In fact, she seemed quite impressed with my insight about the importance of LC broadening its customer base in the current economy.

"Cydney, it's come down to you and another candidate and quite honestly, I'm pretty much on the fence. So, if you don't mind, I have a few more questions I'd like to ask you. First, I want to know how you would suggest that we broaden our customer base with next season's clothing line?"

"That's easy. My suggestion would be through strategic print and video advertising. The internet is a viable, marketing catalyst and can prove to be very valuable by helping to transition the company once utilized to its fullest."

"Okay, and how would you, as head designer, broaden LC's customer base within the design process?"

"I would design a line of price appropriate pieces that would integrate into the customer's existing wardrobe by initiating a trend that's rising like a *Mommie and Me* line at a competitive price point. The trick will be not to design the line in the matchy matchy way like its been done in the past."

"Cydney, I like the way you think! Now, when are you available to start?"

"How soon do you need me?"

"Next week if that works for you, but first let me speak to our human resources department to see what needs to be done before I give you an exact date." Abby's intercom rings.

"Yes?"

"Abby, John is ready to see you now."

"Ok, tell him to give me a few minutes and I'll be right there!" Abby stands up. "Okay, Cydney, let's plan to talk tomorrow, but in the meantime let me unofficially welcome you to Liz Claiborne," she tells me while extending her hand.

I smile but am screaming internally like I did when I got tickets to the last *Oprah's Favorite Things* show! "Thank you, Abby. I'm looking forward to working with you," I tell her as we shake hands.

I'm so excited, I want to scream! As I exit the building still on cloud nine, I want to celebrate! I pull out my cell and start to dial Robyn to tell her the good news but when I see the time, I remember that Omar is coming by. And I'm not sure what how our conversation will go so it may not be a good idea to plan to go *out* to dinner. But after *finally* landing a job there's no way in hell that I feel like cooking. So, it'll make more sense to just pick up something to take home I reason while heading towards Macy*s.

"Cydney, Cydney!" I turn around and see Zoe running across the street toward me.

"Hey Zoe, how are you sweetie?" I ask while we exchange a quick embrace.

"Good, but Cyd I *miss* you. Work is not the same without you. And you *know* Kyle is trippin' ever since Gretchen promoted him to designer and, well, Gretchen is still Gretchen. Oh, and guess who else got fired?"

"Who?"

"Tasha! You know, the model!"

"Why, what happened?"

"Well, when she just got back from her vacation. You remember, that day Omar came up to the office and Tasha was leaving for Dubai for a photo shoot. Well, Tasha changed her return date and stayed several additional weeks for vacation. And you know how things always get back to Gretchen. Well, somehow it got back to the Queen of Mean that Tash's boyfriend went with her and stayed in the room while on company money and needless to say, Gretchen was pissed! As soon as Tasha got back Gretchen fired her butt right on the spot! Gretchen didn't even discuss it with Donna. But that's what Tasha gets for being stupid and charging both *vacation* and work meals on the company's credit card. And not only for her but for *her boyfriend* too!!"

"Yeah you're right, that was pretty stupid. So, how did she take it?"

"Well, I wasn't there when it actually happened but I do know that when she came out, she was totally stunned. But please she'll be fine, those models always are! So, how are *you*?"

"I'm good. And by the way, thanks for the messages that you left on my voicemail. I really appreciate it Zoe."

"Don't mention it. Look I have to run, I'm late for my manicure appointment, but let's have lunch soon!!"

"Okay," I yell as she quickly dashes off. *Dag!* I forgot to ask her if Federated placed an order for the line I designed.

While waiting to cross the street a city bus stops directly in front of me. I'm face to face, with a *larger-than-life* ad on the side of the bus, eye to eye, when something familiar catches my attention. I step back so that I can view the ad and when I do, I cannot believe my friggin' eyes!! *Damn that Gretchen!* The graffiti designs that *I* developed are featured on three models on the side of the damn bus. I cannot believe that conniving, wicked witch!

Forty

Omar should be here any minute now. He called earlier, right before I met with Abby and said that he has something to tell me. I'm a little anxious because this will be the first time that I've seen him since he left for Atlanta after telling him that I was pregnant. I hope that what he has to tell me, is something good because I am not in the mood for any *I'm-not-ready-to-be-a-father* crap! Especially after just seeing what that witch did with my designs. So, today is *not* the day!

After having time to cool off and put things in perspective, like it or not, I guess I can't really blame Gretchen for using my graffiti designs. I mean after all, I did still work at DK when I designed them, besides the company *is* in business to make money. Bottom-line, it was really the timing and the manner in which the Wicked Witch fired me that really upset me. It was just cold and borderline heartless for her to let me go right *after* I presented the graffiti designs to her *trying-to-shine-in-my-limelight* ass. Not to mention this was the launch of the division *I* started and in all reality, DK*Urban* is *my* baby! Whatever. As of now, I'm officially moving on and from this point on I'll just let karma deal with her butt.

KNOCK, KNOCK!

Good, that's Omar. "I'm glad I stopped by Macy*s Cellar to pick food up for dinner," I whisper to myself as I peep out the peep hole and open the door.

"Hello Cyd," Omar says while leaning over to kiss me on the cheek.

"Hi. How ya doing? "I ask semi-guardedly.

As soon as Omar walked in the door, Milo jumped on him while wagging his little tail, then licked his hand after "O" pulled out the little chew toy he bought him.

"I'm good but more importantly, how are *you*?" he asks while affectionately rubbing my bulging belly.

'But more importantly, how are you?' Did someone sneak in and inject him with a nurturing chip? Where did this sudden concern for me and my pregnancy come from? Wow! I don't show my shock but I probably should get an Oscar for hiding it so well! Fully recovered, I answer, "Good, just tired and exhausted from having a baby grow inside of me and all of the things that go along with it. You know, like reading all of the baby books, plus traveling back and forth to my weekly prenatal classes on top of job hunting but other than that, I'm fine," I tell him hoping to evoke some sympathy sprinkled with a touch of guilt for doubting and leaving me so that he could escape the pressure of his new daddy-to-be role.

"Well, hopefully this will make you feel a little better," he says as he pulls out a single white rose from behind his back. "It was between this or a white flag and I figured you'd like this better." I smile as I draw in the fragrance.

"It's beautiful, thank you. C'mon in, let's sit down. Are you hungry?"

"Starving."

"Good, me too. I picked up a few things from Macy*s Cellar. All I have to do is pull out the plates."

"Hey, let me get the food together while you sit down and take it easy. I know where everything is."

I go and sit on the couch and happily put my feet up. I hear the plates clanging and cross my fingers that none of them break.

Meanwhile, I can't wait to tell Omar my good news. But first I need to know exactly where his head is and if he's ready to accept the fact that he's about to become a father. I hear Omar putting the plates on the tray and I make room on the coffee table.

"Okay, here we go," he says as he puts the tray down on the table.

"Thanks," I tell him as I reach over for my plate.

"So, what is it that you wanted to tell me?"

"Well, first I just want to say that, while I was in Atlanta I read the pamphlet, and as crazy as it is, I see how you could be pregnant…"

"*Could* be?"

"I didn't mean it like that. I meant that I know how it happened and that it's possible."

I look down at my stomach and then at Omar. "Possible?"

"Cyd, look what I'm trying to say is that you don't have to worry about me not being there for you or the baby. Okay?"

Ease up Cyd, he's trying. "Okay," I make myself say even though the words, "*The* baby or *our* baby?" hang on the tip of my tongue waiting anxiously with their passport. But I force them back with a large forkful of salted pepper shrimp and rice then mumble, "I appreciate that," while smiling. "So, what else did you want to tell me?" I ask nicely.

"Well, I know how difficult these last weeks have been for you and as you know, I'm still dealing with my own emotional post cartel issues and all that drama with my brother. So, all that to say, I thought that it might be good for both of us if we went away for a weekend."

Wow, I didn't see that coming! Talk about a complete 180 degree turn "Really?" I ask stunned.

"Yeah. So, why don't you think of three places where you'd like to go, then I'll surprise you and take you to one of them soon. Sound good?"

My initial reaction is split. One, *How soon can we leave?* And two, *Slow down, don't rush into anything!* But the truth of the matter is, as torn as I may be about this trip, I have to admit that I have always loved a man who takes charge. And let's keep it real, this will be a nice break from stressing over the pregnancy. And while we're keeping it real, if I don't go somewhere now, I doubt if I will be going anywhere once I'm further along in my pregnancy. And then after the baby is born, I *definitely* don't see me planning any trips in the near future. So now, the more and more I think about the idea, the more excited I am, not only about going but that I also get to choose the three options!

"Yes, actually it does sound good."

Omar walks over to the console table and selects a playlist as he turns on the iPod.

"So do you have any idea of where you want to go or do you need more time?" he asks.

"I have some ideas but before we discuss them, I have some good news that I want to share with you."

"Uh, you won lotto?" he asks with a big grin.

"No silly, I got a job!" I tell him while hitting him in the head with one of my throw pillows.

"That's great, babe! Congratulations, who's the lucky company?"

"Liz Claiborne. And I might start as early as next week!"

"Well, I know how stressed you've been, as well as disappointed with everything that went down with your last job. So, I'm glad you can now move forward without that added stress and will finally be able to put all that negative drama behind you. I'm happy for you baby!"

"Thanks! I don't think that I can even begin to tell you how relieved I am just to know that I'll have a paycheck coming especially now, under these circumstances," I tell him as I look down at my belly. "Then of course, I'm really looking forward to being creative again. I didn't realize how much I missed it or what a big part of my life it is."

"So baby, how is that going to work? Did you tell them that you're pregnant?"

"NO! And why in the hell would I tell them?" I snap.

"Whoa, whoa, time out, I just asked because you'll be showing soon and once they do the math they might not appreciate that you didn't tell them. Cyd, I'm just lookin' out."

I probably need to get a handle on my mood swings but I can't believe he just asked me that!

"Sorry, I didn't mean to snap at you and I know you mean well but I'll have to deal with that if and when it becomes an issue.

The last thing I want to do is deceive anyone but under these circumstances I have to think about my baby first and if I don't take a full three month maternity leave then whoever I work for shouldn't have a problem with it, hopefully.

"Ok enough about all that. Are you ready to hear my three choices?"

"Uh, *you* tell me, am I ready? he asks cautiously. Do I need to brace myself?"

"Ha ha, looks like someone has jokes…okay my first place is the City of Quebec because it reminds me of France, second, Martha's Vineyard because it's close and quaint, and last but not least, St John's in the Virgin Islands because I've never been and it is on my list of places to visit!"

"Okay, I think I can work with those," he exhales. "That wasn't too bad. And as promised, I'll take care of all the arrangements and the only thing you'll need to do is pack."

"When will I know where we're going?"

"On the day we leave."

"Uh, all right. Well, good I can't wait!"

"Ditto to that!" he said as we both laugh for the first time in a loooong time while *Joe* croons through the wall-mounted speakers.

I can't buy you fancy rings
Or all of the expensive things you're used to, baby
No trips around the world, no diamonds or pearls
To give you, baby
But what I've got to give is more precious
Than you'll ever know
My deepest inner feelings, my heart and soul…

Forty One

Omar's efforts continue as we start looking for baby furniture. Omar surprised me by offering to take me when I told him I was going window shopping. I wanted to get an idea of what I'm looking at, cost-wise. Even though I just got a job, I still have to budget since I'm planning for two now. I did however go ahead and get a rocking chair because not only does it conform perfectly to my body but it was on sale! But the thing I love most about it, was knowing that while rocking in it, *during* my pregnancy, that it'll help make my baby's transition into the world much smoother because my baby will already be accustomed to the rocking motion.

My hope is that after today's little shopping trip that Omar will continue being active in his new, impending father role, especially since the baby and I have already begun to bond. And I know to some that it might seem a little early for a mother and child to bond but I definitely feel a special closeness to my baby.

"O" just left *Pottery Barn Kids* to pick up his car from the repair shop so while I'm still in Manhattan I'll continue to shop for our *mystery* trip. It's not going to be easy to shop for a trip when you don't know where you're going. Uh, okay, correction; I do have an idea since I *am* the one that gave Omar three places for our little weekend getaway. But it would *still* help to know which of the three Omar chose. I just want to be prepared so that I can pack everything that I'll need. I hate going somewhere, then realizing that I forgot something. So, now I'm darting from store to store buying basics and all the things that I *think* I'll need. I want everything done today because once my Liz Claiborne paperwork is completed, and if Abby, *God bless her*, wants me to start work next week, all my running around will be done and I can just focus on my N-E-W J-O-B. So far I've picked up a pair of Via Spiga sandals and a pair of True Religions. Milanya swears by those jeans so I'm going to temporarily retire my Levi's and try them out to see what's so great about them! Plus this will probably be the only time I'll be able to fit in them before the baby is born. My last stop is to *LaPerla* to buy some new lingerie. My practical self knows that I really shouldn't spend that much money on something that won't be on very long, especially since I have other financial priorities, but we still haven't *technically* made love yet and what better time to do so than this weekend? After being celibate for five years, being in something new and sexy especially for our *real* first time together will help ease some of my *it's-been-a-long-time* anxiety. Besides, I'll be able to afford it thanks to my new job, plus I'm only buying one set on sale, so I'm good.

As I glance down at my watch I remember that Abby asked me to call her today with a decision between the sportswear design position and a new opening in the men's division. As soon as I left Abby's office after my second interview, Abby called and left a message on my cell. In the message, she told me about another listing for a new sub-division in Claiborne Men which she felt that I'd also be perfect for. She also told me to think it over once I had a chance to check it out on the LC website and to please get back to her sometime today with the position I preferred. Since I'm only a few minutes away, I decided to stop by LC before going to LaPerla and just tell Abby in person which position I was going to accept. I'm leaning more toward the new sub-division, since I started Urban*Chic* and wasn't able to see it through to its fruition.

When I enter the Liz Claiborne offices, the receptionist is on the phone. I smile when she looks up to acknowledge me. She takes a message then hangs up.

"Hello Ms. Rochon, how can I help you?"

"Hello, is Abby available? I don't actually have an appointment but she is expecting my call," I tell her while turning to sit.

"I'm sorry, Ms. Rochon, but Abby no…no longer works here."

Stopping dead in my tracks, my first instinct is to sniff the air a couple of times to determine exactly what this girl's been smoking but I don't.

"Excuse me?" I ask, with a slight attitude. "I was here just two days ago. What do you mean she no longer works here?" I demand while looking around for *Ashton Kutcher* to jump out with his camera crew yelling that I've just been punked!

Just as the receptionist is about to speak, her intercom rings and she promptly repositions her headset back in place.

"Reception. Yes, okay, I will be right there. I'm sorry, Ms. Rochon, but Abby no longer works here, I'm really sorry," she tells me as she gets up and walks rapidly down the long corridor.

Again, I look around, hoping that the prankster behind this sick joke will come out and reveal himself. I wait a few more minutes and *still* nobody!

Forty Two

After my little three hour pity party which mostly consisted of a lot of crying, *Why me? And the very terrifying, what now?*

I forced myself to stop crying by telling myself that I can do one of two things; one, extend the pity party and cry myself to sleep or two, dry my eyes and get back on the proverbial horse and continue my job search before I'm too far along in the pregnancy and *unable* to physically work. I realized during my pity party that it's no longer just about me that now, I have someone else to consider. Bottom line, crying and feeling sorry for myself is not going to pay my bills or provide for my baby!

So, now I'm back to square one as my *one-time-26"* waist begins to slowly expand inch by inch by the damn minute. As for the whole Liz Claiborne situation, I've accepted that *shit happens.* Which of course, would be Robyn's take on it. According to *Life by Robyn*, there would be no valid or invalid explanation. No inane gibberish about karma and definitely no mention of *it-wasn't-meant-to-be.* Just plain and simple, in your face, *Shit happens, that's life. Now deal with it!* I, on the other hand, have always been on the opposite end of that spectrum, courtesy of my mother. Mama always says that with every set back or challenge that there has to be either a lesson or an opening for something better. Or both. The trick, she says is being able to recognize the lesson so that you don't have to repeat it over and over. *Cyd baby, it's just like school, if you don't pass and get good grades, then you will have to stick and repeat that grade until you learn your lessons,* she would tell me.

From my own personal experience, I've discovered that sometimes the lesson is buried in the deep, sub-terrains of the earth, in which case one might need to organize a friggin' digging expedition just to uncover it. However, I do know firsthand, that the lesson *is* always there. It may be down kind of deep, but it is there.

Despite yesterday being a big disappointment, and a *major* setback, I'm trying my best to scrape together a new attitude while psyching myself up for all good things coming my way.

On the up side, I still have resumes out there and will send more out as I resume my search at additional design companies. So, basically all I can do now is maintain a positive mindset with all of my fingers and toes crossed that something else comes along. Something within the broad scope of things, that will be better suited for me. Now, I just have to do my part by sending resumes, staying positive and then waiting it out.

I called Omar and told him that under the circumstances that I wasn't up to going on our little weekend getaway because now I desperately need to refocus on getting a job, ASAP. He really wasn't trying to hear it and told me that is exactly why I need to go and that it's only for the weekend therefore shouldn't affect my job search. The trip, he said will help me refuel and recharge myself which in the long run will actually help me focus on my search. He even played *the baby card* by telling me that the trip will also help relax me and put me in a calm state which will ultimately benefit *our* baby. So, despite everything that has happened, I convinced myself that "O" is right and that going away would more than likely help my state of mind. So after several bouts of vacillation, I decided to go.

I'm almost finished packing which hasn't been as bad as I thought it would be since all of my destination choices are warm at this time of year. Omar hasn't told me anything except that I need to be ready at 10 a.m. sharp. Although that little bit of info was just that, *little*, it at least let me know when I need to drop Milo off at Shaye's.

Just as I am about to put my shoe bags in my suitcase, the phone rings. I check the caller id and it's BCBW, one of the companies that I interviewed with.

"Hello."

"Hello Cydney, this is Faye Gregory from BCBW, how are you?"

"Hi Faye, I'm fine thank you, it's good to hear from you!" *I hope this is good!!!*

"Cydney I'm calling because I was reviewing applicants for the design opening and we would like to speak to you again about the head of design position we were wondering if you could come in tomorrow morning to go over a few things and maybe even sign some papers…oh, but first I guess I should ask if you are still available and even more importantly, if you're still interested?"

Unfriggin'believable! "Well, first Faye, thank you for calling and yes as a matter of fact, I am still interested. However, I'm going out of town tomorrow morning so, would it be possible for me to come in sometime today or perhaps Monday?"

"That shouldn't be a problem, let me check my schedule. Uh…let's see. Hmmm, how about Monday at 3:15, is that okay?"

"3:15 it is. I will see you on Monday. Thank you, Faye."

"No, thank *you*, and enjoy your weekend."

Now *that* was crazy! Wow! Apparently *shit happens* for the good too! BCBW is a solid company and according to my research has many design opportunities in several areas within the company. I laugh and pick little Milo up and twirl him around a few times then sing my way into the shower.

While showering, I'm trying to process everything that's happened. And, I'm *still* very confused about that whole Liz Claiborne debacle. It happened so fast that my brain can't even wrap itself around what in the hell could have possibly happened to Abby for her to no longer be working at the company. The only thing I can pull from that craziness is that Liz Claiborne, Inc. was not the good fit that I thought it would be, which in all honesty is fine, especially with this latest development. And it's better to know now than to find out later. Mama just said last night while we were on the phone that when one door closes, another one opens. But who knew that it would be so soon?

Forty Three

This is the final boarding call for passengers on flight 803. Please proceed to Gate B5 for St Thomas, Virgin Islands. This is the final boarding call……

This must be it! Just about every flight to St John's Island stops in St. Thomas first then proceeds to St. John's. I can't believe we're going to the Virgin Islands I look at Omar and he smiles and winks at me, then turns back to the game he's playing on my iPad. *Oh well, so much for St. John's.* There are approximately six gates in our seating area and he hasn't dropped one friggin' clue. The only two things he's said is that I'll know once we begin to board the plane and just forty minutes ago he told me that our plane takes off within the next hour. So, with twenty minutes to go, the only destination that I can safely rule out is St. John's unless of course there's another flight that leaves within the next twenty minutes, which I highly doubt. So, that leaves Martha's Vineyard and Quebec City.

"Passengers on Flight 286 please begin boarding at Gate B3. Again, passengers on Flight 286 to Montreal please begin boarding at Gate B3."

Omar shuts down the iPad then looks at me and says, "Okay, baby, that's us."

"For real? Montreal?"

"Yes," he tells me while picking up our carry-on bags. Smiling, I stuff my magazines into my DK tote, grab my handbag and follow Omar onto the plane.

The flight was smooth and pleasant but even better, it was *non-stop*. Nonetheless, we're still a little tired, especially with all the airport *customs-passport-security-one-carry-on-bag-no-liquids-over-3-ounces-take-your-shoes-off* rules and regulations! "O" got us a town car as soon as we got to the ground transportation area and now we're headed to our hotel which I'm told is in Old Montreal.

Well, let me tell you, tired just flew out the car window because now that we're here and see how beautiful Montreal is, we've been hit with an unexpected surge of energy. Now, we just want to get to the hotel, drop our bags off and hit the city! Our driver is giving us a mini tour of Old Montreal before taking us to the hotel. Old Montreal is somewhat quaint and village-like, (new village not old village). And as we ride through the city I'm experiencing an instant sense of home, it feels nice. You can't help but fall in love with the city because Montreal is absolutely beautiful! This is my first time here which is exactly why Omar said he chose it over the City of Quebec. He told me on the plane that this weekend is about relaxation and new experiences. I was touched by the fact that he actually put some real thought into where we were going as well as what would work for both of us. That, in itself, is worth a few points.

We just checked into *The Hotel Nelligan* which is a very charming boutique style hotel located on Saint Paul St. in the center of Old Montreal. It's unique and unlike any hotel that I've been to. Our room's walls are beautiful exposed brick and furnished with highly styled Ethan Allen-like furnishings. Our room also has a stone fireplace and a cozy bathroom with double marble vanities as well as its own Jacuzzi and walk in shower. Directly over the fire place are several beautifully framed works of poetry by Emile Nelligan, a noted poet who also happens to be the original owner of the hotel.

Most of Omar's plans for us are centered around tomorrow with the exception of dinner which he planned for this evening. Fortunately, we've caught a second wind as we continue our tour via foot. We walk around the area before heading to the restaurant for a quiet and romantic dinner.

Forty Four

Cyd, Cyd….."

I don't want to open my eyes. I hear my name but am not sure if I'm dreaming or if someone is really calling me.

"Cyd, baby wake up!"

Ughh!! What is that smell? I grudgingly open my eyes while covering my nose with the sheet and see Omar standing over me with a huge white wooden tray. As I rub my eyes, I wiggle to prop myself up.

"What's all this?"

"This is what you call *breakfast in bed!* So check this out, we have banana walnut pancakes with syrup…"

"Oh my God, it's got to be the syrup! Get that syrup out of here, NOW!"

Omar looks at me like I'm one of those Atlanta housewives then quickly takes the syrup and puts it outside on the floor in the hall. He comes back looking confused and guilty.

"I'm sorry Omar, I don't know what kind of syrup that was but whatever kind it was, made me sick to my stomach! I didn't mean to yell."

"No it's okay, you can't help how certain smells affect you..."

"No, you're right but you don't know either so I just have to handle it better. Okay, so what else do you have here?"

"Uh, let's see, scrambled eggs, toasted English muffin, a bowl of fresh fruit, a glass of ruby red grapefruit juice *and* a cup of Earl Grey tea with lemon."

Fully recovered and fully propped up, I ask "Is, all that for me?" *I can't believe it, these are all of my favorite breakfast foods…*

"Well, not *all* of it, the cheese omelet and protein shake are for me."

Impressed and hungry as hell, I peck him on the lips then carefully jump out of bed and head for the bathroom.

"I'm just going to brush my teeth then we can dig in and enjoy this wonderful breakfast in bed!! Seriously though, thank you "O", this was very thoughtful!" I yell from the bathroom. "Just give me two seconds!" I shout as I squeeze toothpaste on my toothbrush.

I can see Omar smile in the mirror's reflection as he places the tray on the end of the bed and slides the table over to the side where I was sleeping. Then he pulls a piece of paper out of his pocket and begins to read it. As I wipe the toothpaste from my mouth and head back to bed, Omar glances at his watch then crawls on the duvet before stuffing the paper back into his pocket.

"What's that?" I ask as I sit next to him.

"What?"

"This," I tell him while pulling the paper out of his pocket."

He looks at it, then clears his throat. "It's just a letter from Brendon."

"Oh. Is he okay?"

"Yeah, he's fine, go ahead you can read it."

Unfolding the letter, I read it out loud.

Hey Bro,

I'm not that good at writing and even worse at expressing my feelings but I want you to know how glad I am that you had my back as my brother and my friend. I don't know if I'll ever be able to forgive myself for being the reason you got hurt. I should have listened to you when you told me to be careful with who I hang out with. I've definitely learned my lesson and I just want to thank you for being there. Moms always tells me I should be grateful that I have a big brother to look out for me. And I am, I really am

Thanks again,

Love, Bren

P.S. Tell Cydney "hey" for me.

"Ohhhh, that was sweet," I tell him as I kiss him on the corner of his eye catching a tear right before it rolls.

"Yeah, he's a good kid. Ok, not to rush you baby but we have just enough time to eat and shower in order to make our 9:30 appointments."

Chewing, I ask, "What appointments? Mmmm these pancakes are good!"

Omar looks at my pancakes and makes a face.

"What did you do, put the fruit on top of the pancakes?"

"Yes, it's healthier that way. Remember, I *am* eating for two! Wanna taste?" I ask him, while offering a forkful.

"Nooo thanks. We have appointments at the *Rainspa*."

I stop chewing. "As in the spa, *Rainspa*?"

"Yeah, that's it," he says somewhat surprised but seemingly happy that its reputation had preceded it.

"That's so funny because just a few months ago I read about *Rainspa* in a *Departures* magazine and called Anya to see if she wanted to go for a spa weekend. I'm speechless!" *This is almost too good to be true!!*

"Good I'm glad that it's something that you'll enjoy."

"Are you kidding me? I can't think of a better way to de-stress and unwind!" Omar smiles while we continue eating. I can't help but wonder what else he has in store for me uh, *us* today!

This day has been absolutely perfect! The Rainspa was exactly what I needed and then some! I had no idea how much stress I was holding in my body. At first, I was worried that I wouldn't be able to have any of the spa's services because of my pregnancy but Omar had called ahead and checked their specials before booking me for their pregnancy package. Please, by the time we left, I felt like a completely new woman!

After a light lunch at the cutest sidewalk café, Omar surprised me with a choice of a Jean Paul Gaultier exhibit at the Museum of Fine Arts or a street car tour of the city. I chose the exhibit because JPG is one of my favorite fashion designers. And I'm glad I did because the exhibit was *beyond* incredible. I got enough inspiration for designs for the next three seasons!

We didn't leave the museum until a little after five pm and I was exhausted! I didn't want Omar to know, how tired I was so I suggested that instead of the hotel restaurant that we have dinner at a nearby eatery. Then Omar explained that we already had reservations and didn't feel comfortable cancelling them. So, as if reading my mind, he promptly hailed a taxi so I, we wouldn't have to walk to the metro/subway. Needless to say, my feet and I were both *very* happy.

I'm glad Omar insisted that we keep our reservation at *Verses* because the dinner was superb and the restaurant's ambience is like no other. It's open faced brick walls and large windows exude a warmth and charm that can't be duplicated.

After Omar signed the check, we stopped by the concierge to arrange for a car to take us to the airport in the morning. We then headed up to our room. As we approach the door, there is a lovely fragrant scent coming from inside. I know the scent is coming from our room although Omar doesn't smell it. During my entire pregnancy, my nose has been extremely sensitive, and tonight is no different. When Omar opens the door, I look inside and see *at least* 100 lit candles throughout the room. I can't believe it! Then on top of that, there are apricot colored rose petals on the floor leading to and on top of the bed.

"Wow," I hear myself say before turning to Omar. "Did you do all this?"

"Not *physically*, although I did arrange it."

"I, I don't know what to say, everything is so beautiful."

"And so are you. Now, babe why don't you slip into something more comfortable while I take care of one last thing."

While I'm in the bathroom, I hear Omar taking something out of the desk drawer. I smile as soon as I realize what it is when I hear him opening the room door.

Ne pas déranger!

Do not disturb!

Forty Five

Yesterday was perfect! In fact this whole weekend, although short, has been exactly what the doctor ordered. Omar really went above and beyond to make sure that everything was as much fun for us as it was relaxing. Right now he's in the lobby checking out while I'm in the steam shower taking full advantage of every second I have before having to leave.

As the warm water massages my face, my mind flashes back to last night and how amazing it was. Not to take away from the day or suggest that it wasn't great also because it was, but just in a different way. Suffice to say that the evening was *indeed* well worth the wait romantically speaking, not only for moi but for Omar as well. There was not a detail, area or inch that my baby skipped from music by *Luther* and *Robin Thicke* to white chocolate covered strawberries complete with a warm oil leg and foot massage!

As I close my eyes and revisit the *hour* that followed the fruit…a slight gust of cool air brushes across my bare, wet back. Shivering, I turn to see if I accidently pushed the shower door open, but before I'm able to turn around, suddenly a pair of large hands cover and overtake my hands while being firmly placed against the wet shower wall. I'm immobile as he presses his strong, damp body against mine.

"I didn't scare you, did I?" he whispers in my ear.

"Mmmm, no you didn't," I say softly while feeling his moist lips nibbling on my lobe. His body melds onto mine, creating a corporeal union.

"Ahhhh, you feel good." I whisper to him as he loosens the grip around my hands allowing them to drop from the wall while slowly turning me around. I part my lips in eager anticipation of a steamy, torrid end to an incredible and most memorable weekend.

Forty Six

I hear the phone ringing from the hallway. And of course, as soon as I walk into the apartment the friggin' thing stops ringing. The light on the handset is flashing, summoning my attention. I drop my suitcase, take Milo's leash off, then go over to the light's base and press **PLAY**.

BEEP

"Hi sweetheart, it's dad. Just checking to see how the job search is going. Okay, give us a call."

Good ole dad! He's always there for us. I'll call him and let him know about BCBW a little later.

BEEP

"Hey gurl, I'm tired of this phone tag. Will you *please* call me and let me know how you're feeling and what's happening with you? I know that you're about to go away or maybe you and Omari already left. And if my memory was functioning correctly, you told me that you'll be working at, I believe Liz Claiborne, but that's all I know. So call and tell me what else is going on with you...

Meanwhile, I've got a lot to tell you so call me, okay? Call me!!!"

For the ninety ninth time, it's Omar! And Liz Claiborne is out and BCBW is in! Hmmm, I wonder what news she has.

BEEP

"Hey Cyd, it's me. How was Montreal? Look I want to hear all about it but you have to call me ASAP. Que is taking me to Bora Bora!!!! I can't believe that we are finally going!! We've only been talking about it forever and a day! But anyway call me because I want you to check in on the girls while we're there. Giselle will of course, be with them plus my mother is coming down but I know that they would love talking to you while we're away. Okay, call me. Love you!"

Bora Bora? Are you kidding me? Damn and I thought Montreal was great! Wait, I don't remember telling her that I was going to Montreal, I didn't even know until we were at the airport??? I wish I could fly down to be with the girls but now I can't with my new job. But I will definitely call my godchildren daily and check in with them!

Forty Seven

Will texted me earlier today while Omar and I were on the plane returning from Montreal. He asked if he and Dev could stop by my apartment to share some *can't-wait-til-tomorrow* news. Although I'm tired, I have to say that I'm curious as to what news they have to share. Maybe they're gay and getting married! Or even better, they won lotto and want to share their winnings with me! Seriously though, all kidding aside, I can't even begin to imagine what they have to tell me but one thing I do know is that lotto win sure sounds pretty good. Meanwhile, I just finished walking Milo and now I'm juicing lemons, raspberries and limes for raspberry lemonade for the three of us. Omar went back to his apartment to catch up on things, which is just as well because now that we're back in the real world, as soon as Dev and Will leave, my butt needs to prepare for the week. But not before I return daddy's and Anya's call!

BUZZ BUZZ…BUZZ BUZZ. My intercom rings and after I buzzing Will and Devin in, I rush back into the kitchen to finish arranging the fruit platter. Once all the slices are arranged, I hear a triple knock on the door.

Devin always knocks three times so I'll *know* it's him! Go figure!

"Hey Dev! Hello Willie! Come on in and make yourselves at home," I tell them while I go and get the platter.

"You look good. Looks like you put on a little weight." Dev says as I walk in with the fruit.

"Uh, I'm not too sure how to take that!"

"No, I meant that as a compliment. The weight looks good! So, how was Montreal? Devin rebounds, still smiling from his *attempted* save while helping himself to a slice of mango.

"It was great. The city is absolutely beautiful, and Omar surprised me with all kinds of wonderful plans. Old Montreal reminds me a lot of the Left Bank in Paris and you *know* how much I love that side of the city. But I have to say that Montreal has its own little charm apart from the city of lights. But enough about me and my little getaway. What's going on? What's this news that couldn't wait?"

"Well, you know that Devin and I have been doing our consulting thing with a few clients…"

"Yes and if I'm not mistaken, you just got a new client last week that Devin met with, right Dev?"

"Right," Devin echoes as he drops a strawberry on the floor.

"Damn man, can't take you anywhere," Will mumbles to Devin before continuing. "Well Cyd, while you were in Montreal we moved into our first office space!"

"Get out! That's great! But wait, did I miss a couple of pages? I didn't even know that you guys were looking for a space!"

"We weren't, it was just fate, karma or whatever you want to call it."

"The father of one of my friends," Devin jumps in to elaborate,. "has office space that he isn't using and fortunately for us, isn't quite ready to sell. So when my friend told him about our life coaching business, his dad offered the space for us to use for the next year or two or until we're ready for a larger space."

"Well, that was pretty generous. How big is the space?"

"It's a little under 800 square feet with two rooms—."

"We're going to use one of the rooms as a conference/meeting room," Will interrupts, "then a general office area plus there is a bathroom and a kitchenette. But the best part is that we only have to pay for the utilities."

"You definitely can't get a better deal than that. I'm really happy for you two! So it looks like *Strategies for Life* has finally found a home. We'll have to celebrate. And of course if there's anything that doesn't involve painting or moving big, heavy objects that I can help you guys with, just let me know," I tell them while laughing.

Smiling, Will tells me, "Of course," while grabbing a few more strawberries as he rolls off the couch, "we just wanted to share the good news with you since we all share a common journey."

"Speaking of journeys, Cyd," Devin begins while getting up from my shabby chic leather chair, "you texted us that you put all the pieces together but you never did tell us what you came up with."

"You know what? I think you're right, I don't think I ever did!"

"No you didn't, so what do we need a drum roll or some sort of special permit to hear what this secretive, ambiguous purpose of yours is?" smart ass Devin asks.

"Ha, ha, no, there's no secret, I just wanted to take some time to let it digest and marinate for a little bit. But now that I have and you're both here I can actually tell you about it now. All right, so remember the exercise when we had to delve into our parents characteristics and personalities and then try to connect the dots and put all the pieces of the puzzle togeth….?"

"Yeah, yeah we remember," Devin impatiently interrupts in his attempt to rush me.

"So, as I was saying, after connecting the dots and verbalizing the finished puzzle, it became clear to me that my purpose *is to help introduce people who have yet to be awakened, to the infinite possibilities that lie within each and every one of us. And to communicate it in a relatable, easy to understand way!"*

Devin and Will look at one another as if waiting for the other to respond. *Their expressions show a feeling of pride and surprise all wrapped up in one cohesive look.*

"Sounds good," Will finally says approvingly.

"Yeah, it sounds great. Have you thought about how you're going to accomplish this? And even more importantly, how are you going to fit this into your schedule while working 9-5?" Devin asks.

"I'm not sure. I didn't get that part of the memo yet, but my guess is that it could be anything from radio, television, writing or even, one on one, one by one. I really have no idea. And as for how I will incorporate time to fit with my career. I guess I'll have to work it out or it will work out on its own, as it always does."

"Well, the most important aspect has been communicated so now just prepare for when the rest will be revealed to you," Devin says while getting up and walking toward the door.

"Well, congrats, Cyd, and good luck with your newfound purpose! I know that you'll not only fulfill that which was revealed to you but even more as well," Willie adds.

"Thanks, guys. I appreciate your support. However, I am curious about one thing."

"What's that?"

"What's the timetable for this kind of stuff?"

"Timetable for what stuff?" Devin asked.

"For the *rest* of my purpose to be revealed? Like when will I know how I'm supposed to fulfill it?"

"There are no timetables. When the time is right, then it'll be revealed, and you'll know, just as you knew with this. But only when the time is right," Will answers, "then and *only* then!"

"Ok, we're outta here. Keep us posted!" Devin says as they walk out. "Patience, Cyd, patience!"

"Not exactly my strongest trait but okay I'll do my best! Later guys and congratulations again on your new space!"

After I clean up, I pour myself another glass of iced tea then plop down on the couch and hit the phones speaker button. "Call Anya" A few seconds later Anya's phone rings through the speaker.

Forty Eight

The BCBW offices are nice, somewhat industrial although sleeker with a touch of sophistication. The elevators, like those at Liz open directly into their showroom. The first thing I see are miles and miles of clothes along the perimeter of the exposed brick walls.

"Good afternoon, can I help you?" the Anniston-ish receptionist asks.

"Yes my name is Cydney Rochon and I have a 3:15 appointment with Ms. Gregory."

"Ah, yes, Ms. Gregory is expecting you. Please have a seat and I'll let her know that you're here."

"Would you like coffee, tea, Perrier?" the other receptionist offers.

"Herbal tea if you have it, thank you."

"Sure, I'll be right back."

"Thank you."

Four or five models get off the elevator and head into the expansive showroom. I can't really see their faces but from what I can see, a couple of them look familiar. As I'm contorting to get a glimpse of their faces, a short red haired woman walks swiftly toward me.

"Hello, Cydney. How are you?" she asks, smiling broadly.

"Hello, Faye. I'm great and you?"

"Good. C'mon let's go to my office."

I smile at the receptionists as I get up and follow Faye into her all-white office. Even the floor is white.

"Please have a seat," she motions. As I sit in one of two white crocodile embossed leather chairs finished with white nail heads, I admire the sepia toned family photos on her desk, which of course, are also framed in white. Faye reviews the job description again then briefly recites the company's policy which prompts me to ask a few questions after her obligatory company spiel. Just minutes after agreeing on a salary, Faye's assistant brings in the paperwork along with my cup of herbal tea. As I carefully peruse the contract and am about to sign, Faye's door abruptly opens. I look up and it's Les, Faye's boss. I met him briefly during my initial interview.

"Hello, Cydney. It's good seeing you again!" he bellows while extending his hand.

"Hello, Les. It's good seeing you as well," I tell him as I shake his hand.

"Well, I hope you have suntan lotion!" he says while eyeballing the paperwork.

Suntan lotion? Why the hell is he asking me about suntan lotion? I glance over at Faye and she seems to be just as confused as I am. "Uh, I believe I do, but why do you ask?"

"I just got word from the CEO, and it looks like BCBW is going west! We're moving our offices to Los Angeles with the exception of a small office here in New York, but all of our designers will now be based in Los Angeles."

What the hell? Needless to say I'm totally stunned! Faye didn't say anydamnthing about the offices moving to LA during the interview. I turn back to Faye hoping that she will say something, *anydamnthing* but her expression is blanker than a chalk less blackboard. *Are you kidding me? Is this some kind of a joke? Friggin' Los Angeles?*

Forty Nine

While playing with Milo, I see the flashing light on my phone. I take Milo's little paw and press **PLAY**.

BEEP

"Hey woman! Just wanted to holla at you. I know we've been emailing and texting each other but every now and then it's nice to hear a voice. And in case it's been too long, this is Ty. All right, I guess you're not in so I'll try you later, but just wanted to let you know that I'll be in the states for some meetings and interviews in a few weeks. Tell you more when we speak, Hope all is well. Ciao!"

Good, I could use a distraction right about now. It'll be good to see Ty, I kinda miss him!

BEEP

"Hi Cyd it's Zoe. Look, I'm calling to give you a heads up. Donna asked me for your number since the company deletes former employees' info from the main database after thirty days. And who knows, she might not even call but in the event that she does, I didn't want you to be blindsided. Oh, and a Gail King called. Hey, is that Gail, Gayle, as in Oprah and Gayle? Anyway, she wants you to call her; she said that you have her number."

Oh cool, Gayle called, it'll be nice to talk to her again. Hmmm and Donna wants to talk to me? I wonder why?…

BEEP

"Hey Cyd, it's Devin. Look, Will and I have a proposition for you. We talked after leaving your apartment on Sunday and we know you're about to start a new job, but before you make any final decisions we want you to think about coming aboard with us at SFL. Our client base is growing and having you, we think, can bring something different to the table. Different enough to put SFL ahead of our competition. We have a great office space that is more than sufficient for the three of us. We can work out the logistics later but just think about it. It could be a good thing. No, it could be *great* thing! I'll call you in a couple of days and we can sit down and discuss it. Think about it, Cydney, we're serious!"

What? Are they pay-me-a-salary serious? Truth be told, I have always felt a part of SFL from the start with input for planning and developing it. But me as a life coach? I don't know about that. Maybe with some type of twist. And as my main source of income? Hmmm, I don't know, I love designing although it could be a nice change plus provide me with a sense of fulfillment. I don't know, I'll still have to really think about this…

BEEP

"Hey gurl, I'm tired of this phone tag! Call me. We need to catch up, okay? Call me! I don't even know how your new job is going! Call me, gurl!!! Oh and how are you feeling? Oops my bad, I probably should have asked that first!"

Yeah, you should have but that's okay, I'm doing good and we'll talk soon. Life has just been a little crazy, but soon! Promise!

Fifty

I'm relieved that Donna wanted to meet me at a restaurant instead of at the office. Quite frankly, with the exception of Zoe, I really wasn't up for chit chatting with anyone and I *definitely* was not up to running into the Wicked Witch and Toto!

As I walk into the restaurant, I see Donna talking on her cell seated at one of the back tables. I walk over to her as she ends her call and stands to greet me.

"Cyd, thank you so much for meeting me especially with such short notice," she tells me while we exchange a quick employer to employee embrace.

"No problem, Donna. I of all people know how crazy your schedule is!"

"Yes, *crazy* is the right word. So, Cydney, how have you been? Are you working?"

"I'm good, thanks, but Donna I must admit that I'm curious as to why you wanted to meet with me."

"Fair enough. Let me get right to the point. First, you should know that I fired Gretchen last night. I've not been happy with the way she, hmm how can I say this—*interacts* with people. Nor have I been comfortable with certain decisions she's made. So, to cut to the chase,

Cydney, I would like you to return to the company in a new position that I created just for you. You will have a few more responsibilities in addition to having an assistant as well as another designer under you. And *this* time you'll be reporting directly to me. And of course, if you accept the position and I hope that you will, it'll be at a higher salary. We can talk about the numbers later. So, tell me what do you think so far? Are you interested?"

"I, I don't know what to say, I wasn't sure what to expect when you asked me to meet you, but I didn't expect this. Donna, can I think about it and call you before you leave for Bali?" I ask her as the waiter brings our drinks.

"Sure, that will be fine," she said glancing at her diamond and black leather custom made watch.

After about five or ten minutes of small talk over tea and cappuccino we say our goodbyes.

While still trying to absorb what just happened, I walk as quickly as I can, up 7th Avenue to get on the uptown subway to meet Shaye for a late lunch.

Fifty One

Who was it that said when it rains it pours? Well, whoever it was got it right! Who would have thought that I (or anyone for that matter) would have three good job opportunities thrown at me (or them) at once? After taking time to revel in my good fortune, I weighed the pros and cons of each one, then did some serious *what's-best-for-me-and-all-concerned* meditation afterwards. Within a short time my reasoning was crystal clear.

As I reviewed each one, all three had different pros and cons. But Donna's offer in particular, seems ideal because not only is designing my passion but I would have more money but more importantly, job stability along with a new promotion. I would also have the added bonus of the Wicked Witch gone and Toto very possibly, once again, working for moi! Now, *that's* what I call karma and/or sweet revenge. It's just a matter of how you look at it. I pause briefly before dialing the number.

"Hello Faye, it's Cydney Rochon. Before I say anything, first, I just want to thank you for giving me a few more days to think about relocating to L.A. And well, after much thought and deliberation, I decided that I'm not quite ready to leave New York. At least not at this time."

"Well, Cydney, the move did come up rather abruptly and I can't say that I blame you but I am disappointed as I'm sure Les will be."

"Well, hopefully our paths will cross in the future but in the meantime, thank you again, I really appreciate the offer."

Okay, one down and one to go. Although I pretty much know which job I'm going to accept, I still want to run it by my mother for her input. Just as I'm about to call her, my phone rings. I look into the phones monitor and see that it's Omar.

"Hello."

"Hey Cyd, are you hungry?"

"Is grass green?"

"Funny. Wanna go to dinner?"

Smiling I ask, "Sure, Vietnamese or Soul?"

"You decide, I'll pick you up in forty five minutes, cool?"

"Ok, see ya then!"

I have just enough time to jump in the shower and get dressed so it looks like mama's insight will have to wait until tomorrow.

Omar and I are at Soul 2 Soul which is a great new soul food fusion restaurant/lounge that just recently opened. Robyn, Shaye and I have already been here at least three times, but who's counting? S-2-S specializes in soul food with a little twist. This is Omar's first time here although he's known about it because I've been talking about it ever since it opened.

"So what's good?"

"Everything."

"Okay, then hmmm, let's see, I'll try the blackened catfish and why don't you just order the sides for me while I go to the men's room. I'll be right back."

"All right."

Omar excuses himself just seconds before our waiter comes to the table.

"Good evening. Can I get you a drink or are you ready to order?"

"Yes, I'm ready. My friend would like the red blackened catfish, collard & cornbread pudding and the lobster mac & cheese. And let's see, I would like the fried chicken and waffle sliders and a side order of fried cheese-drizzled macaroni balls and…"

Suddenly I hear shouting. A man and woman. The woman sounds familiar and I think that the man's voice is….It can't be. *What the hell is going on?*

"Uh, and…that's all. Thank you," I tell the waiter, then quickly scramble out of the booth to see what all the commotion is about. I stand behind one of the walls and peep out from behind it. I can't believe this. It's Robyn and Omar! Robyn is in his face with her neck going back and forth like a chicken on steroids while her index finger is waving in his face! Omar *looks* cool but I can tell he's pissed as hell!

"…IF YOU WERE HALF THE MAN YOU SHOULD BE, YOU WOULD HAVE NEVER DENIED WHAT'S YOURS!

"And you need to MIND YOUR OWN DAMN BUSINESS!" Omar retorts.

"FOR YOUR INFORMATION MY FRIENDS *ARE* MY DAMN BUSINESS! Just man the hell up and take responsibility for your actions…"

"Just stay the hell outta *my* business! And while you're at it, stay the hell away from *my* woman too! And for the record, I could care less if women are your thing, but just get your own AND LEAVE MINE ALONE!"

"I *KNOW* you're not trying to say, that I'm gay!'

"Hey, if the SIZE 12 shoe fits. WEAR IT!"

"Look, Oreo, Omareo or whatever your damn name is, for *your* record not that it would matter if I was but I'M NOT GAY! But think what you want because from the moment I met you, I knew that your golden brown ass was shady! And just in case you think you fooled somebody, I know that there is *no way* in hell that your ass was kidnapped by some damn drug cartel! You need to STOP LOOKING AT THOSE "CSI" EPISODES and start living in the real world and take responsibility for what's yours!"

Robyn walks away as she flips her hand in Omar's face. He stands there with his teeth clenched while I rush back to our booth. I cannot believe those two! Robyn was clearly out of line, actually they both were. All I know is I am not going to be put in the middle of their nonsense so I'm not going to say anything to either one of them unless one of them says something to me first.

Omar returns to the table and sighs deeply then signals for the waiter. The waiter quickly obliges and comes right over.

"Give me a gin and tonic. And make it a double."

◊ ◊ ◊ ◊ ◊

Robyn just called. This will actually be the first time Robyn and I have spoken since her little shouting match with Omar, several nights ago.

"I have a confession," she begins.

"I'm afraid to ask," I respond naively as I switch the phone to **SPEAKER**.

"I think you should know that I ran into Omar several nights ago at Soul 2 Soul."

"Okay, and?" I ask while circling items for my boogala from the *Land Of Nod* children's catalog.

"We got into an argument and I let him know what's up."

"And what *is* up…exactly?"

"My feelings about that whole *it's-not-my-baby* bull. Look Cyd, bottom line I don't like him, I think he's a big phony and I really believe that in the beginning he just told you what you wanted to hear so you would fall in love with his ass. And I still can't get over that he didn't believe you when you told him that you were pregnant and that he was the father. I mean c'mon he should know you well enough to know that you don't lie! *Especially* about something like that."

"Robyn, please don't think that I don't appreciate you having my back, because I do but this is really between Omar and me. Right after our trip to the clinic, I decided that it would be best for everyone if I didn't involve you or anyone else with Omar's and my issues. And just a FYI, he's actually coming around. I guess it takes some people a little longer to digest things than it does for others. But, the good thing is that he's finally on board with the pregnancy and has even gone with me to look at baby furniture…"

"Oh and uh… let's see, looking at what, a cute pink crib, is supposed to make up for him making you feel like crap while carrying his baby? Gurl, please don't tell me that you're regressing back to one of those HEA women, again!"

"Excuse me?" *I can't believe that Robyn just said that!* HEA is the acronym for happily ever after, as in the ending of most, if not all, fairy tales. Robyn made it up and uses it to refer to women whose mindset is fairy tale based and somewhat removed from most forms of reality. Robyn believes, and I agree, that a lot of women in relationships refuse to let go of their *happily ever after* ending no matter what their situation or circumstances are with their so-called prince charming. The syndrome's premise is that it's not the man that the women are holding onto, it's the fairy tale ending that women can't seem to let go of.

"I can't believe that you think that I would try to hold onto Omar or any man for that matter because of some story book fantasy," I tell her as I close the catalog. "Now, that may have been the case several years ago, but it certainly is not the case now. This has less to do with happy endings and more to do with second chances. And who knows, maybe I am wrong about Omar. But if I am, I'm sure in time, I'll figure it out. On my own! Look, uh…I gotta go. I'll talk to you later," I tell her then hang up, cutting her off before she has a chance to come back with a signature Robyn-esque retort!

Fifty Two

I am just now meeting with Donna although I decided several weeks ago which job offer I was going to accept. Donna extended her trip to Bali and just returned yesterday. It was important to me to speak to her before telling Will and Devin my decision. When I asked the dynamic duo if they could wait, they both told me "no problem."

"Cydney thanks so much for coming to the office. And I have to tell you that I'm truly looking forward to working with you again. Hopefully, this new arrangement will make up for some of what you went through with Gretchen."

"Thanks Donna, I appreciate that. And I'm looking forward to working with you as well. I'll call you next week to discuss my start date."

"Perfect, I'll talk to you then."

As I cross Seventh Avenue to the 40th Street subway entrance, I call Devin.

"Hello."

"Hi Devin, it's me."

"Hey Cyd, what's going on?"

"I'm heading home now and want to know if you and Willie are still coming over at five thirty?"

"Uh yeah, as far as I know. I'll text him and have him meet us. I assume this is regarding your decision?"

"Yes."

◊◊◊◊◊

"Thank you both for coming over, I just want to talk to you about *Strategies for Life*, even though I've already made my decision."

"No problem, we're glad you called," Will said as he props his leg up on the edge of the couch.

"So what's on your mind?" Devin asks.

"I'm curious as to your thinking in respect to me joining SFL especially since I don't have the degrees and experience that the two of you have. The only thing I have is a BFA in fashion design and industry experience. I mean, Will, you were a human resources manager for four years and before that you were a high school career counselor. And Devin you majored in psychology and practiced as a psychotherapist for five years."

"Okay, now tell us something that we don't know. Cydney, we asked you to join SFL not because we want someone like us but because we want someone that's different, someone who can bring something new to the SFL table. As you know, Will and I play by the book and inside the box, but you play *outside* the box and you *write* your own book. Plus, you're still developing spiritually which automatically gives you and the client a commonality. We believe that, that alone will make the client feel more comfortable and open to the whole SFL process."

"Exactly," Will cuts in, "you're still developing as will be most of our clients which we feel will help them relate to you more so than if you weren't."

Then if you come on board with us, once Will and I complete the reorganization of SFL you'll be able to see how all of our roles will complement one another."

"Can you define these roles?"

"Well, I'll primarily focus on career guidance and transitions while Devin will deal with general life and social issues. And our plan for you is to focus on helping clients explore and develop their inner strength and spiritual side. That will be their foundation, and once that's completed, they will continue with Devin and me for their career, life and social issues."

"So, with you in the SFL equation, a solid foundation will be in place for our clients' life coach requirements."

"And/or issues," Will adds. "So, bottom-line with you on board, we will be an unbeatable team and unlike any other life coaching business."

"Exactly," Will quickly throws in."

I smile and could tell by the look on their faces that both Will and Devin not only want me to join SFL but in their minds, they *need* me to. And listening to them explain how I would fit in with the company just further confirmed what I was already feeling internally. I'm glad that I spoke to Donna first. It was only fair, not just to her but to me and my long time passion. When I told her of my decision Donna was not only understanding, she was very gracious.

Anyone that knows Donna, knows that she is very much in tune with her spirituality and has made it a part of her day to day routine. And for that reason alone, I wasn't at all surprised at how totally supportive she was of my new role as a SFL consultant. In fact, she was so supportive that she actually revised her original offer so that my schedule would not conflict with my position at SFL. Instead of working full-time, Donna proposed a part-time schedule where I would design two major lines annually on a free-lance basis in addition to overseeing DK*Urban's* creative team via monthly meetings. I really couldn't ask for a better set-up because not only will I be doing what I love but it'll allow me to honor and serve both of my passions! After working out all of the particulars, I didn't really need to think about it so I just gladly accepted.

◊◊◊◊◊

Since joining *Strategies for Life*, I've been on several appointments with Devin and am learning quite a bit.

During one of our last appointments in my final training phase, Dev asked me to briefly explain to the client how I would help them tap into their inner strength before proceeding to whatever life issues they have. I'll be the first to admit that I started off a little shaky but all in all I think I came through pretty well at the end.

Right now I'm waiting for Devin in front of one of our new client's buildings when my cell phone beeps. I look down at the screen and see that it's a text from Willie. *This can't be good.*

As luck would have it, within seconds I'm now on my own. The original plan was that Devin would start the consultation with the foundation's director, Carole Brown and once he completed his segment, I would then join in and talk to Ms. Brown about the seminar and laying the foundation for her employees. In his text, Will explains that SFL had a last-minute appointment with a follow-up client in New Jersey and Will felt that Devin should go, since he was the one the client initially met with. Well, that's all fine and dandy except for the little, teeny ass fact that Devin knew all the particulars for this new client and had *only* asked me to prepare the preliminary paperwork for this meeting. I've tried his cell more than a few times hoping to get some additional information but it keeps going into voice mail. From the short time I've been with the company Devin and I have met and consulted with clients during my training phase as a *team.* Of course, I knew that *soon* I would be on my own once I completed the training. But not today, I'm not prepared! I can hear Robyn's voice now, *Gurl, shit happens! Just roll with it!* So, I guess I'll just have to pull a friggin' rabbit out of a hat and wing the entire consultation by myself. And not making things any easier, as I approach the building, I see that the exterior is so badly dilapidated it looks as though it should be on some sort of emergency brick life support!

As I enter through the dirty, smudged glass doors I see quite a few cigarette butts, several mouse traps and a greasy, balled up McDonald's bag on the lobby's worn linoleum floor. It's obvious that the floor hasn't been mopped in weeks, probably even months. I didn't expect plush but I sure as hell didn't expect this! I walk to the double elevator bank and see a handwritten, cardboard "**OUT OF ORDER**" sign on one of the doors. I cautiously knuckle-press the **UP** button as I contemplate taking the stairs. Reaching in my pocket, I pull out the paper to see which floor the client is on. "Damn," I hear myself say, "they would be all the way up on seven!"

Just then, a pizza delivery guy enters the building, walks over to the elevator bank and presses the "up" button several times, even though it's already lit. It amuses me when people do that as if pressing the lit button *again* will actually make the elevator come faster. However, oddly enough, the elevator comes. Accompanying the elevator is a loud and extremely annoying, screeching sound. I glance at *PDG* (pizza delivery guy) to see if he looks the least bit concerned and, surprisingly, he doesn't, so I assume that this isn't the first time he's been on these elevators. The doors open and two chatty women get off. *PDG* gets on and I cautiously follow. The screeching resumes and I quickly "knuckle" 7 while *PDG* thankfully presses 8. There is no way that I wanted to be on this screeching elevator by myself!

I get off on my floor and unexpectedly the hallway is fairly clean. Well, let's put it this way: the floors could definitely use a good mopping, but I don't see any nasty nicotine butts, mouse traps or balled up bags. I walk over to the floor directory and follow the gold and black peel and stick arrows to Suite 703. The door is unlocked so I slowly walk in and to no surprise, there's no one sitting at the worn, wooden desk. Just as I begin to look around the dismal surroundings, I hear someone coming and brace myself— for what, I'm not sure.

"Who's there?" A deep, raspy voice bellows.

I look to see who's asking, but the stack of boxes is blocking the raspy voice's carrier.

"Uh, I have an appointment with Carole Brown," I say as I look above the boxes, curious as to who the hell I'm talking to.

Then suddenly a 60 something, Whoopi-look-alike minus the locks and plus a few pounds, makes her appearance from behind the cardboard blockade.

"You Devin?" raspy asks.

"No, I'm Cydney Rochon, Devin and I work together but unfortunately he couldn't make it." I tell her while managing a smile, "Are you Ms. Brown?"

"No I'm Jackie, have a seat, honey. Carole will be out in a minute," she says as she presses the grimy button on the phone's intercom.

"Okay, thanks," I say, looking for somewhere to sit. I see an old, tattered, plaid upholstered chair across from the boxes with a large crate on top of it so I move it, brush the dust off the seat and sit down. To say that the office looks as though it's been deserted for quite some time would be a friggin' understatement! Practically everything in the office is covered in dust, and needless to say the entire place is in dire need of a good cleaning. I automatically start digging in my purse but before I can find my pocket size *Purell,* the sound of irregular footsteps are nearing, someone with a slight limp is approaching.

"Hello, Cydney. I'm Carole Brown," she says, extending her hand.

"Hello Carole. It's nice meeting you," I tell her as I quickly withdraw my hand from my handbag excavation."

"Why don't we talk in my office? Follow me."

I jump up and follow her down the soiled and scuffed corridor. Carole Brown is a short, slightly round, attractive Black woman, I would guess in her mid to late 50's. Her short silver hair shimmers in the fluorescent light as I follow her into the oddly shaped room. There are three chairs in her office, all mismatched. I sit in the poorly patched, brown leather one in front of her desk. Of the three, it seems to be the least dusty.

"Thank you for making the trek up to Harlem and please excuse the condition of the office. My foundation is actually in the process of moving, and a good friend was nice enough to offer this temporary space so that we could continue to work during the transition."

"No problem," I lie, while trying not to show my apprehension.

"It's no *Trump Tower*, but it serves the purpose and I'm very grateful. But that's neither here nor there....I want to hear more about your company, *Strategies for Life* and how my employees can benefit from your services."

"By all means but first Ms. Brown, may I ask how you heard about our company?"

"Please, call me Carole. One of the contributors for *the Metro Newspaper* mentioned *SFL* in an article titled *"Uncork Your Genie."*

"Oh yes that was just several weeks ago. Okay so now, to answer your question, *Strategies For Life* is a small company that focuses on strategic solutions for life, such as career and family transitions, while helping our clients build a foundation based on the enlightenment and development of our client's inner spiritual power."

Carole stares at me for a moment before responding. "That *sounds* pretty impressive. But truthfully, Cindy, this whole spiritual thing is relatively new to me;

so can you *please* explain that enlightenment power part in layman's terms so I'll know exactly what it means?"

Damn, somehow I unconsciously memorized Devin's little convoluted spiel and like a mimicking parrot I repeated it verbatim!

Now nervous, I laugh trying to stall, filching whatever time I can in order to quickly regroup. Now, somehow I need to explain this to Carole in a way in which she can grasp what SFL is all about. While regrouping, my eyes are drawn to a DSW shopping bag in a corner next to what looks to be a relatively new canvas Coach handbag.

"My apologies Carole, obviously I've been around Devin and Will too long because now, I'm even beginning to talk like them. Let me try to rephrase that in a way that hopefully will be more relatable. Okay," I tell her before taking a deep breath. "Quite some time ago I was told by a wise woman that we all, only use a small portion of our inner power, a portion that has been reported to be as little as one eighth of our full potential. Now, Carole, that's *seven eighths* of our potential inner power that is unused, dormant and essentially inactive. Just imagine having *DSW, the Designer Shoe Warehouse* at your total disposal and being able to select anything from the store. You can have as many shoes, handbags, pantyhose, tights or socks in whatever quantity of *DSW's* merchandise that your little heart desires. For free! You can select from any price point, any style or in as many colors as you want. And with all those choices, all you end up with is two pairs of shoes and one handbag!"

"Now *that's* something I can definitely relate to. But Cindy, I know one thing, I wouldn't walk out that store with one measly ass handbag and just two pairs of shoes, not as much as I love shoes and handbags!!" Carole says, laughing.

"Exactly, and why would you when you have total access to an entire store full of merchandise? Personally, I would be all over the designer shoe section, Italian handbags, tights, socks, house shoes, running shoes and well, I'm sure you get the idea. Bottom line, to have an incredible opportunity like that and to leave the store with, as you say, one little ass handbag and just two pairs of shoes would be totally lax on your part not to take full advantage of what the *entire* store has to offer. So, to summarize, one of *Strategies For Life's* focus is to help our clients obtain more than one handbag and two pairs of shoes by not only letting them know that they have total access to the store but by also *showing* them the steps to gain access. And once that foundation is laid, we'll move onto the client's life issues So now, simply speaking, are we good?"

"Yes, I think we are…So, before dealing with the life, family and career issues, SFL helps their client's to access, explore and utilize the 7/8 of the dormant power which you're saying, is in each and every one of us. Then once accessed, we will be able to tap into our full potential, then move on to the other issues at hand."

"Exactly!"

Carole smiles while leaning in to me then gets serious and whispers, "So, Cindy, what's the secret to activating this power? Honey, I want to get in on this!" Carole said, as if wanting in on a *guaranteed-not-to-get-caught* multi-million dollar bank heist.

"Great question, Carole, but I've got an even better answer: there is no secret. In fact, there's only one crucial thing that you will need to do along with several other key components which go hand in hand with this newfound revelation. Those key components are needed to activate your inner power while also raising your level of consciousness but these are things that we will go more into during the actual seminar. And Carole, it's *Cydney*."

"Oh Cydney, I'm sorry! Okay now, that you've got me *totally* intrigued, *Cydney,* how do we get started?"

"Well, first we schedule the group seminar followed by private individual meetings with each participant. Here, I put together some literature for you to review. When you're ready to schedule the seminar, just call either Devin or me," I tell her as I hand her the SFL pamphlet.

"Great, I'm excited! This will be perfect for the foundation and our employees, myself included. Technically I cannot speak for them, but I'm sure the Board of Directors will all be on board for this, but as I told Devin, knowing them, they will probably want to call or meet with you and ask a few questions of their own.

You know how that goes. I'll contact you to set the seminar up as soon as I get the green light."

"That's fine, just let us know once you have a day and time."

As we walk to the door, we shake hands and say our goodbyes. Waiting at the elevator, I'm using every bit of strength I have to stop myself from jumping up and down. I am ecstatic! And not because I'm leaving this brick nightmare of a building (although that is something to jump up and down about) but because, numero uno, Carole got it! She actually got what I was saying! And two, if all goes as planned and it looks like it will, then I would have accomplished the exact reason why I joined the company — to help enlighten small groups of people to the unlimited possibilities that lie within them, that lie within all of us! Which, in turn, will help them begin the journey of a lifetime and ultimately make an incredible impact on their lives, forever! And the best thing is that I, *moi,* would have had a small part in it.

I press the "down" button and get on the screeching elevator, totally unfazed and smiling all the way down.

"YESSSS!" I yell!

Brrnng, brrnng…

"Hello?"

"I just called you, I guess you were still with Carole Brown."

"Uh, no, I was in the elevator and probably didn't have reception."

"Well, how'd it go?" Devin asked.

"All and all, it went pretty well," I tell him as I rub my hands vigorously with *Purell.* "Carole is a no nonsense woman with a brain *and* a heart. I like her."

"Good, good, glad it went well, I'll follow up with her in a day or two and try to secure a date. Then you and I, if necessary can meet with the foundation's board or move forward to the employee seminar."

"Great, I'm looking forward to it."

"So am I. I want to see you in action because if you handle it the way Will and I think you will, then we'll be set to proceed full speed."

"Thanks for the pressure!" I tell him sarcastically.

"No problem! Catch you later!" he laughs.

"Yeah, later gator!"

Fifty Three

"Damn gurl it's about time you called me back! You know I …"

"No, let *me* finish…uh let's see, you were going to say how much you breathe and thrive on our little catching up sessions and…"

"Looks like *Clair Voyant* strikes again!" Robyn laughs.

"Ha, ha! But seriously didn't I just see you in *Lula Mae's* night before last or was that a hologram?" I remind her, picking Milo up and putting him on my lap.

"Yeah but you know how much I enjoy giving you a hard time! But if you remember, we really didn't get a chance to talk that much because James and Black came over to talk, and then as soon as they left, Shaye's friend stopped by to say hello to us. Uh, well, really to *you.* Which reminds me, when did Shaye and Jackson break up?"

"They didn't!" I smiled. "They're still together and FYI Alex is actually Shaye's boyfriend's friend, not Shaye's! And while on the subject of friends, did I tell you," I quickly segue, "that I spoke to Gayle King?"

"No, not since you had dinner with her and Ty. Did you run into her again?"

"No she called my old office and left a message with Zoe for me to call her. Turns out that, *Miz* King wanted one of the *O Magazine* writers to do a story on me and the division I started. However, since I'm just there on a free-lance basis, we spoke mostly about my new role at *Strategies for Life*. And well, long story short, after I told her about SFL she wants to feature Will, Devin and me in the magazine's October issue!"

"Damn, gurl, that's great! You've barely been there a month and you already got the company in *O Magazine!*"

"Yeah, how 'bout that? Will and Devin are too excited. Oh and before I forget, guess who's going to be the Clippers new coach!"

"Who Hershey?. Now maybe we can finally get some decent seats at the Garden! And hopefully the Clippers can win some games!!"

"Yeah, wouldn't that be nice, as long as they don't win while playing the Knicks! But this is what Ty's been waiting for so I'm happy for him. So what's happening with you and what's his name, Kwame?"

"Gurl keep up, Kwame is yesterday's news! See what happens when we don't talk?" Robyn asks facetiously." Today's news sista gurl is that I'm in love and unofficially off the market!"

"Shut up! For real? Who's the lucky man?"

"Gurl it's still hard to believe that I finally met my match *and* someone that frankly, I didn't think existed! Cyd, between Steve Harvey's book and your *write-all-the-things-you-want-in-a-mate* list, I am with the man of my dreams! And gurl, he even has money, although that's no longer important to me anymore."

Yeah, right and I'm Michelle Obama! "That's great Robyn! So, does Prince Charming have a name?" *This is the first that I've heard of Robyn not believing that she could have any man that she wanted. Well, I'm glad the book and list helped to boost her self-confidence!*

"Yep, Chauncey!"

Chauncey, Chauncey? As in I-found-an-open-box-of-Extenze-in-his-medicine-cabinet Chauncey? Wow, even little Milo looks surprised!

Fifty Four

I love my new work schedule. Depending on the day's client appointments, I typically go into the office two or three days during the week, then I work the balance from home which has me working a four day week! This schedule will allow me to be more of a hands-on mommy and eventually, once I begin, it will also allow me time for my free-lance work with Donna. Needless to say, the freelance work will definitely help compensate for my slightly below average salary and put me back in the game. Although, today is my day off, Willie called and asked me to come in for a brief meeting.

Devin and Will have done a great job with the SFL office space. However, according to them, there was not much to do. Will's cousin is an interior designer so she did most of the work and created the perfect office space. Will and I are in the freshly painted conference room which has been hand-stenciled. After Will told his cousin what type of atmosphere he wanted, she came in on the weekend Dev and Will moved in and repainted and stenciled one of the walls with various affirmations that Will provided. I'm reading and admiring the wall while Will and I wait for Devin. Will wants us to review the seminar material for Carole Brown's employees and the foundation. Devin finally joins us and takes a seat across from me.

"Devin and I both agree that for your last day of training that you should handle the seminar in the way you feel most comfortable. We have a basic outline that we've used in the past, but since this is your baby and area of expertise, it's your choice to use it, not use it, tweak it or dump it. It's totally your call. You have complete control of the seminar and how it will be conducted."

"And you won't be by yourself. Will and I will both be there for your first few seminars to see firsthand how the participants receive the presentation via their questions, comments, body language etc. And of course, we'll be there in case you need us for anything, but we know you'll be okay."

"I appreciate the vote of confidence," I tell them while looking over the outline. "Well, the good thing is that I have a week before we meet with the foundation's employees so that…"

"Uh," Devin interrupts, "That's why we wanted to meet today, Carole called this morning and she wants to move the seminar up to the day after tomorrow."

"The day after tomorrow?" I repeat while staring at Devin like he just lost complete ownership of his mind. I glanced at the outline briefly, and it is not at all something that I would be comfortable using. The last thing I want is to make the same mistake twice by using

Will and Devin's words or spiritual jargon. Been there, done that. I will definitely have to create my own wording.

"Are you serious?" I ask convinced that this must be some sort of *welcome-to-the-company* joke!

"Yes, but I'm sure you'll be fine. Don't worry about it. All you have to do is share the information that's already in your head. Now, how difficult could that be?" Will asked.

"Just sharing what's in my head? I can't believe you just said that!" I get up and start heading for the door. "Are you kidding me? It's more than just sharing my knowledge! First, I have to digest this," I tell them while waving the outline in the air. "Then I need to figure out how to communicate it sensibly and effectively."

"You'll be fine, trust us. You can do this," Devin reassures.

I hear him but choose not to respond.

"Do you at least have information about the employees or even the age range of the group?" I ask, stuffing the outline in the back pocket of my metallic tote.

Will looks at Devin for an answer. "Uh, yes, I believe Carole said that the age range is 25-42. There are sixteen people and of those, three or four are men. I believe that's what she said."

"Okay, well, that helps a little as long as the information is accurate. If you find out anything else please call me. And can you, text me the time and address?"

"Done."

"All right. Gotta run," I say as I head out of the office, "I've got to get started on this, like yesterday!"

Humph. Now, this should be interesting!

Fifty Five

As I'm about to jump on the train to go home and prepare for the seminar, my phone rings. It's Milanya.

"Hey Anya!"

"Hi Cyd, where are you?"

"About to get on the train to go home. Why?"

"Que and I are in New York. Can you meet me in Soho?"

◊◊◊◊◊

"I still cannot believe that you're here! So tell me, what brings you two to New York? And don't get me wrong, I'm happy to see you even if it's just for the day but you usually call me so we can make plans…"

"I know, I know," Milanya interrupts my run on banter. "Que had to fly up for a last minute meeting so I decided to come with him so that I could see my best friend!"

I'm glad I have my oversized tunic on because Anya's certainly not blind and if she got one good look at my stomach, she would definitely suspect something!

"Okay, that's sweet and I love you too but I *know* you and there has got to be more to it than that!" I tell her as we walk along Mercer Street.

Slowing down she smiles, "As I said, *to see you* as well as to get a jump on things."

We're directly in front of the *Monique Lhuillier* shop and before I can respond Anya pulls her hand out from her pocket then slowly waves it in my face! Notice anything?"

"Get the hell outta here. I can't believe it!" I am blinded by a perfectly cut four or five carat diamond ring. "OMG! Quentin proposed! Wh…when did this happen? Congratulations! I can't believe it, I'm so happy for you, for you both," I tell her as we hug in the middle of the sidewalk.

"Thanks Cyd, I can hardly believe it myself! Quentin proposed while we were in Bora Bora under the moonlit sky. It was actually quite romantic. He arranged for a small trio to play music while we sipped champagne and ate shrimp, crab and lobster. And, he had these gorgeous exotic flowers for me. It was totally unexpected and a night I'll always remember!"

She holds her hand out again to admire her flawless ring.

"He did good, didn't he?"

"Yes he did," I say, adjusting her hand so the rays from the sun can pick up the facets of the ring. Anya, I am really, really happy for you! Have you set a date yet?"

"We don't have an *exact* date but it will definitely be within the next six to eight weeks. Cyd, I don't want to wait any longer. You know that I've wanted to marry Que from the moment I first saw him. So, tomorrow when Preston flies down with one of his assistants we'll *officially* start planning. And today, you and I are here because I spoke to Monique and she pulled a few dresses for me to look at because unfortunately, I don't think I'll have time for a custom designed dress. So she'll just alter and customize one that has already been made," she tells me, as we head into the shop.

"Hey, when did you meet Monique Lhuillier? I don't ever remember you mentioning that you two met!"

"We met at that charity dinner in Florida last year. Remember, I'm sure I told you?"

"Oh yes, you sat next to her during dinner," I vaguely recall, as a well-dressed woman approaches us.

"Hello, welcome to *Monique Lhuillier*, how can I help you ladies today?"

"Yes, Monique is holding a few dresses for me."

"Oh yes, you must be Ms. Milanya?"

"Yes and this is my best friend and Maid of Honor, Cydney."

I look at Anya and smile. She remembered. We made a pact in college that we would stand up for one another when we got married.

"Nice to meet you both, I'm Veronique. Ms. Lhuillier sent several dresses over from the studio for you, please come with me and I'll get them for you."

As we follow Veronique through to the back, I can't help but think of how much Anya has been waiting for this day. I am so excited for her. I know that she is okay with living with Que and would have continued to do so. But deep down I also know that she really wanted to marry him not only because she loves him but as an example for the girls. She wants Kai and Nico to marry their Prince Charmings and not settle for living together, unless that is something that *they* choose to do and not something they do because mommy and daddy did it. She always says that 90% of all children live by example and that is one example she didn't want to pass on to them. But she loves Que so much that she was just going to deal with it and discuss it with them when she felt that they were old enough to understand her choice.

Veronique rolls out a small rolling rack with seven or eight dresses.

"All right, Ms. Milanya, these are the dresses that Ms. Lhuillier sent over for you to choose from."

"Thank you Veronique."

We both go over to the rack and start looking through the dresses.

"I hope you don't mind," Anya said while turning to me.

"Mind what?"

"Well, I always had in the back of my mind how nice it would be for you to design my dress whenever I got married and now with such short notice, I just thought that it might be easier for everyone if I bought one."

"Girl, please, don't be silly! I'm flattered that you even thought of having me design it, but you're right; it would have been difficult with such little time. Besides, it's more fun for me to go shopping with you!"

"Thanks for being here with me."

"I wouldn't be any other place," I tell her, searching through the rack of wedding dresses.

I stop when I come to one in particular.

"Anya, how about this one?" I ask as I pull out one of the most beautiful dresses that I have ever seen and hold it against my body. Anya turns to look at it and immediately smiles.

"Oh my God! Cyd, that's it! I love it!"

Fifty Six

"Juice, coffee or both?" I yell into the bedroom.

"Juice, no coffee!"

"Breakfast will be ready in three minutes. So you have just enough time to brush your teeth!" I yell.

I hear the rustling of sheets followed by a long drawn out stretch. I haven't seen much of Omar this past month. In fact our rendezvous' have only been averaging about once a week. I've been really tired, not to mention crazy busy with work, and it's only going to get busier once the *O Magazine* article runs, which should be very soon.

There's no doubt that our business will triple. And quite possibly, quadruple! So, in anticipation and/or smart planning, we decided yesterday to start interviewing several more people to join the company. This way, Will can return to the field and leave the *behind the scenes* work to someone else. The plan is for that person to be in an administrative position and be responsible for most of the scheduling, billing and miscellaneous paperwork while the other person will be training out in the field with Devin and me. Down the road we will hire another trainee but our goal is to grow slowly even if it means turning some clients away, something that we don't want to do but feel will be necessary for the sake of quality service and longevity. The additional staff will be a huge relief for me especially since I've yet to tell Will and Devin about the baby. I know that I'll have to speak to them soon so that we can plan for the time that I'll be out of the office once my little angel's born. My decision to join SFL was partially made because of the time flexibility it offers and with a small baby, Lord knows I'll need as much flexibility as I can get!

After a rather noisy gargling serenade, I hear the toilet flush soon followed by the sound of slow dragging feet. Omar comes into the kitchen from behind and snuggles up behind me, his arms around my expanding waist as he kisses my neck. I turn my head so that our mouths can touch then peck him playfully several times on those *supplelicious* lips.

"Did you wash your hands?" I whisper between pecks. This pregnancy has made me a lot more anal than usual. Just the mere thought of germs makes me nauseous.

"Of course., don't I always?" he whispers back while turning me around as he lowers his hands onto my buttocks and pulls my hips closer to him. I smile as my oven mitt falls on the floor and he starts nibbling on my lips, kissing me passionately for several minutes before I pull away, reluctantly.

"Babe, our food is going to get cold. Shouldn't we save *dessert* for later?" I ask while rubbing his tush.

"What's wrong with having dessert first?"

"Nothing," I tell him as I kiss him softly on the lips, "it's just that pancakes aren't as good re-heated. Besides I only have a couple of hours before I have to start getting ready for the seminar." *Fortunately after I left Anya, I decided that the most effective method would be for me to format the seminar similar to the meeting I had with Carole Brown. I made a few additions but all in all if it worked for Carole, it should work for her employees.*

"Okay, cool, but can we at least have breakfast in the bedroom?"

"Okay," I tell him pretty much knowing what he has in mind. Especially since we haven't spent that much time together, Omar desperately wants to make up for lost time and so do I, but only if we can do it within the next two hours! For some reason, with me slightly showing, Omar seems to be surprisingly turned on to me physically more so now, that I'm prego! Although, I enjoyed the intimacy, I had to get used to making love with a baby growing inside of me. I had several appointments with my doctor, one by myself and another one with Omar so that we, rather I, would feel comfortable making love without feeling like we were harming the baby (It was mostly me that needed the reassurance). And the doctor did assure us, me that it was safe and actually beneficial for my well-being which ultimately will be good for the baby. So, ever since our visit to the doctor, Omar hasn't missed a beat!

"O" takes his tray as I follow him into the bedroom. As soon as I place my tray on the bed, Omar goes into my night table drawer and pulls out my leopard silk eye mask. He kisses me on the forehead then carefully places the mask over my eyes while kissing me on my cheek then sensually on down to my waiting lips before making the mask nice and snug.

Omar is no longer touching me. And I don't hear anything except for the ticking of the clock. At this point, I'm not even sure if Omar is still in the room…Then, out of nowhere I feel something on my lips. I part them just wide enough to let whatever, slide through. It's soft and spongy and has a nice taste to it. Mmmmm. It's a piece of pancake. I take it in and while chewing it, I feel Omar's finger slowly circling my lips. There is something on his finger. It's sticky. Whatever it is, "O" has smeared it all over my lips. I slip my tongue out and slowly lick the top of my lip. I run my tongue seductively along the perimeter of my smeared lips as I take the syrup in for the remainder of the pancake lingering in my mouth. Just as I chew and swallow what was left, Omar slides his *maple* coated tongue in my mouth. Soon after the sweet encounter, he recoils his tongue and brushes my lips with something kinda rough and hard. "O" pulls it away and replaces the piece of toast with something round and thick on my lips before slowly pushing it all the way in. I lick it while savoring it's surrounding juices, quickly realizing what it is, I bite it. As I chew the beef sausage, Omar massages something wet and cold on my breasts, before kissing both, one twin at a time. I fall back onto the bed as "O" slowly rolls on top of me then slowly continues to kiss his way up to my lips. So much fo… for uh, the rest of breakfast…… Mmmmm…auhhh yesss!!!

Fifty Seven

I just met Will and Devin in the lobby of the foundation's new office. The lobby has an Asian, zen-like look. The entire length of the wall facing the street is a genormous charcoal grey, stacked stone waterfall with it's water flowing gracefully into an Asian rock garden. In the center of the garden sits a large, intricately carved stone Buddha. As I stand within ten feet of the stone wall, I'm filled with an unexpected sense of calm and tranquility. If the lobby is any indication of how Carole's foundation's new office looks then that little transitional period was well worth the wait, even if they had to temporarily work in that sad excuse of a building and inside that dusty ass office!

"So, are you ready, Cyd?" Dev asks as we get on the elevator.

"As ready as I'm going to be," I tell him while fumbling through my purse for my small pack of saltine crackers.

"Is there anything we can do?" Will offers.

"Yes, actually there is," I tell Will while munching on the crackers.

"What do you need?"

I wipe my hands then pull out a stack of stapled papers and hand them to him. "If you could pass out this literature along with these questionnaires that would be a big help."

After wiping a cracker crumb from my mouth, I quickly pop an *Altoid* in my mouth. I don't want to worry Will or Dev about this, but truth be told, I'm still slightly anxious about today although my nervousness seems to be dwindling. Will and Dev have a lot of faith in me and my ability to share and communicate to others everything that I've learned and experienced. They know how important this first seminar is and they've made no secret in letting me know that they believe in me 110%. Now, I just hope that my little *Carole Brown* strategy works…for everyone's sake!

As the three of us enter the light and airy reception area, I check out the loft-like space as Carole swiftly walks up to us, irregular gait and all.

"Hellure, hellure," she says in a questionable *Madea* impersonation while rushing over to us. She sounds like she's ready to get this party started. I can tell from her body language and enthusiasm that she's looking forward to the seminar and I'm sure, to what SFL can do for both the foundation and its employees. I'm just keeping my fingers crossed that I don't let my nerves get the best of me. The last time I spoke in front of a group was my presentation for Federated. And we all know how that turned out.

"Welcome to our new office! You're right on time. C'mon let me give you a quick ten cent tour, then I'll take you to the conference room," Carole tells us as we begin to follow her down the bamboo wood corridor.

I check out the huge sky-light which is situated right in the center of the spacious office. Underneath are these incredible large, twelve foot bamboo trees which are placed throughout the space which surprisingly, has erased whatever threads of anxiety that were remaining. The entire space exudes peace and serenity. Whoever they hired as the designer did an exceptional job. I remember hearing someone say when I was at their temporary office that it was the same designer that designed one of music mogul Sylvia Rhone's homes. As we look around, and I'm admiring the open loft like space, I notice a small and cozy meditation room complete with floor pillows, candles and soft music piping through the built in speakers. *Are you kidding me?*

As we enter the decent size contemporary conference room, I feel relieved. It's not as big as I imagined. Translation; *there won't be as many people as were in my dream last night.* Devin told me that there would be about 15 or so employees participating but I dreamt there were at minimum 60-70 people!

Carole informs us that the employees are on their way. Devin is checking the microphone although I don't think I'll need it. Not for just 15 people. Will is positioned at the door preparing the literature I put together. And Carole is there greeting the employees as they enter. Once everyone is in and seated, Carole gives me the *ok-to-start* nod. I immediately look at each person and size up the small crowd while clearing my throat before speaking.

"Hello everyone, my name is Cydney, and I'd like to welcome you to the SFL seminar along with my two associates, Will and Devin, who are to my left."

Will and Dev smile and nod as all eyes momentarily fall on them.

"I'm sure most, if not all of you are probably wondering who we are and what SFL is. Well, what we're not, is a new football league although a few have thought so. And no, we're not located in south Florida nor are we a flooring company.

SFL stands for *Strategies for Life.* And the three of us are life coaches who help individuals and groups with general life issues, but not until we *first* help our clients establish a solid foundation to work from. This foundation stems from an inner power which lies within each and every one of us, a power that *Strategies for Life* will assist our clients to access and tap into. Or as the title of the Metro's news article on SFL puts it, we assist our clients to *uncork* their inner genie.

Once the clients are able to tap into their inner power and the foundation is laid then Will and Devin will proceed with the client's general life and career issues. This inner power I'm referring to is not an exertion of our physical strength but is actually a powerful, unique part of our subconscious mind that, in most of us, is asleep or dormant but can be and is *waiting* to be awakened, tapped into or *uncorked* by us at any time. Scientists and others have said that we only use 1/10 of our full potential which essentially leaves 9/10 of our inner power unused. And *SFL* wants to show you exactly how to gain access, tap into and uncork it."

A hand goes up.

"Yes sir, what is your question?"

"I'm satisfied with my life as it is so why would I need, as you say, to uncork this so called power?"

"Because it's an integral part of you. In order to operate and function to your fullest potential, you need to utilize all that you are and all that you have. Tell me this, if this untapped power can assist you in achieving any and everything you desire then what reason could you possibly have for not exploring it?"

Another hand goes up.

"Yes, the man in the denim shirt."

"I'm not sure that I understand this whole untapped power thing…"

"Okay, then let me give you an example. Imagine owning a Ferrari, which to those of you who are familiar with this sports car probably know that they have the potential to go up to, what, 180 mph? They're fast, extremely fast. Now, this might be difficult to imagine, for some of you. But let's say that each and every time you drive your Ferrari, for whatever reason, you never drive it more than a measly 50 mph! That's no more than 50 mph each and every time you drive it. Although the car is functioning, it is not functioning to its maximum capacity or full potential. Not *even* close to it. But once you tap into its maximum capacity then and only then will you see what the car is really capable of! Does that help to put it in perspective for you?" I ask the man in denim.

"Yes, it definitely does. And for the record that wouldn't be me because I would drive it to the max!" he bragged.

"You got that right, it wouldn't be me either," a man in the front adds.

A man in racing-car red smiles and nods in agreement with his male counterparts. "I mean why even have a Ferrari if you're not going to drive it the way it was built to be driven?!"

"Exactly! And why have this extraordinary power if you're not going to use it the way it was meant to be used? Especially, if it can help you," I reiterate.

Several hands go up.

"Yes, the young lady in the brown leopard shirt."

"In what ways has this power helped you?"

"This power can help you do anything you want and with anything you need. It can help you with something trivial and/or life-changing. The list is endless. But to answer your question; it has helped me with things ranging from finding my misplaced watch to landing my ideal job *with* all of my criteria. It's has actually become second nature to me and now helps me regularly on a day-to-day basis."

Carole clears her throat and waves her hand impatiently to get my attention.

"Yes Carole?"

"Cydney, give them that DSW one!"

I smile and turn back to the group of employees.

"During my first meeting with Carole I asked her to fantasize about having total access to her favorite store and now, as Carole did, I want all of you to do the same. Imagine for a minute, having total access to *Neiman Marcus, Macy's, Bloomingdales, H&M* or Carole's favorite, *DSW*. This access will provide you with anything you want, at no cost to you! And once you've shopped the entire store, you've only selected five items. Imagine, just five items from an entire store full of merchandise. Crazy, right?"

"Yeah, that's crazy all right," a young woman in the front mumbles.

"So, the point I'm trying to make with these examples is, that we all have access to much more than what we're actually using. We have more power than what most of us are aware of which is just waiting to be tapped into and utilized. And *not* to utilize it or take advantage of our full potential and power is the same as owning a *Ferrari* and *not* driving it over 50 mph, or having total access to everything in an entire store and leave the store with only five items. And *Strategies for Life* wants you to use much more than a small fraction of your full potential, we want you to explore and enjoy *all* that you are and all that you have. All 100% of you!! Trust me, it's there and now all you have to do is tap into it. And once you do, we promise you that the rewards will be amazing!"

Several hands go up.

"Yes, the young lady in the blue and gold tunic?"

"This sounds great but how do we start? Is there a manual or a set of instructions that we can take with us?"

"No, there isn't a manual but there are plenty of books that can guide you through this process. In fact, I included a suggested reading list in the literature that was handed to you as you came in. The books listed will help you uncork and gain access to your inner power. A few of my personal favorites are *Your Subconscious Mind, Real Magic, You'll See It When You Believe It, The Power of Intention, Creative Visualization and The Celestine Prophecy and the companion workbook*. But keep in mind that not every book on the list will *speak* to you so my suggestion is to read the back cover and/or the first few pages to see which one piques your interest before you purchase it.

More hands go up.

"Yes, the young woman in black?"

"Sometimes when I say someone's name, that person calls. Am I using my inner power when that happens?"

"Good question! Yes, most people chalk it up as a coincidence but in actuality you have tapped into your inner power *subconsciously*. My goal is to help you tap into your inner power *consciously*!"

"And how do we do that?"

"At some point or another, all of us have tapped into our inner power *subconsciously* but in order to tap into it consciously, there is one prerequisite and that is that you must change your current pattern of thinking. So bottom line, when *you change your thoughts, you change your life!*"

"What do you mean by change our pattern of thinking?" A young woman blurts out.

"Our thinking patterns have been influenced and formatted by the environment in which we live. And that environment and the people around us have shaped and molded the way we think and pattern our thoughts. I call those thought patterns the *old school* mentality so *now* we need to erase, update or change that old school mentality to a *new school* mentality and to a new or different way of thinking. Thinking without negative external influences. Changing your thinking patterns is as simple as shifting your thoughts from old patterns of thinking to new patterns of thinking and first and foremost, being open and willing to make the necessary shift."

"What are some examples of old school mentalities?" a woman in red asks curiously.

"An old school mentality is comprised of various influences including all negative thoughts and behavior, ignoring and not trusting your instincts, lacking confidence, being afraid of taking risks, being unappreciative and closed-minded, spewing hatred etc.

And new school thought patterns represent positive influences and thinking. It's the exact opposite of the old school mentality; listening to and trusting your instincts, being confident and not afraid to take risks, being open-minded and going with the flow. And of course, being loving."

A hand goes up.

"Yes sir, the young man in the pin stripe shirt?"

"Let me get this straight. So, if I stay positive, keep an open mind and go with the flow, I can change my life?"

"Let's just say you'll be on your way. Throw in some affirmations, consistent visualization and belief and you should be good to go."

"Before I take any more questions, I just want you all to know that this power is about you being all that you are and all that you can be. And nothing else. Believe me, I know this is a lot to take in and I was slightly skeptical too, initially. But what I've come to realize is that it's difficult for most people to understand the new school mentality with their old way of thinking. Once you openly accept the NSM and the shift takes place, you will be exposed to a whole new world filled with extraordinary experiences. This is very much a part of each and every one of your journeys and as soon as you open yourself up to it and believe in the possibilities, you will immediately see amazing changes in your life!"

I glance at the clock on the wall as another hand goes up.

"Yes? the young man in the plaid shirt."

"I looked at the list of books and was wondering if any of them have *Cliff Notes* to help us get started?"

"Wow, it's been a long time since I've heard anyone mention *Cliff Notes*! Do they still publish those? I turn and ask Will and Devin who look at one another as they shrug their shoulders. I turn back to the man in plaid. "Okay, so basically you just want to cut to the chase and get results ASAP, am I correct?"

"Yeah, I guess you could say that."

"Well, I can't say that I blame you. Actually there are several things that I can suggest, although neither are *Cliff Notes*. My first suggestion is meditation which is a very valuable and reliable method. It is highly effective as it serves as an open communication portal from your inner power. My other suggestions are creative visualization and or a vision board which are also very effective, although with these methods, an open mind, trust and patience are crucial. There is also an amazing experiment from one of the books on the list, *The Magic of Believing* that I have shown friends and if we have time during the second part of the seminar, I can demonstrate the extraordinary power that I've been telling you about. I also want to discuss the importance of clearing the past. So, why don't you grab a snack and stretch your legs then we'll meet back here in 15 minutes!"

Fifty Eight

The seminar went a lot longer and much better than I planned. Unfortunately, we didn't have time for the experiment I mentioned to the group before the break but I asked them to check out the book and try the experiment on their own. I still don't know how I was able to squeeze in as much as I did *and* maintain my high energy level. From a physical standpoint, I wasn't even sure if I would have the stamina to endure half of the seminar let alone *finish* it along with an extended session! In a word, the whole experience was surreal. Within minutes of me starting the seminar, I felt a wave of calmness coupled with what seemed like a magical inner strength emerging from my body followed by this sense of knowing that all was right and as it should be. After that, everything and I mean *everything* fell into place. Whatever nervousness I was experiencing, completely vanished. Whatever I wanted and needed to say, came out smoothly, stutter-free and on point. It was like being in the zone. Kinda like *Michael Jordan* back in the day when he was on the court and could do no wrong. Whatever blocks he attempted were blocked, whatever free throws went up, went in and whatever dunks were tried, went down not only dramatically but with a flair that only *Michael* could pull off!

I went into the seminar with the intention of igniting a spark of motivation in order to prepare the employees with what was needed to lay down their foundation before proceeding to the next step. And once I conduct the individual interviews, I'll know if sparks were ignited. And if they were, then the seminar would have been successful.

However, three things that I didn't plan for was that there would be *three times* the amount of questions asked during the Q & A segment and that Carole Brown would want to schedule a separate seminar just for the Foundation's board members! From that alone I knew that, at least with Carole, that more than a spark was ignited. With all the questions, including Carole's, I almost didn't have time to complete my little *Clearing the Past* spiel and speak on how vital it is to removing old school blocks in order to make room for the new school mentality. I really think that everything I said during the first half of the seminar must've sunk in because during the fifteen minute break when everyone returned, they were all on fire, bombarding me one after another with questions and more examples. It was great because it showed me that they were listening and actually got what I was saying. Their enthusiasm was somewhat surprising primarily because most people aren't open to change and different ways of thinking but when you have nothing to lose and everything to gain, how could you not be open?

Once we finally left the foundation I was on a cloud so high that I couldn't comprehend one thing that Will or Devin was saying to me. Not one damn thing. Hell, they might as well have been talking friggin' Chinese because that's what whatever the hell they were saying sounded like.

Once I got home and replayed everything in my head, a bizarre and wonderful thing happened; an indescribable feeling of completeness flowed through my body like a warm, gentle, waterfall. And what followed next, made the barely visible hairs on my arm stand up. As soon as the feeling of completeness flowed through me, that pesky feeling that something was missing in my life, totally vanished! Poof! Gone and nowhere to be found. And the strange thing is, is that I knew exactly what it was. I knew that the emptiness I had felt for so many years was now filled. I just *knew* it. And it wasn't the *usual* "I know"; it was that *undeniable* feeling of knowing.

For the first time in my life I felt complete from within, now *knowing,* that all was, as it was meant to be. With Milo peacefully asleep on my lap, I sat quietly on my couch feeling for the first time in my life, a sense of wholeness paired with a feeling of divine triumph and supreme accomplishment. A feeling that I have never, *ever* experienced and one that I *know*, will always be a part of me.

Fifty Nine

I'm still enjoying my high from the seminar while running a few errands. Just as I leave the pet store, I get a call from Shaye. She wants me to meet her in Tribeca for a quick lunch. As soon as she told me she wanted to talk to me, my mind, of course went straight into a hormonal panic. I immediately start wondering, if somehow, she guessed that I'm pregnant. Although, I must say, I've been pretty good at hiding the extra seven pounds I've gained, but not quite as good at controlling my being tired or my dramatic reaction to certain foods. So, I guess I can't be too surprised if she suspects that I'm expecting. I mean, it's not rocket science! Actually, it's probably better if she knows because it's time that I start to tell people before they figure it out on their own. At least this way they'll hear it directly from me.

Now, I'm in *Pottery Barn Kids* trying to finally decide on a color scheme for the baby's room. Initially, I was using the room as a small guest space but now I'm transforming it into the perfect baby's room. I've already packed up most of my stuff to make room for my little boogala's furniture. I know everyone says that mommies-to-be shouldn't start buying anything for their baby, at least, not until the second trimester. But I've never been one to buy into that old wives tale stuff plus, I want to get everything ready now because once I'm further along, I know me and I'm not going to feel like doing it. My plan is to buy the big ticket pieces at *Target* then a few accessories here at *PBK.*

I quickly glance at the clock and realize that if I don't leave now that I'll be late for lunch.

◊ ◊ ◊ ◊ ◊

The new Tribeca restaurant that Shaye selected is quaint and fortunately at this time of day, it's only half full. I see Shaye at one of the back tables, texting. Probably to Jackson and his fine Boris-Kodjoe-looking-self! When she sees me approaching our table she finishes her text then gets up to hug me.

"Hey Cyd, perfect timing. Our food should be here any minute!"

"Great 'cause girl, I am starvin' like marvin! Smart move to call me to see what I wanted so we wouldn't have to wait long," I tell her as I sit down after re-adjusting my top so its fullness will hide my little *baby* bump.

"So you look cute and all glow-y! Are you wearing that new MAC luminescent make-up?" she asks.

No girl, it's not MAC, it's called MPG. my pregnancy glow! "Uh, yep, it sure is," I lie. *Sorry but I'm not spilling any beans until I find out what she wants first* "Who are you anyway, MAC's new product expert?" I ask sarcastically.

"Actually, that's not a bad idea, I should send them a resume. But no, in fact, I had planned to buy some later today," she tells me as the waiter comes with our food.

My blackened salmon, garlic mashed potatoes and grilled asparagus look almost too good to eat but forget that! I'm so hungry that I could eat a horse *and* his damn saddle! As soon as the waiter places our plates on the table, it's off to the races! Shaye and I both immediately dig in. After inhaling several forkfuls of everything on my plate, I come up for air and notice a familiar face walking toward our table. The tall, statuesque woman is smiling at Shaye.

"Hello Shaye!"

Shaye looks up and returns the *happy-to-see-you* smile. "Hey Wendy, how are you? What are you doing on this side of town?" They share a quick embrace.

"I'm looking at restaurants for my girlfriend's surprise birthday dinner."

"That's nice and something that I'm sure she will definitely enjoy! Oh, Wendy meet my friend Cydney. Cydney this is Wendy Williams and Wendy this is Cydney Rochon."

I quickly swallow my food. "Hello Wendy, it's nice meeting you! Girl, I just want you to know that I was rooting for you on DWTS (Dancing with the Stars)!"

"Thanks, Cydney, but honey let me tell you that was some hard work! It was a work-out times ten!"

Shaye and I laugh, and then I continue eating.

"So ladies I have to run but Shaye, let's try to get together soon. I know both our schedules are crazy but maybe you and Jackson can come to the birthday dinner."

"When is it?" Shaye asks.

Suddenly I feel a sharp pain; it feels like someone just stabbed me…

"Sometime next month, it depends on the *blah,*, that I *blah, blah* select but *blah* will send you *blah* invitation, cool?"

"Cool, looking *blah* forward *blah* it!!"

"*Blah, blah BLAH…..blah…*okay Wendy…*blah…*"

"Aaaggghhgghhh!" I double over gripping my stomach and…"THUD!"

I've fallen on the floor and can't move! The pain is getting worse and worse….I want to scream but can't….Somebody please stop the pain, please!!

"CYDNEY! CYDNEY, WHAT'S WRONG? TALK TO ME!"

I can hear Shaye and I'm trying but I can't talk, no words are coming out! The pain is unbearable! Aaagggh, what's happening to me?

"WAITER, WAITER! SOMEBODY CALL 911! HURRY!"

Sixty

I hear voices but I'm too drowsy to tell who the voices belong to. I'm trying but I can't seem to open my eyes. My eye lids feel like two pound slithers of lead. Wait a minute, where am I? Uh, wait, I was having lunch at a restaurant in Tribeca...with Shaye. Maybe I'm at home or maybe Shaye took me to her place? I try to open my eyes again. This time they open just enough for me to see two blurred figures sitting next to me. I try to "will" my eyes open a little more so I can see who the blurs are. The faces are still slightly out of focus but I recognize the black and lime green scarf. It was a gift I gave mama and that must be Jordyn sitting next to her.

"Cyd, baby, good you're awake. Can you hear me?" mama asks as she squeezes my hand.

"Ungghl!" I groan as loud as I can just to let her know that I can hear her and that I'm alive.

"Cyd, how do you feel? Are you in pain?" my sister asks.

"UNGGHH!" I moan slightly louder in a higher pitch to let them know that YES, I'm in pain!

"Baby, go get the doctor," mama orders. Jordyn leaves as mama scoots closer while still holding and stroking my hand.

"Baby, everything is going to be okay. Your sister just went to get the doctor," mama tells me as she kisses my forehead.

The nurse comes in first and puts a cup of water to my mouth and has me sip from a straw as she proceeds to examine me. Several minutes later my sister returns with the doctor. I'm still somewhat drowsy but at least now I can open my eyes fully.

"You're going to be fine," the doctor smiles while reassuring me. All of your tests came back and in a few days, you'll be almost as good as new!"

"Wa..was it food po…oisoning?" I manage to ask even though I already knew it had to be the salmon.

"Ms. Rochon, no. I'm sorry I thought you were told, you had a miscarriage and unfortunately lost the baby."

WHAT? NO, THERE MUST BE A MISTAKE! Mama please tell me that he didn't just tell me that I lost my precious little boogala! Pleeeeaase tell me my baby is alive and okay!!! I look at mama and pray that she'll tell the doctor that there has to be some mistake and that my baby is all right. However, when I look at her, she's not saying anything. All I see are tears rolling down her face. Somebody pleeasse, tell me that my little boogala is okay!! Pleeeeease!!!

Sixty One

Omar brought me home from the hospital several hours ago. Although it was nice that he offered to stay with me I really wasn't up to any company so after I got settled I told him that I would be fine and that he didn't have to miss work because of me. At first, he hesitated but after making a large pot of tea for me and me telling him that I needed to get some rest, he gave in and left. Quite frankly in my current state of mind I really wasn't up to talking to or even looking at anyone, then or now.

As soon as Omar left, I turned the phone off then rolled off the couch and immediately closed all the wooden blinds. Seeing the sun shine just seemed to make everything worse in my mind because internally I was going through my own personal storm of sorts. For me, it was a cloudy, dismal, depressing day and to look outside and see the sun shine was a cruel and heartless oxymoron. After I closed all the blinds I lay back on the couch and cried as the images that I had been carrying around in my head for the last several weeks, returned. The first image was of me coming home from the hospital carrying my little boogala wrapped in her little quilt. The second was a scene with Anya and the girls meeting my angel for the very first time and Nico and Kai arguing over who was going to hold her first while she looked at them and smiled. That would have been my little angel's first smile. In the scene I see myself reaching for the camera to capture it so that I could put it in her little *All of my Firsts* scrap book. The book was actually Milanya's idea. While in college, Anya and I always talked about how nice it would be if our children (me with two and Anya with three) were close the way she and I are. Don't ask me how but I knew, deep down that they would have been. That was something that I was really looking forward to. That and Anya and I putting our scrap books together. Anyway, it was those two scenes that I replayed over and over until my tears dried and I eventually fell asleep.

I woke up an hour later and heated up some soup and made another pot of tea. On my way to the bedroom, I couldn't help but stop at the entrance to what was going to be the baby's room. I hesitated for a few minutes, then took a deep breath, before going on in. As I looked around the room, I felt a deep sadness. Deeper than what I've ever felt.

There were *Benjamin Moore* and *PBK* paint chips spread out on top of several baby catalogs which were stacked on the small round table which Robyn and I just painted buttered cream. Next to the table, was the new rocking chair Omar and I bought with the beautiful, handmade quilt I got on sale draped on its arm.

There were all the boxes that I had packed my things in so that I could make room for the rest of my baby's furniture. Just looking at everything knocked the wind out of me almost as if someone had kicked me in the stomach. Hard! It was at that precise moment that I knew that I had no business being in there. It was way too much to deal with. *And* it was way too soon.

Despite feeling overwhelmed, along with my emotions going in every which way, I sat in the chair clutching my boogala's quilt against my cheek. Rocking back and forth rhythmically the exact same way I imagined I would with my little angel, night after night. As I rocked and rocked I held onto the quilt for dear life while hearing myself whisper, "Why? Why did this happen?" as my eyes began to tear up I kept repeating over and over again, "Why? Why did this happen? Why?" again and again as tears streamed slowly down my face. "WHY, why, WHY?" I asked, no longer whispering.

Sixty Two

Six weeks later…

To cope, I threw myself into my work. After the "M" (it's still hard for me to say the word), I felt that the best therapy for me would be to keep busy, which I also believed was the best way to keep from feeling sorry for myself and sinking into a dark depression. But even with keeping busy, it's still difficult because not only is there a deep sadness there is now a permanent hole in my heart.

Omar, however seems to be okay. I think the first week was hard for him, and although he hasn't said so, I believe there is a small part of him that is relieved, but I also know there is a part of him that feels bad for me and everything that I've gone through these past weeks.

My mother has been very supportive and nurturing as most moms would be. I really don't know what I would have done without her love and support. We were both in agreement that keeping busy would be therapeutic but mama also felt that it would be beneficial for me to go to therapy as well. It wasn't easy at first, to accept that I needed therapy, then even harder to find time in my schedule to actually go. But I soon realized that it was something that I not only needed to do but it was something that I *had* to do. For my own sense of well-being. So now I see the therapist once a week and when I can, twice. Although tiring, keeping busy with work along with therapy has definitely made an impact on my healing process. It's been six weeks and I've already made tremendous progress. Each and every day I'm feeling better and finally getting back to my old self. And for the record, getting back to me doesn't mean that I don't or won't miss my baby because I do and will from now to eternity. In fact, it's my little angel who is helping me through all this. She has let me *know* that she's with me in spirit and forever in my heart, and that, she always will be.

Sixty Three

Since my big debut, I have independently conducted two other seminars and have several more scheduled within the next two weeks. In addition to that I'm also conducting another group of individual interviews for one of Devin's clients. Speaking of which, Carole Brown's foundation interviews were a complete success; in fact a couple of their employees were so inspired with the seminar and their individual interviews that they volunteered to work part-time at SFL! I call them our little *strategic-consultants-in-training!*

Our little SCIT's were also pretty impressed with the article that ran in *O Magazine* and the small gathering we had to celebrate its running. The party, which was held at *The Smythe Hotel* in Tribeca was Will's idea, especially since we never had a chance to celebrate our official opening. Devin was sweet and made a touching toast to me for making it possible with my "O" connection. Our volunteers could not have started at a more perfect time because when the *O Magazine* article hit the stands last week our phones were ringing off the friggin' hook!

Meanwhile, I've been trying to get out of the house for the last hour so that I can run by the office and take care of a few things before meeting Omar for lunch. This is the weekend of Milanya and Que's wedding and I'm heading to Florida tomorrow a few days early to help keep my BFF stay cool, calm and collected before her big day!

Brrnng, brrnng… *Why is it every time I am trying to get out of the house the daggone phone rings?*

"Hello."

"Hey *Ms-too-busy-to-return-phone-calls!*"

"Oh, hey Rob, sorry about that. What's going on girl?" I ask while putting on my jacket.

"You've been back almost two weeks now and I still haven't heard one damn thing about Milanya's bachelorette party in South Beach!"

"It was great. Que came down too with his groomsmen-to-be for his bachelor party. He got two suites at my new favorite hotel, *The Setai*, for both his and Anya's parties. Then after their separate parties, everyone met at the *Club Mansion*, and then later we all gathered at Que's suite to keep the party going."

"Damn, you guys really partied! I hear that *The Setai* is slammin'! So tell me, anything good happen?"

"Girl, you're always looking for something scandalous. All I'm going to say is that the future is looking better! In fact, it's a future that I'm finally looking forward to."

"Hell, with all the partying you all did, I would be looking forward to the next party too! So tell me, was Mr. Hershey there?"

"Yes, Robyn Ty was."

"That's all you have to say is, *Yes, Robyn Ty was?* she mocked.

"Well, you know what they say," I begin to tell her while looking through my handbag for my cell phone, "what happens in South Beach, *stays* in South Beach!"

"Gu-url, that's Vegas, *not* Miami!"

"Well, bitty *now* it's South Beach!" I find my phone. "Ok, Rob, I gotta go, I was just leaving to go to the office. I'll call you later."

"Ok, wait, what time is your flight tomorrow?"

"1:25, why?"

"Do you need a ride to the airport?"

"Sure, if you don't mind!"

"Ok, I have to drop Chauncey off at the doctor which is in your area then we can go to the airport. Is 11:00 okay?"

"Perfect. Thanks, girl! See you in the morning!"

Sixty Four

I just finished reviewing the questionnaire forms for the next group of individual meetings with one of our clients. As I glance at my watch, I see that it's two fifteen. Omar and I were supposed to meet here *between* one forty five and two o'clock and I have yet to hear from him. This is not like him. After the whole *model/cartel* drama and during the time I was pregnant "O" promised that unless it was physically impossible, that he would call if anything came up to prevent him from meeting me. Even though, he's coming to Florida for the wedding this weekend, I still wanted to see and talk to him before I left. I check my phone, to see if maybe, he called my cell instead of the office. I scan my phone's menu for *missed calls* and nope, nothing. I dial him again and once more it goes directly into voicemail.

"Hey Cyd!"

I jump. "Dag, Devin you scared me! Didn't your mother teach you not to sneak up on people?"

"No. Should she have?" he asks sarcastically.

"Yeah, it would've been nice," I tell him equally as sarcastic. "What's up?" I ask as I get up to gather my things.

"Just want to know when you're coming back from Florida. Your friend's wedding is this coming weekend, right?"

"Yes. I return Monday evening. Why? Do we have a new client?"

"No, but it has been pretty busy and we need all the help we can get."

"I know, and I'll be ready to pick up from where I left off as soon as I return," I tell him while grabbing my bag and walking as fast as I can toward the door, "so don't worry because I'm up to speed with all of my clients."

"Okay, good, that's all I wanted to hear. Have a great time and give the bride and groom my congratulations."

"Okay. Thanks, Dev. Talk to you when I get back."

I rush out before he thinks of something else. I love Devin but today is *not* the day for problems or any added stress. Now, where the hell is Omar? I'm pretty sure he told me that he was going to meet me here at the office. I send him a quick *Where are you?* text, then dial his cell and *again,* it goes straight to voicemail. Oh, shoot I always forget that he has a landline! I find that number and dial it. It's ringing!!!

I'm sorry, the number you have dialed has been disconnected.

Sixty Five

Surprisingly, Robyn is on time. I roll my bags out to the car as Chauncey jumps out to help. Smiling, he holds the front door for me then chivalrously puts my bags in the trunk. We've talked on the phone and caught glimpses of one another across a crowded dance floor but this is the first time that I've met Chauncey in person. Now, that I see him up close, Chauncey is attractive and holds his own in the looks department. To me, he looks like a younger version of Forest (*not* Gump, Whitaker!) sprinkled with touches of Will Smith. But if you ask Robyn, she'll tell you that he's *all* Will. 100%! After several minutes of skillful maneuvering of Robyn's junk in her trunk, Chauncey manages to fit my bags inside then hops into the back of *Toya*, Robyn's three year old Camry.

"I don't think you two have officially met, so Chauncey, this is Cydney; Cydney, Chauncey."

I turn and smile. "Nice to finally *officially* meet you, Chauncey. I've heard a lot about you."

"Well, I hope all good things," he laughs, "and yes it's nice meeting you too. Sweet pea, it's the next block on the right side," he directs.

"Okay honey boo," she tells him while slowing down. Then before I know it, *Honey Boo* jumps out as he says good-bye then gives *sweet pea* a sensual peck on her lips.

"Thanks, pumpkin, I'll see you later!"

Robyn watches him for about seven or so seconds before driving off.

"Where in the hell is Robyn *sweet pea, pumpkin* or whatever your name is, where is my friend and what did you do with her?"

"Gurl, I know, tell me about it! I don't know where Robyn is. Apparently, this is what happens when you fall in love. Gurl, he has brought out a whole side of me that Cyd, I never even knew existed! And the best thing is, is that he really does love me," she states with the utmost of confidence.

Wow. I've searched but I have no words. Not even one! It's hard to believe that Robyn's in love. In the ten years that I have known her, she's only been in love once, and that was five years ago. That's one of the few things that Robyn and I have in common. Kind of. Neither of us is one to fall for just any ole man. Not anymore. There's got to be something there, something real. At least for me. Rob on the other hand, may be *physically* attracted to someone then act accordingly but unless there is some strong, sort of mental connection, it stops there. Chauncey however, seems to be more than a physical attraction and I'm truly happy for her however, there is one little thing that I am curious about.

"Can I ask you something?"

"Gurl, puh-leeze since when did you start asking me if you could ask me something? You know that my life's an open book. Wassup?"

"I'm curious, what did *honey boo* say about the box of *Extenze* you found in his medicine cabinet? Does he, uh, actually use it and does it really work?"

Damn! As soon as the words left my mouth I wanted to snatch them back because immediately I thought that, that may have been a little too personal to ask someone, even to Robyn! Once my words were airborne, Rob's head whipped around and looked at me like I just attacked her man. Then suddenly, as if she was just told that I was no longer a suspect, she starts laughing!

"What's so funny? I wanna laugh too!"

"Gurl, I had forgotten all about the *Extenze!* But I thought I told you, didn't I?"

"Tell me what?" I ask as we merge onto the Brooklyn Queens Expressway.

"What Chauncey does. Honey boo is the marketing director for an advertising agency and the *Extenze* I found in his medicine cabinet wasn't his *personally*, it was one of his client's products. Chaunce volunteered to try it *purely* for work purposes. And gurl, trust me, my man does NOT need *Extenze* or any other male enhancement product. Mr. Big is just fine with what the good Lord gave him!" she preached proudly like she was standing on her daddy's pulpit on one fine Sunday morning.

Both relieved and somewhat embarrassed, I start laughing. "Amen and good for him and good for you too! I just remember when you saw it in his medicine cabinet and at that time it was a definite deal breaker. So, good then it's a non-issue, but, girl, that'll teach your butt not to be snooping around in your man's stuff!"

Robyn starts laughing with me. "I know that's right! Gurl, I think I learned my lesson!"

My cell phone rings just as we change into the airport lane. I look at the screen, it reads **PRIVATE.**

"Hello…." I hear nothing but static. "Hello, hello.." The static stops.

"Hi… hel-lo Cyd." A male voice says in a low, barely audible voice. "Cyd it's me, sorry that I didn't call you earlier… I left my apartment so fast that I forgot my phone."

"Omar?"

"Yeah…"

"You don't sound so good, where are you?"

"I.. I'm in Atlanta."

"What are you doing in Atlanta? Is everything okay?"

"No, there's been an accident. It's my…brother Brendon..."

Sixty Six

There is just too much going on especially with Anya in wedding la la land and the last thing I want, is to upset her beautiful *it's-about-damn-time* weekend! I'm sure she would want to know about my pregnancy and the baby but I don't have the heart to tell her. At least, not now. There's no doubt that we'd both be crying which is something neither one of us needs right now. Meanwhile, I'm also dealing with Omar's brother's tragedy that I should probably keep to myself as well.

Although I'm not going to say anything to Anya about Omar's brother, I still can't stop thinking about him. Life can be so unpredictable; one minute you're fine and the next minute all hell breaks loose; as in the case with Brendon.

But these next few days are all about Milanya and I'm going to try my best to keep it that way. But, if Anya mentions Omar's name *one* more time I think I might just lose it. There's only so many times that I can change the subject when she asks when he's arriving. At this point, she probably thinks that we've broken up, especially with the way I've been dodging any sentence with his name in it! All of a sudden my door swings open.

"Auntie Cyd, Auntie Cyd, Mommie needs you," Kai and Nico both squeal while each pull an arm.

As I enter Anya's and Que's large bedroom, Anya is standing in front of her full length mirror with her veil on.

"That's pretty!"

"Oh good, exactly what I wanted to hear. Although I'm still torn between these two," she says, turning around and pointing to another veil draped on her tufted silk bed. "Pretty is nice but is it *the one?*"

"Let me see the other one on first."

Anya quickly changes veils then turns for me to see it.

"I love that one!"

- She smiles. "Me too, I just wanted to make sure that this one goes with my dress. Please tell me it does."

"You know, I actually think it adds a special edge to your look without taking away from the elegance of the dress, I think it'll be perfect!"

"Good because that's exactly what I want, to have a slight edge while still maintaining the elegance of my dress!"

"Then ding, ding, ding that's it!"

Anya walks over and hugs me. "Thank you, Cyd, for coming early and being here for me. It means so much to have my best friend by my side."

"Please, Anya, you know I wouldn't be any other place!" I tell her while my mind flashes back to Brendon and Omar and what happened.

Several days ago Brendon was with friends at a neighborhood skate park in Atlanta when he had a freak skateboarding accident and sadly, now is paralyzed from the waist down. Needless to say, Omar and his mother are heartbroken, we all are especially with having just dealt with that life threatening episode involving the drug cartel. They thought that the worst was over and that life was finally getting back to normal and then this heartbreak. I feel horrible because there's not much I can do especially from Florida. That family has been through so much lately. Actually we all have.

"So what else do we need to do?" I ask Anya.

"I just checked with Preston and everything seems to be under control. I still feel bad that I asked him to pull this off in six weeks. Especially when I know he usually meets with clients *six months* prior to the wedding or special event."

"Look, that's what challenges are all about. At least now he can say he pulled together an amazing wedding in just six weeks!" I tell her, "and Anya, from the way your grounds look, it *will* be amazing! He has literally transformed the entire outside area into a beautiful enchanted forest!"

"Good point but now I can't wait to see it! After Preston showed me the sketches for his design, I signed off on it, then told him that I didn't want to see it until it was completed!"

"Well, he has done an unbelievable transformation, girl, you won't even recognize it!"

"Then it's exactly the way we had hoped because it was the girls and Que, and, a part of me, who wanted to have the reception at the house instead of at the Ritz. It was an easy decision since we love what our home has come to mean to us with all the fond memories. And of course, you know that the girls were really looking forward to having their home turned into an enchanted forest!"

"Of course, what kid wouldn't want that? I'm looking forward to it and I'm no kid!"

Laughing, Anya agrees. "Exactly, so as soon as Preston showed me his sketches, I called the Ritz and cancelled my appointment."

"Well, you made the right decision. Hey and speaking of the Ritz, where are your parents? I saw them for a hot minute when I arrived and then they disappeared. Did they go back to the hotel?"

"No, I sent Mom and Lillian, Que's mom to the spa for the day and our dads are playing golf with Tiger."

"Tiger, *Tiger*?"

"Yep! Que set it up a couple of weeks ago when he ran into Tiger on the Windermere golf course."

"Wow, that's great! I know your dads are thrilled!"

"Yes indeed. Daddy took two cameras *and* his pocket camcorder!"

"Well, good for them, oh and while on the subject of parents, mommy and daddy send their love and blessings!"

"I know I received their gift along with a note from your mother. That was very sweet of her."

"You have no idea how sick mama was that she was going to miss your wedding! But as I'm sure she's told you, she and daddy have had their tickets to Africa for seven months and there was no refund and believe me, you know that my mother tried!"

"No I know, I told her that we will make sure she sees the video and all of the photos!"

"Yes, she will appreciate that! Okay, so what's next on the list?"

"Being pampered! Our masseuses are coming after dinner at eight o'clock. Then we'll have our mani-pedi's in the morning followed by hair and make-up. And I think that's it unless we need to arrange for more out-of-town guests to be picked up…Will Omar need to be pick..."

"No Anya," I cut her off, "he's not coming…..," I begin to tell her. Then *she* cuts me off.

"Oh, Cyd, I'm sorry! I was afraid that this was going to happen, when did he tell you?"

"What are you talking about? Afraid that what was going to happen? And what was Omar supposedly telling me?"

Sixty Seven

Anya has got to be the most beautiful bride that I've ever seen! And of course Quentin is extremely handsome and quite the distinguished groom in his custom made suit. Que decided against the traditional tuxedo and opted for a tailor made dinner suit instead. I was flattered and a bit surprised when he asked *moi* to look at the design before his tailor made the final pattern.

"Tell me what you think," he said while handing me the sketch and fabric swatch. It looked fine except for one teeny little adjustment but other than that, I thought it was perfect. It's usually Anya who asks for my design input and advice, not Que. His suit is very similar to a tux but not as formal which is actually more in line with Que's personality. Classy minus the stiffness and hard lines.

The church is packed with family and friends as we all look on as the vows are exchanged. Milanya and Quentin look perfect together as the minister proudly pronounces them husband and wife. Que kisses Anya, and then to her surprise, he literally sweeps her off her feet and starts carrying her up the aisle while a flurry of white rose petals drop from the church's arched ceiling. I glance up, curious to see how Preston pulled that one off. Unfortunately, I couldn't see anything with the petals falling from practically every inch of the church's ceiling! Nico and Kai throw more little handfuls of petals at their parents while giggling as they follow them up the aisle. Rose petals are everywhere as Anya laughs as she's being carried off by her new hubby. While applauding, everyone follows the bride, groom and the wedding party outside as Jax, Que's son leads the rest of the guests outside to a white and gold horse and carriage. The house is a short ride from the church so the carriage is a perfect touch and the perfect ending for a perfect wedding.

When we pull up to the house, we're absolutely blown away! All of the guests are greeted by two life-size white horses situated on each side of the walkway leading to the reception. The horses are made of white roses from hoof to mane. I have never seen anything like it. As we continue past the rose covered horses down to the reception area, it is as if we are actually walking through a magical forest! Trees, trees and even more trees are everywhere, as are a flood of flowers, in every imaginable color — colors that I never knew existed in flowers were absolutely everywhere. Preston's team also erected an open wooden twig pergola leading from the house's entrance on the small cul-de-sac on around to the back of the house. It is positively breath-taking! My favorite though, is the monogrammed dance floor on top of the pool that Preston and his team built. And there are at least ten white cabanas with lit lanterns placed sporadically throughout the grounds and four bar stations placed strategically around the area — two main stations serving any and every drink imaginable and two smaller ones which serve the couple's signature drink along with white and red wine.

As we take it all in the band is playing instrumental songs by *Kirk Whalum, Eric Benet, Robin Thicke, Kenny G, John Legend, Dave Koz, Gerald Albright* along with a bevy of others. And if the evening isn't perfect already, no one, not even Al Roker could not have ordered better October weather! The temperature is around 76 degrees with not even a thought of humidity.

After we all eat in the airy glass dinner house, which was erected next to the lake and comfortably holding all 300 of Anya and Que's guests, we are ready to test out the dance floor. The bride and groom have their first dance which to all of our surprise, is sung by Jennifer Hudson! Apparently Preston likes to surprise his clients with something that they would love but might not have the resources to get or something that, like in this particular case, is Preston's special gift to the host and/or hostess. So, Jennifer is Preston's surprise gift to Anya and Quentin, mostly to and for Que because a few of us know that Anya secretly wanted Maxwell to sing on her special day. Me too for that matter! But for Anya, it was actually a toss-up between Maxwell and John Legend. Although, I know she's also a big fan of and absolutely thrilled to have Jennifer! As the dee-jay plays *Usher*, I feel a tap on my shoulder.

"Would you like to dance?"

"Yes," I say smiling.

I can tell that this is definitely going to be a night to remember!

Sixty Eight

Is it me or is not the world getting smaller and smaller? Have you ever met someone within a certain circle and then you go outside that circle into another circle of friends then run into that *same* someone in the second circle?

It's Monday night and I just boarded the plane heading back to New York. As I check my boarding pass for my seat number, I look down the aisle for my row to see who my potential "air neighbor" is. I see several prospects. A gray haired woman clutching a photo album and the back of a tall, muscular man…who actually reminds me a little of...wait it looks like…..no it can't be! OMG it is! Damn, it really is a small world. I thought he was going back to New York tomorrow. I can't believe that Alex (Shaye and Jackson's friend from New York) is on this same flight. This is crazy! I was *just* dancing and talking with him at Anya's wedding. As happenstance would have it, Alex was also in Anya's wedding, as one of Que's groomsmen. Apparently, he and Que have been friends for quite some time. I found that out at Anya 's bachelorette party in South Beach when I saw Que talking to someone who looked familiar. Then once I moved closer, I saw that it was Alex.

As I approach my, *our* row Alex is now seated in the aisle seat with his eyes closed.

"Excuse me sir, I'm in the window seat," I say in my best southern accent, eager to see his expression once he realizes that it's me. On cue, he opens his eyes then grins like he just won the million dollar Power Ball!

"Cydney! This is a nice surprise. So, what do you know, dreams do come true!"

We both smile as he gets up, lifts my leopard print carry-on bag effortlessly while slipping it carefully between two bags in the overhead compartment. Impressed with Alex's take-charge move and his manly prowess, I smile and tell him, "Thank you."

"Hey it's the least I can do for keeping me company on the flight," he smiled back.

"Presumptuous, aren't we?" I ask teasingly.

"I'd prefer to think of it as optimistic."

Ladies and gentlemen, the captain has turned on the ***FASTEN YOUR SEAT BELT*** *sign. Please take your seat and fasten your seat belt…*

Grinning, I scoot over to the window seat as Alex stands until I'm situated. As I reach for my seat belt, he sits back down while reaching for his book from the center seat then stuffs it into the outer pocket of his black leather messenger bag, I contort my neck while fastening my seat belt to see the front cover and surprisingly recognize it. I smile and ask, "Is that *Your Journey, Your Purpose*?"

"Yes," he responds with a look of surprise. "Have you read it?"

"Yes, it's one of my favorite books."

"Me too," he tells me smiling. "In fact, this is the third time that I'm reading it."

At this time, we request that all mobile phones, laptops, iPads and any other electronic devices be turned off until we notify you that it's safe to use them….

Alex reaches back into his messenger bag and slides his iPhone out just far enough to turn it off.

"So if you don't mind me asking, are you in the process of trying to figure out your purpose or are you one of the lucky ones that has already been, hmm, *enlightened*?"

"No, I don't mind you asking," he smiles while exhibiting all 32 of his pearly whites. "Luckily, I have, as you put it, been *enlightened.* I'm actually highlighting key points for a seminar that I'm conducting at the camp I sponsor for inner city teens."

"Wow, that's great. What's the title of the seminar?"

"*The Purpose of Your Life.*"

"I'm impressed. When did you start the camp?"

"Three good friends of mine and I started it about four years ago. We practically grew up in the Boys & Girls Club and since then have always wanted to create a place of inspiration for inner city teens as our way to give back to the communities we grew up in. But enough about me, I want to hear about you. You've read the book so tell me are you one of the lucky ones?"

At this time, make sure your seat backs and tray tables are in their full upright position. Also make sure that your seat belt is securely fastened. And at this time, all electronic devices must be turned off. Thank you.

Smiling, I tell him, "funny that you should ask…"

Flight attendants and cabin crew, please prepare for take-off…

Sixty Nine

It feels good to be home although the wedding was a great time squared. Just for me, to be able to witness firsthand, the happiest day in my best friends life was by far a moment that I'll always treasure. Admittedly, I'm tired from the festivities but now, even more so from having to recap the *entire* weekend for Robyn's *got-to-know-everything-wish-I-could-have-been-there* ass! As tired as I am, I really don't have a problem with recapping and replaying the wedding for Robyn especially Que's gift to Anya. As I revisit the moment for Robyn, she almost rams *Toya* into the car directly in front of us!

"No he didn't," she screams.

"Yes he did," I tell her, laughing and reliving it again in my head. After Jennifer sang, Preston snuck in Milanya's gift and surprised her and everyone with Maxwell! Girl, Anya almost fainted! In fact, we all did.

"Gurl, quit lying! Maxwell was NOT there," she insists.

"Girl not only was he there but he sang not one, not two but three of Anya's favorite songs including Pretty Wings!"

"Shut up, shut up," she keeps saying over and over.

"Yes he did and you know that I was front and center! Girl, Anya was so happy her face lit up like the Christmas tree at Rockefeller Plaza!"

"Don't tell me that there were white doves flying while he was singing?" she asks still begging for more.

"No, they didn't but Preston had several large standing gilded bird cages with two doves in each one. They weren't flying but Master P didn't miss a single beat and actually replicated one of Maxie's BET Awards performances. Instead of doves PB had a zillion white feathers floating from the sky while Maxwell was singing."

"SHUT the front door!"

Robyn is so taken with the wedding and everything that I'm telling her that for the first time she hasn't asked one word about Ty. Not that it would matter because there really isn't much to tell since the basketball season just started which had Ty only in Florida for about three hours total. Just enough time for the wedding plus an hour or so for part of the reception before he had to fly back out. Luckily, we were able to spend some time together although not as much as either of us would have liked.

While in the car recapping the wedding for Robyn, I receive a text from Omar saying that he was going to come by my apartment in about an hour. To save time and an extra trip for moi, I asked Robyn to swing by Shaye's so that I could pick up my little Milo.

◊ ◊ ◊ ◊ ◊

Now that we're home and I've given Milo water and fed him, I'm making a large pitcher of pomegranate ginger martini's. I know that I can use one or maybe even two and I know Omar will definitely want several. I glance down at my watch. He should be here any minute. I really want to talk to him face to face although we did speak earlier today when I called from Florida to get an update on Bren's progress. We didn't talk long because he had just returned from ATL last night. During our brief conversation he told me that Brendon is still in the hospital and will be for a while until he's ready to be released to the rehabilitation facility. The doctors are saying that his brother will never walk again but Omar said that Bren is extremely optimistic and hopeful and continues to tell him, their mother *and* his team of doctors that he'll be up and walking this time next year. If not sooner. In fact, he even has the hospital staff placing bets on his recovery date! That's Bren for you.

I look to see if there's anything in the fridge for me to quickly throw something together just as the intercom rings. I answer it and it's Omar. When I open the door he's standing there with a bag.

"Hi," I say in my best nurturing voice. "You look tired and like you could use a hug!"

"Yeah, I'm okay; it's been a long four days but a hug sounds good." He says as he walks in and straight into my arms.

"Look, I'm sure Brendon is going to be all right. We just have to stay positive and keep praying." I reassure him as my arms loosen to help him take his jacket off.

"I know you're right," he says slowly pulling me towards him. We hug again as he kisses me on the top of my head.

"Is that what I think it is?" I asked while eyeballing the bag.

"Well, if you think it's food, then you're right!" he tells me as he pulls out a small bakery size box from behind his back.

"What's that?"

"Dessert!" he proudly announces.

"Wow, you must've read my mind. Thank you!" I tell him as he hands me his jacket. Milo doesn't miss a beat as he runs up and sniffs the take-out. Omar hands me the food and I take it into the kitchen while he plays with Milo.

Once we finish the scrumptious jerk chicken with rice and peas, Omar takes the black lacquer dinner trays into the kitchen while I finish my drink. "O" returns with the martini pitcher and the cake box.

"Let me get some plates and forks" I said while getting up.

"No, you sit. I've been sitting all day. Let me get them."

I fill our glasses with the remainder of the Pom-Gin martini. After a few much needed sips, I start to untie the string on the dessert box, as Omar returns with the plates.

"You know, Cyd, this thing with the baby and now Brendon's accident…you know it..it's affected me. It's given me a whole new perspective on life," he tells me while I struggle with the string. The stupid thing has a knot that's tied so tightly that I can't even slide the daggone thing off the box. Omar pauses while watching me as I struggle. He's not offering to help so he must be waiting for me to stop with the ridiculous string and give him my undivided attention.

"I'm listening, you said that you have a whole new perspective…," I parrot while still struggling with this stubborn knot.

"So, as I was saying," he continues, "just seeing you laid up in the hospital after the loss of the, uh *our* baby and then watching Bren lying there and possibly never walking again forced me to examine my own life. So, baby, I guess what I'm getting at, is these tragedies have taught me that we are not promised tomorrow and if we know what we want then we need to go after it 'cause life is short…"

It's about time! I finally got the stupid knot out! "I know, you're absolutely right, none of us are promised tomorrow," I concur as I open the box.

"Baby, so what do you think?" he pressed as I look inside the box at my second favorite cake, *Chocolate Brownie w/Nutty Praline icing.* Auhhh, the chopped nuts are sprinkled in the cutest little design…uh, wait a minute… I look at it again and they look like… like words. The nuts spell something….Will… uh wait, Will… you marry me? *Oh my God! I can't believe it! Omar just asked me to marry him!*

Seventy

Five weeks later…

"Cyd, are you sure he's the one? I'm only asking because a lot has happened during these last few months and Lord knows that you've been through a whirlwind of emotions. So, baby, as your mother I have to ask."

"Yes, mama." I switch the handset to speaker, "A lot has happened and yes, you're right, my emotions have been all over the place but everything in me tells me that we *are* meant to be together. So yes, for the first time in my life, I can honestly say, I *know* he's the one!"

"So then you're happy."

"Extremely!"

"Good then I'm happy too! Now, should we alert Father Arnold so that he can put you two on the church's calendar?"

"Yes mama but not yet, we want to take our time. But before we talk about wedding stuff, I really want to thank you for suggesting that I see the therapist. I'm pretty sure that I wouldn't be this happy if it hadn't been for my sessions with Dr. Newton. At least not without a lot of guilt."

"Honey, that's what mothers are for. And baby taking your time sounds like a good idea."

"I know mama, but it'll be hard because we're both really excited, although, we know we really shouldn't rush either."

"So, then I take it you and Omar have talked?"

"Yes, he's in Atlanta helping his mother take care of Brendon. They're moving him into the rehabilitation center tomorrow. Thankfully, he's coming along. Slowly but surely."

"Good, then it looks like our prayers have been answered."

"Yes they have."

"So honey, I don't think you told me what Omar's reaction was after you told him."

"Well, I guess he reacted like anyone would under the circumstances, speechless at first, then questioning my motives before we were able to discuss all of the events that led up to this point. But later he was able to process it a little better. I mean, don't get me wrong we still care about each other and I would like for us to remain friends but that's it, nothing more."

"And he's okay with that?"

"Yes mama, but it really wasn't a case of multiple choice. Now, it may still take him a little time for it to actually sink in, but I know that he knows that this is what's best for both of us. And I also know that he'll be better off with someone who he's truly meant to be with."

"And that person is *definitely* not you?"

"Like I've said before, although our connection was real, it wasn't a true *love* connection in the, *I-want-to-spend-the-rest-of-my-life-with-you* sense. There's no doubt that Omar was a significant part of my journey, but he was more of what I see as a *spiritual helper or facilitator.*"

"A spiritual helper, facilitator? I don't think I ever heard of that one…"

"In other words, he *facilitated* the process of revealing something that I needed to know, which in my case, was my purpose. All along I thought that his love was the answer but mama it wasn't. However, I needed Omar's and my experience in order to help me realize that it wasn't his love or anyone's that I needed. And my experience with Omar *helped* me in discovering that.

So no, mama, I'm 100% sure that Omar is *not* the one that I was meant to be with. But rest assured, he's going to be all right. In fact, Omar and Brendon will both be fine, just fine. And the truth is, we *all* will be."

I pause for a few seconds before saying good-bye. Through the silent stillness, I can hear mama smile through the phone. It's a sound filled with pride, one that my sister and I hear often. I breathe slowly while basking in the silence, then I smile back *knowing* that somehow, mama can hear my smile too.

Epilogue...

Six months later...

As we reach the end of the workbook, we are also marking the end of a chapter in our amazing journey together. A journey which has affected the three of us differently but has also affected us the same as each of us have come full circle, as one. Especially you Cydney. I don't think I have to tell you how proud Will and I are of you. Your open-mindedness and tenacity throughout these past years have resulted in tremendous growth and an emergent desire to explore all facets of Cydney Michelle Rochon which ultimately *opened* your pathway to full potential. You have not only enriched your life but in a lot of ways have broadened Will's and my perspective. And for that, we're grateful."

"Since we've completed the workbook, I want to take this opportunity to talk about our nine year experience in whatever way you would like to express it. So, are you guys up for that?" Dev asked Will and me. Will and I nod.

"Okay cool. Will, why don't you start?"

"Well, what can I say? It's definitely been an interesting journey. I came into this not knowing what to expect and now after this experience I know not to expect anything other than, to live in the moment and embrace all, both good and bad."

"Okay, nicely put, brief but carrying great weight. Cyd, what would you like to say?"

"I want to say firstly that, for me, today is bittersweet. It's hard to believe that this is really our last first Sunday. Nine loooong years of pulling issues and facts from our past to make sense of the present and to embrace the future. This has not only been an incredible experience but a journey that has helped reveal the person that I am today. However, to answer the question; on how the past nine years have affected me…"

"Yes, we're all ears."

"Well, as I'm sure you remember I came into this whole thing as a naïve, *it's-all-about-me-gotta-have-the-best-of-everything* girl and now, am leaving as a *knowing it's-not-just-me-it's-about-all-of-us* consciously evolved individual. And please don't get me wrong, I still love nice things but now material things are no longer my focus whereas say, five to eight years ago that's all I wanted, Gucci this, Prada that, Donna, Ralph, you name it, and if it wasn't *on* my body, it was in my closet or on my *got-to-have-it* list!"

"Yeah, you're right about that," Devin jokes.

"*As* I was saying, the events in this past year have revealed a very important path in my journey. Events that at the time I had no idea were part of a bigger picture or a part of, my *puzzle*. As I kept an open mindset and continued going with the flow while each piece was played out, it gradually hit me that all of the pieces were instrumental in bringing me closer to my what, as what was revealed later, as my purpose."

"For the sake of closure, what were the exact pieces or events that you believe led you to your purpose?" Will asked.

I never did tell Will or Devin about the baby and the miscarriage because, one, it's personal, and still emotionally painful and two, I know they would have insisted I take time off to heal. Work and therapy was actually what kept me sane. And closure or no closure, I'm not about to bring it up now, because there are other pieces and events that are more relative to my purpose.

"The first puzzle piece or event was Omar's disappearance from my office which was extremely stressful and eventually culminated into me getting fired. Following that I went through the ups and downs of job hunting which eventually led me to SFL which directly correlates with my purpose as it was revealed. Now, with the restructure of SFL I am fulfilling that purpose by helping others recognize and access their inner power and utilize it to its full potential."

"Good, good. Now, since Omar was a piece of your puzzle, I'm curious as to where he falls in regard to the poem you emailed us several days ago?" Devin cross examined.

Did someone put me on the witness stand and forget to tell me?

"Which email? Will blurts out."

"She sent it to you too, you know the Reason, Season one."

"Funny that you should ask," I tell Devin, "that's actually something that I thought about when I emailed it to you guys, but just never articulated. So yes, I have to say that Omar definitely came into my life for a *reason.* And before you ask, Ty came into my life for a *season.* The way I see it, he was placed in my life to help him open his awareness."

Devin smiles, then walks over and hugs me.

"I can see how much this journey means to you and believe it or not, going through it with you means almost as much to me."

"I second that," Will promptly adds.

"These past nine years, for all of us," Devin continues, "has been an extraordinary experience. One that I personally will cherish and forever hold close. I love you both and am without a doubt looking forward to the next chapter in all of our lives. But before we end, I'd like to ask one last question."

"And what might that be? Will asks.

"Now, that we're ending this leg of our journey, I'm curious if either of you still feel that something is missing from your lives."

Will smiles then responds, "No man, I can honestly say, no. Especially now that my body is in total alignment. So, Devin, what about you?"

"I'm good, nothing is missing. As you both know, I recently met someone who is also on her spiritual path. And it's working out pretty well. Cyd, what would you say is missing from your life?"

"Brace yourselves! I can honestly say, nothing. Absolutely nothing!"

"Well, I think that officially closes this chapter of our journey," Devin smiles as Will gets up and joins us with open arms for a group hug. The three of us embrace. For several minutes there are no words spoken.

"Okay, enough of this," I said softly while pulling away from our little *Kumbaya* huddle, "I don't want to cry, I'm gonna mess up my make-up!" I whine just as my eyes begin to water.

Will and Dev look at me then at each other and start laughing. As I carefully knuckle-dab my eyes, I join them in their little laugh-fest until the phone rings and interrupts our little gleeful threesome.

"Excuse me," I tell them as I head towards the phone.

"Cyd, no go ahead, take your call, we'll catch up with you tomorrow in the office." Milo escorts them to the door as Will and Dev let themselves out.

◊◊◊◊◊

Milo runs back then jumps in my lap. "Hello," I answer into the speaker while hooking the phone to the top of my True Religions.

"Congratulations! So, you're officially engaged!"

"Yes, I'm still pinching myself! It still hasn't sunk in!" I tell Anya while extending my arm to once again admire my beautiful engagement ring. I can't stop looking at it! (not because of its size and beauty but for what it symbolizes, although it really is a beautiful ring!)

"Cyd, before I uncork the *Cristal*, I just need to know that you are 100% sure that this is what you want and that this is the man you want to spend the rest of your life with."

"Anya, you sound like my mother! And look I know you're asking because you think it's partially your fault that Omar and I are no longer together but I assure you that I am 200% sure that I'm with the one I want to spend my forever with."

"I am so happy to hear that, I really am! But what if I never told you that Omar borrowed money from me? Would there be any chance that you two would still be together?"

"Did he ask you to talk to me?"

"No, no but I'm sure he's just as curious as I am. And before you say anything, don't forget that the reason he called me wasn't for money, it was for suggestions to help create a special weekend for you in Montreal, I just spontaneously offered to loan him the money when he mentioned that his money was tight. Cyd, all he wanted to do was to impress you."

"Okay, first of all, even though I love nice things and places, that is *not* how I want a man to impress me and second of all, you *did* tell me about the money but neither matters because they have nothing to do with why he and I are no longer together. Omar and I discussed your phone conversation and the whole money and impressing me thing and although I didn't like the way he handled the situation, I also told him that I appreciated that you both wanted me to have an enjoyable and relaxing weekend. I mean, it was very sweet."

I hear Anya about to speak but I keep talking.

"So, bottom line, loan or no loan, Milanya, he's just *not* the one! And that's not to say I don't still care about him because I do, but *now*, only as a *close friend.* So girl, quit beating yourself up about this because I'm happy, I really am! I have never ever felt this, this… *deep* sense of *knowing* that I am with the person that I was meant to be with!"

"Okay, okay, I got it! I just wanted to make sure that you're sure..."

"I am. I swear!" I cut her off. "In fact, I have never been surer of anything in my entire life!"

"Well great, that's all I needed to hear! I just needed to get everything out in the open and now that we have, Cyd, I am genuinely happy for you, for both of you! So now, that I know that you are truly happy and I do, Que and I want to give you and your *fiancé* an engagement party!"

"Oh, Anya I don't know what to say! Thank you, thank you, and thank you! You guys are the best!"

"That's what best friends are for! I'll call Preston this week and have him start on some ideas and then I'll fly up to New York so we can make sure that we're all on the same page. And, I'm telling you right now that we're not going to tell you *everything* because I want us to still leave some of the details as a surprise! So, BFF congrats again and I'll talk to you later in the week! Love you!"

"Bye Anya, and thanks again! Love you too!"

I can't believe this! Not only have I found my soul mate but we're get-ting ma-ar-ried! And my best friend is giving us an engagement party!

I have so many things to do that I don't even know where to begin or who to call first! I should probably start with calling Shaye and ask her if she will....wait, what's this? I see a package on the floor next to the chair where Devin was sitting. *I swear that boy would forget his head if it wasn't connected to that neck of his! That's funny though because I don't even remember seeing him bring anything in.* It looks like it's a gift for someone...probably that woman he just met! Fortunately, there's a card on top, which I open.

"To Cydney,
Love Will & Devin"

For me? As I untie the ribbon, I'm thinking, it's not my birthday or any other special day not that I know of…or is it? I open the box and OMG!…I cannot believe this. How did, when did they…I don't even have words. Those guys are too much. Still stunned, I take the gift out of the box to see if it's the same one. It's been so long since I've seen it. I hold it up and look at it. Inspecting it, front first, now the back…yes, it is, this is definitely it! I jump up and slide it on as I sprint to the mirror. After several minutes in the mirror and remembering everything that I loved about it, I slip it off my shoulder then slide my hand under the monogrammed tissue paper and pull out the Gucci dust bag. A piece of paper falls out of the cloth bag…

"Just a little something to remind you of our journey together, from the very beginning!"

Smiling, I admire it once again while noting the beautifully, polished antique brass nail heads and that kick-ass trademark stripe strap, before slowly sliding the handbag into its cloth dust bag and gently placing it in between my other bags on my closet shelf.

It seems like an eternity to have gotten to this point but I must say that everything that I have gone through, (well, *almost* everything) was more than worth it to be where I am, right now, in this moment! And yes, I have *definitely* come full circle. In fact, interestingly enough, Alex and I *both* have!

Reason, Season or Lifetime?

People come into your life for a reason, a season or a lifetime.
Once it's revealed why they're in your life, you will act accordingly and instinctively know what to do with or for that person.

When someone is in your life for a REASON, it is usually to meet a need you have expressed. They have come to assist you with that need or desire, to provide you with guidance and support, to aid you physically, emotionally or spiritually. They may seem like a godsend and truth is, they are. They are there for the reason you need them to be.
Then without any wrongdoing on your part or out of the blue, this person will say or do something to bring the relationship to an end.

Sometimes they walk away. Sometimes they act up and force you to take a stand. And in some cases they may even die. It's important to realize that at that time, your need has been met, your desire fulfilled, and that their work has been done. The prayer you sent up has been answered and now it is time to move on.

Some people come into your life for a SEASON, because your turn has come to share or teach. Their gift to you is an experience of sharing knowledge and teaching the lessons you've learned. They may also teach you something that you need to learn or fulfill. With this person comes an unbelievable amount of joy. Believe it, it's real. But only for a season.

LIFETIME relationships, teach lifetime lessons, things you must build upon in order to have a solid emotional foundation.

Your job is to accept the lesson, love the person and put what you have learned to use in your other relationships and areas of your life.
They say that love is blind but it appears that friendship is clairvoyant.

Whether it's for a Reason, a Season or a Lifetime, be grateful to that person for being a part of your life.

Anonymous
(Amended by C.J.L.)

Made in the USA
Lexington, KY
06 June 2012